A Lake's End

Bert Jordan

PublishAmerica
Baltimore

Hardcover 978-1-4512-9792-8
Softcover 978-1-4489-4224-4
PUBLISHED BY PUBLISHAMERICA, LLLP
www.publishamerica.com
Baltimore

Printed in the United States of America

Table of Contents

Chapter 1
The Campout

He walked through the water, a bewildered look on his face. "We used to camp here," he thought. There were open spaces that had marked the areas where tents were pitched when it was dry years ago. He waded on and stopped at what was a tall Maple even fifteen years ago. Its bark was crumbling and the look of rot was all over it. He walked around it looking for something and finally, looking up a little, he found the crude knife marks, L T; Luke Thomas.

"Man! I really chewed him out when he carved up this tree," he muttered. But, this was the place they had camped fifteen years ago. The initials in the tree proved it.

Luke and his sister were happy to be camping with their dad, even though their mom had died the year before. It was the first outing for Bill and his two kids since the accident; a car crash on the passenger side when a drunk driver ran a stop sign.

Bill planned the trip when Luke told him about studying National Parks in school.

Neither father nor son could recall how they chose Yellowstone Lake to visit when they lived in Minnesota, but the trip halfway across the country seemed to order the chaos they all had been living with. The painful memories took their place in the back of their minds and the trip of a lifetime was planned and lived till on the way home they felt healed and ready to take on life again.

At age eight, it was a tougher trip for Becky than for Bill and Luke, but she tried hard and by the time they left for home, she enjoyed camping as much as her older brother.

Once back home, an injury fighting a fire caused his department to force Bill into early retirement and he moved his family to Augusta Wisconsin to try small town living. The decision wasn't easy, but once made the changes in location and life style came easier than feared.

"This was a great campsite," he thought. "But, where did this water come from?" He was right in thinking it couldn't have been a bad rain storm. The water had to be several inches deep and when they had camped here fifteen years ago it was an easy step down to the canoe when they fished.

"Grandpa Bill," came a distant voice. He looked around almost expecting to see Luke, but the voice was too young. He peered through the trees and saw a young boy waving from the lakefront campsite he had his RV parked in. It was Luke Jr and behind him two worried parents chased his younger sister who wanted to meet this man called Grandpa Bill.

He called back, "Hey Lukey! I'll be right there. And don't let your sister fall in." It was a short wade to the inflatable boat he bought for the trip.

He settled into it thinking he should have gotten a smaller one, or a bigger motor. But, a larger boat just seemed more safe for grand kids than that old canoe he thought was safe enough for he, Luke and Becky.

A quick pull on the rope and the ten horse outboard motor came to life. The boat felt more like a barge with such a small outboard motor. But, the sight of two tiny fishermen on shore made him sure the safety factor was more important than speed. "I'm coming, I'm coming," he called even though no one could hear him.

He floated up to the shore and Luke reached for the bow rope and pulled the inflatable to the dock. "Boy, what a boat!" Lukey yelled. "Can I get in?" "Sure," said Bill with a big grin as he watched the five-year-old half jump and half tumble in. He rolled onto the floor with the biggest smile a boy could have and said "what a great boat. Can we go fishing now?"

"Well, I think I better meet your sister first and say hello to your parents too," Bill replied.

"Aww," said Lukey, with his best disappointed voice. "Meet me again, first," and threw himself into Bill's waiting arms. Being a grandfather had become his greatest joy in life and he was more than happy to hug wrestle with a grandson.

When the boy was satisfied with his hello Bill got out of the boat and crouched down to meet his new grand daughter. She was three and clung to her mother's leg. They looked at each other, Bill grinning broadly and she smiling shyly. She knew this big man from family pictures and stories, and even though he looked like someone she should love, it would take a little time.

"That's O.K." laughed Bill. "As far as grandpa is concerned, you can be shy till you're thirty." She looked away.

"I'll have you know I am not raising any old maids," laughed Sarah.

Bill stood up and opened his arms to welcome Sarah. "The best thing I ever did was to give my blessing to Luke getting married." He had never talked about his earlier apprehension when Luke came home from his Freshmen Year in College and announced he had met the girl he wanted to marry. And marry they did just before their sophomore year.

They seemed to be a good match. She had a single mother and needed a good man as much as Luke needed a good woman. They attended a small College and faith combined with good advisors saw them through to graduation in five years. Of course, gifts from God named Luke junior and Rachel slowed them a little, but the love in Luke's eyes told Bill it was right and there would be more kids as time went on.

Bill and Luke hugged with back slapping and an affection that was real. "How you been?" they asked together, and then laughed. They proceeded to talk to each other at the same time to get their "hellos" said. They laughed at themselves, then Bill turned to Lukey and asked if he'd said hello to his Aunt Becky yet?

"No," he replied. "When can we go fishing, Grandpa?"

"Right after we eat," Bill replied. "Right now your grandfather is hungry enough to eat the backside of a road kill skunk. How about you?"

"Grandpa!" protested little Rachel.

"I don't know about that," said Lukey, "But chocolate cake sounds good to me."

"Judging on the smell from the RV I think you will get your wish, Lukey. We'll have to wait for that skunk till later."

Bill's daughter, Becky was the image of her mother; both in a sweet disposition and graceful beauty. She was comfortable around men, used to their banter and knew their tastes. She had married young as had Luke, but her husband had not settled into married life as well as her older brother did. Fast cars and fast times overtook him just before their child was born. Then came the drugs and there was no coming back. Early one morning a call came in and she had to fly to a druggie hell-hole to identify his remains. Bill had to be both father and grand father to Kiia, a good boy who was now at the end of the terrible-twos.

One day when Kiia was shredding Bill's new magazine Bill came up behind him and took his hand gently, but firmly, and said "No." When the other hand tore a page Bill grabbed it and said, "No." But, when a third hand seemed to come in Bill decided to get another magazine later. He decided it would be easier to love him rather than figure him out.

The camper was packed pretty tight with family and the promise of a good dinner. Bill had filleted some fish caught earlier and Becky fried some and baked the rest. After the adults talked a little and the kids stared at each other, the table was set and the campout officially began.

Luke and Sarah talked a lot with Becky about all that had happened to her. They had watched with hope as the marriage came together, and from across the country ached when it came apart. For the most part, Bill was silent. He watched his kids and his grandkids with a love that made everything in his life feel good.

At the right moments he teased Lukey about every fillet he ate. "You should have seen the fight that one put up before I got him in the boat. I think that one was its uncle."

"Bill! You are going to make him sick with that kind of talk," said Sarah.

"Aww," said Lukey, "I just want to be a good fisherman like Grandpa."

"You will be," said Bill. "And I think there will be enough light after dinner for the men to cross the lake and fish the other side. You ready to go?"

"No one will eat the cake while we are gone, will they?" asked a worried Lukey.

"We'll save your cake." Sarah and Becky chorused.

"You just get us some nice fish for tomorrow," laughed Sarah.

The men started moving the dishes to the sink and then turned toward the door. Fishing had already taken over their thinking.

"You got enough bait, Dad?" asked Luke as they walked out the door.

"I bought worms and night crawlers and they will do for now," said Bill. "You grab your old pole and whatever you think Lukey can use from the storage locker and let's get going!"

"Yay," cried Lukey. "Hey, what can I carry?"

"You run ahead and pull the mooring rope so the boat is real close to the dock," Bill said, knowing it would be easier if he and Luke carried the supplies. Lukey ran ahead and did as he was told. But, in little boy fashion, he tugged the mooring rope and promptly pulled himself off the dock and into the boat.

"Lukey! Called his dad.

"I'm O.K.," came a muffled voice.

"That's why I bought an inflatable boat," chuckled Bill, "a little bounce in a rubber boat shouldn't hurt him." The two men reached the boat and began stowing gear. An easy step down into it and they cast off. Luke used the small paddle to put a safe distance from the dock and Bill pulled the starter rope. The little motor came to life and they were off.

Luke couldn't resist a few remarks on the way. "Are you sure the motor is running? If this thing went faster we could get there before the fish die of old age."

Bill took it all with a laugh knowing it was slow, but safe for a man who was more concerned about his grand kids than speed. Soon, they arrived in a small deep cove they had fished years earlier. Bill slowly lowered the stern anchor and when Luke lowered the one for the bow, they tied off so the boat wouldn't move. There were plenty of lily pads and a few old deadhead trees sticking up from the water. It was enough cover for a school of pan fish and their prospects looked good. Bill set to work on Lukey's pole right away. He was just as impatient as his Dad was at that age.

"Find a nice looking worm, Lukey," said Bill as he handed him the bait box. "The fish here are really particular about what they eat."

Lukey took the bait box and began his search with the intensity only a trusting youngster could. It didn't take long to find a worm he was sure no fish could resist.

"Try this one, Grandpa," he said. "If I was a fish I'd like this one."

Bill took the worm and said, "Now, watch this because a real fisherman baits his own hook. And you are on your way to becoming one." Lukey beamed at his Grandpa considering him to be a real fisherman.

Bill baited the hook, set the bobber and cast the line a short distance from the boat. Luke had his line in the water also and was leaning back on the side of the inflatable.

"What happens next, Grandpa," Lukey asked, impatiently.

"Well," you watch the bobber and when it moves up and down or starts to go somewhere you give the pole a jerk upwards and reel in a fish. It's that simple."

Bill reached over the side to wash his hand after baiting his own hook. He gave a small start when he discovered how warm the water felt. Only Luke noticed his dad's reaction, but waited till he finished his cast to say anything.

"What's up?" he asked quietly.

"Rinse your hands," said Bill as he watched for his son's reaction. Luke put his hand in the water and looked over at Bill with a questioning look on his face.

"What do you think?" he asked.

"I'm not sure, but I think I will look around a little tomorrow while the rest of you sleep in."

"Hey! Where did my bobber go?" exclaimed Lukey. Equally surprised, Bill and Luke began calling out so many instructions it was a wonder Lukey started to reel in his catch. Bill reached for the net. Even though the fish would be small he knew a fish flopping around in the boat would scare a little boy. He wanted to train a future fisherman, not scare the sport out of him.

"Wow, he's a beauty, isn't he?" said Lukey as he took in the excitement of it all. "Do you think he is related to the one I had for dinner tonight, Grandpa?"

Bill chuckled. "If he isn't, I'm sure he went the same school."

"Oh, look at this," called Luke as he set the hook and began to reel in his catch. Bill got a bite about the same time and it was all he could do to keep worms on Lukey's hook and his own. They had anchored over a small school of pan fish and for a half an hour they were too busy to talk.

When the fish stopped biting, Bill suggested they "call it a day," and head back across the lake.

"Aww Grandpa, are you sure?" Lukey protested.

"Yes, I am. We have enough to clean for breakfast and lunch tomorrow. To catch more would only cause us to waste them." The men started to secure their tackle for the trip back while Lukey fished for a few more minutes. When finished, Bill and Luke washed their hands in the lake. Their eyes met and Bill said, "I'm definitely going to look into this tomorrow." Lukey was too interested in the pan fish in the live well to notice the talk between the two men.

They pulled up the anchors. Bill started the motor and started back to the women who were waiting at the campsite. Thoughts of the change in the water temperature weighed heavily on his mind. He knew higher water at one end of the lake and the change in temperature at the other had to be related, but how? Tomorrow, he would stop at the local Ranger's office for a chat. This had to be something they were aware of.

They were nearing the boat landing now and the women had gotten up from their chairs to come and see the catch. Lukey was so excited he tried to catch a fish barehanded from the live well to show his mother. Luckily, he got a splash of water from a fish, and not a spiny poke from a dorsal fin.

Luke pulled his son away from the live well as they reached the dock.

"Well, how did my little fisherman do on his first time out?" Asked Sarah.

"Oh Mom, come and see. We got some big ones and some bigger ones and a really big one, but it got away and Daddy sweared and Grandpa laughed and…

"And, and slow down," said Sarah. "Show me what you caught."

With a little help from his Dad, Lukey handed the live well up to the dock. The women looked in it and registered enough approval to please the youngest fisherman. He was wound so tight with the excitement of catching his first fish he was about to name them and assign their capture to himself and his boat mates when his mother suggested a bath and fresh pajamas before bed.

"Bath?" questioned Lukey. "Who takes a bath on a camping trip?"

"Ask your Dad," laughed Becky. The memory of tent camping and a cold water bath in the lake came to her mind.

"Sorry, Son, but Grandpa's motor home has everything; even a bathtub."

The look on Lukey's face was one of disbelief. His mother reached out and picked him up. Knowing these types of hugs would grow few and far between in a little while she felt them deeply.

"Aw, Mom," said Lukey, although his protest wasn't as deep as the comfort in his mother's arms. She let him slide to his feet, picked up Rachel and then took his hand. They walked to the RV talking about a piece of chocolate cake after the bath.

"Why don't you take the fish up to the picnic table while I secure the boat," said Bill. He told Luke where the filleting knives were and began to tie the boat to the dock.

Luke poured the excess water from the live well and walked up to the table.

It didn't take Bill long to tie up the boat and secure the rain cover. He joined his son at the table. Luke had started on a nice Bass he caught and Bill grabbed one of the pan fish Lukey got. They used a filleting style that evolved from many fishing trips. It wasn't fancy, but it did get the fish ready for the frying pan quickly. They made small talk as they worked, but Bill could sense he was the only one still thinking about the changes in the lake since the last time they were here.

"So," asked Luke, "how are you getting along with the women in Augusta? Have you found anyone special?"

Bill laughed in spite of his thoughts about the lake. "There is the one I'm seeing now. Becky knows her. But, there are a couple drawbacks that I'm not sure I can work out."

"What kind of 'drawbacks' can ruin a good relationship, Dad? Sarah and I have worked out any number of problems in our lives."

"I'm glad to hear that son. But Marge comes with two really big issues," and Bill explained them as they worked. He had never met a woman whose teenaged daughter was as precocious as Marge's was. She had made remarks leading Bill to believe she was as available as her mother, and much better at that. Marge's son, in his early twenties, had made a pass at Bill shortly after meeting him. Bill was sure he didn't want see a woman and both of her children at the same time. His plan was to see Marge when he returned and try to make a clean break then.

"I think I would too, Dad."

"Everything started out O.K., Son, but after a few weeks went down hill quickly. But, enough is enough and I going to look for someone else."

They finished cleaning their fish, cleaned up and went inside the RV to put them in the fridge.

Chapter 2
THE RANGER'S OFFICE

In the morning Bill sent his family into town for supplies while he went for a walk. He felt a talk with the park ranger would be easier alone. As He walked past campsites with every manner of tent or RV, his mind went back to the time he was here when his kids were young. They had started with a tent and then went to a trailer before the kids were college age. The magic of camping was still the same and these roads and trails were just as he remembered them. He came over a rise and caught sight of the Ranger's office. The staff was just arriving as he walked up. It was eight o'clock when he walked in behind two secretaries who looked like they could kill for a cup of strong coffee.

"What can we help you with?" asked one of them.

Bill explained he wanted to talk to one of the Rangers about a geological map of the park and the lake. He said the campsite was great, but would like to check out some better fishing hoping he didn't sound like he was interested in something else.

"Sit down," she said, as she took the cover off her computer. "The ranger on duty will be here soon."

Bill sat down near the doorway to an office near the secretary's desk. He looked for something to read that looked local. As his eyes swept the room, he noticed some geological charts on the wall in the office. Instinctively, he knew they contained the information he wanted. He kept an eye on the still sleepy secretary hoping for a chance to check out the charts.

"Coffee's ready," Came a call from a back room.

"Want some?"

"No, thanks," said Bill. "Already had mine. I'm just going to read till the Ranger comes in."

He watched her as she grabbed her coffee cup and left for the backroom. As an old Firefighter, he had learned how to "read" a room so he knew all he had to do was step inside the Ranger's office, take one step to the side and he wouldn't be seen by the secretary if she returned to soon.

He stared intently at the charts and saw more than he wanted. There was a new survey map beside an earlier one and a third one strangely colored. The newer map showed a portion of the land at the north end of the lake was now higher than it had been fifteen years ago.

"That's impossible," thought Bill. "Land just doesn't change position like that." He then looked intently at the third map. The colors showed red at the north end and he knew it meant a great mass of heat below the surface. Quickly he stepped out of the office and back to his seat.

The secretary returned with two cups of coffee and put one on her desk and walked to the Ranger's desk with the other one. She glanced at Bill without speaking. He was glad for her silence because he needed some time to order his thoughts and formulate some questions. While he pretended to read, his mind raced to questions about how hot were the red parts of the map, how long has anyone known about the red, what is the red and what will it do?

The Ranger was predictable because he came sauntering in before his coffee had a chance to get cold. He glanced at Bill and went straight to his office and closed his door. Bill glanced at the secretary and said, "Let him have his coffee before you announce me." She just smiled and went back to work.

Bill shuffled the magazines again without finding anything that looked like it had been written and printed locally. In due time the intercom sounded on the secretary's desk and she turned to him.

"He'll see you now."

Bill walked to the door and since it was still closed he used the military knock; one rap with his knuckles.

"It's open." Came the reply.

Bill walked in and stopped in front of the Ranger's desk. He introduced himself and thanked him for seeing him.

"I'm the Ranger, in charge of the Park," he said as he stood up.

Bill and decided to get right down to his questions.

"Well, Sir," he started, "I've returned to the Park after 15 years and I found my old campsite south of the Lake under water."

Before he could continue, he noticed an obvious increase in the Ranger's discomfort. "And, when we fished the North Side, the water was noticeable warmer than the South Side..."

"Well, ah yah," he stammered. He coughed, cleared his throat, "Well you know, things change a lot in fifteen years."

"That's true," replied Bill, his mind racing, fearing a quick end to their talk. "When I drove in day before yesterday, I noticed a number of State and Federal cars around your building, and..."

"Yah, um, we had a big type POW WOW with the high-up mucky-mucks and, uh, you know how that kind of stuff goes." He was really uncomfortable now.

"I understand," said Bill. He got up from his chair and walked to the maps hoping for a detailed look at them. "I was really interested in lake maps because I have my grandchildren here this weekend and really want to show them a good fishing and camping trip."

"Well, you know, uh, those aren't really fishing maps." He stammered.

"Oh?" I thought they were." Bill tried frantically to memorize what he was looking at so he could draw them later and understand all he was seeing, especially the third map with the changes and red color on it. The Ranger strode across the room quickly and started taking the maps down.

"Actually, these were supposed to come down and the geological maps showing the fishing holes were to go back up, but, ah, well, you know how it is with the "Brass," they forgot to bring them and..." he rolled them up quickly.

"We, uh, I'm sure we have the fishing maps in the tourist section, and, uh, let me show you where that is, and, uh," he turned and opened the office door. "Yes, yes, we have those maps right out there." He gestured to Bill who followed him out of the office.

Bill had twenty years in the fire department and had retired as a Battalion Chief. He could "burn" a blueprint into his mind and years later fight a fire in that building keeping his firefighters safe while trying to minimize the loss for the owner. But, it was still time to continue the game and try not to arouse any suspicion or anxiety in the Ranger.

"I sure appreciate you taking the time to show me where the fishing maps are," said Bill, "I mean this is really a trip of a life time for me and my family."

"Well, that's what we're here for, and uh, oh yah, here they are, right here in the gift shop. You look these over and I'm sure you will find the good fishing you want. Pay the cashier, over there." The Ranger slapped him on the back and turned back to office quickly.

"Thank you, again," said Bill, keeping up pretenses. The Ranger pretended not to hear as he closed his door.

Bill found some maps that he felt he could draw the land changes on later and walked to the cashier. He made small talk with her even though he wanted to run from the shop to get away from what he had learned. Right now it seemed wiser to pretend to know as little as the people around him appeared to.

He tried to stroll back to his campsite, but his mind raced so fast he didn't even remember the walk back.

Once in side his RV he slammed the maps on the table and visualized the large wall maps over them. What he saw was an enormous lifting of the earth's structure at the North end of the lake. It may have only been a couple of feet, but for that to happen in fifteen years betrayed a disaster in the making. Only a huge magma deposit could cause the land to rise and spill a lake away from it. He sat in thought for a few minutes, and then realized he was looking at more than a possible volcanic eruption. This one would be so big it would it would be cataclysmic. The ash cloud would be so great it would take only weeks to cover the entire globe. The ash would be so dense it would suffocate anything that breaths within a few days of the eruption and even as it fell it would block the sun and cover all plant life. If it didn't cause another ice-age, it would certainly plunge the earth into a dark winter sure to last one or two years before winds and rain could clear the atmosphere. He didn't mark the maps and put them in the middle of the table for the others to find when they came back from town. They didn't need to know what he'd discovered until he had some time to understand it all himself. He left the RV for a walk. He knew he needed some time to calm down and get his mind back to his family and the fun he knew the little ones needed to have. When he finally sorted out what he had learned he could tell them everything. But, not now.

He walked quickly from trail to trail trying to understand what he'd learned and hoping he could get away from it. After two hours he was bathed in sweat and found himself approaching his own campsite. Luke and the others drove up in their SUV right then so he put on his game face.

"It's about time you got back," he called to them. "I had time to get the maps and go for a good long workout!" Once again, he was Battalion Chief Bill Thomas with everything in control and no one was going to know otherwise.

"Grandpa!" Lukey, Rachel and Kiia came running to him.

Chapter 3
Filling in the Gaps

It always amazed Bill how his children and grand children could so invade his being that they forced out anything he had on his mind. All three kids hit him with a "crash" hug. It seemed like they didn't really want a hug, but were sure they weren't going to let the other kids get one. Bill managed to touch them all and get in a hug and a tickle and enough eye contact to say "I love you."

"Hey, you three wild ones," called Sarah, "why don't you stay outside and play with Grandpa while we get lunch on the table?"

"Sounds like a good idea," replied Luke. "I'll stay outside too and make sure they don't gang up on Grandpa too badly."

So they read the new books that were bought with the groceries and when that was finished they modified a bean bag toss into Bochi-Ball. Just before ideas ran out, the call came;

"Lunch is ready; everyone come in and wash up."

After lunch, the littlest ones were put down for their naps and Lukey given something to play with in hopes he would sleep too. The adults talked and caught up with the events from the last year. Becky and Sarah talked about their kids while Luke and Bill talked work and retirement. Luke occasionally picked up one of the fishing maps without opening them. Finally, when the conversation lagged he opened one and said he was going to find the spot where the "big ones" were.

After a few minutes, he exclaimed, "Hey, didn't this one spot here seem a little deeper the last time we were here."

Bill pulled the map closer and looked. "It may be. Do you suppose it just silted in?" he asked.

"I suppose it did. Look at this Dad," he continued. "If we were to troll around the west end of the lake, up to the North we could hit this one spot. If there isn't a big one in there I'll eat my hat."

Bill laughed and took the map. He noted the location of the trolling route Luke pointed out and said, "Let's give it a try. I'll start tying some trolling rigs right away."

He folded the map, glad that there would no more study of the lake today. Outside, he and Luke tied some trolling rigs and went down to the inflatable. It was a little early in the day for fishing, but Father, Son and Grandson needed some fishing time. The fishing was good, but the trophy fish eluded them. Luke did catch a large Bass! Bill photographed it just before the release and they had their proof for Luke's co-workers. Lukey was sure his dad was the greatest fisherman in the world, right up there with his Grandpa.

When they returned to the campsite they pulled the inflatable out of the water, opened its valves and rolled it up for storage. Putting the boat away signaled the end of the campout and sadness descended on the adults. They talked about trying to get this campsite again next year. Bill had a strong feeling this was the last time they would be here, but said he would see to the reservation in the morning. That night, he sat up alone making survival plans he didn't want to make and not knowing they would work even if he did have the nerve to execute them.

In the morning goodbyes were said, hug and kisses exchanged and Luke, Sarah and their kids drove off.

"Don't forget to reserve for next year," called Luke as they left. Bill waved and said he wouldn't forget. He felt good that even though they would never be here again, this was a first step in making the plans to keep his family safe.

"Lets load up, Becky. I'll reserve the campsite on the way out."

Basically the RV was all ready loaded and all they had to do was secure everything on the inside. Kiia sensed the other kids were gone and he had Grandpa for his own again. He bounced around the RV, in and out of Grandpa's arms till he was tired. Becky got him into a secure bed and began to read to him. Bill got into the driver's seat and started for the Ranger's Station.

It didn't take long to get the reservation and when he got back into the driver's seat he felt better. He pointed the RV toward home and got down to the business of driving. It didn't take long for the magic of a vehicle moving to put Kiia to sleep. Becky joined her Dad in the passenger seat.

"Do you know the route," she asked?

"Yes; anything east will get us home."

She noticed a touch of sadness in his voice. In fact, she had noticed some sadness in his voice and eyes over the last two days. It was as if her dad knew something that he wasn't ready to tell anyone. But, since she had no way to know the seriousness of what was troubling him she let it go.

It took about three days to get back to Wisconsin where they had moved after Bill left the fire department. They had set a good pace, stopping only to sleep at night and whenever it was necessary to get Kiia out of the vehicle for some exercise. Becky spent some time at the wheel. At first she didn't want to, but after a few minutes of keeping it between the lines on the interstate highway she found it easy.

They arrived home about three o'clock in the afternoon and Bill parked the RV beside the garage. They had been keeping it clean while they drove so it didn't take long to unload and lock it up. When they were finished, Becky took Kiia to see some friends.

Bill wandered about the house for a half an hour or so and finally decided to stop over and see Marge. Before he left he had told her he would return about this time, and had asked her to have dinner with him. There had been no answer when he called on his cell phone earlier so he decided to drive over.

After ten days in a big RV he decided to pull the cover off his 1934 Ford 3-Window Coupe. It was old and slow, but the local car enthusiasts knew it was one of the best. He slid behind the wheel, inserted the Ford shaped key and stepped on the starter. In true 6-volt fashion, the old starter engaged, slowed and then sped up when the engine started. Bill eased the manual choke back in to slow the RPM. After waiting a moment to let the oil pressure come up, he eased out the clutch and smoothly left his garage, frontward. Old firefighters like to park their own vehicles facing out.

It was a cool summer afternoon and perfect for "exercising" an old Ford. The wind moved through the old coupe making the drive comfortable. However, in a small town, it was also a short drive. He slowed in front Marge's house and turned into her driveway. The back door was open.

He shut the old flathead down, swung the front opening door out and stepped onto the gravel. The sound of music he didn't understand and was sure he couldn't dance to nearly knocked him down. He knocked loudly on the screen door.

"It's open." Came a voice Bill knew to be Marge's daughter, Beth. She was a senior in High School and a lot more precocious than Bill could deal with.

He stepped through the screen door and stopped at the large bulletin board in the hall. There was picture there taken a few weeks before the trip. It was of Bill and Marge at an outdoor party. He didn't want to admit it was a good picture of them and it showed that something had come alive in him again. He hadn't met Marge's kids yet and the possibility of all that love could bring was there. He stepped into the kitchen.

"Oh, it's you."

Bill stopped in his tracks. He knew Beth was enjoying being a woman, but he wasn't ready to see her in a skimpy bikini. Totally lost for anything to say he blurted out; "It isn't hot enough for a swim suit like that!

"It depends on who's wearing it," she replied.

Feeling his face grow red, Bill asked if her mother was home.

"Not for you. You've been gone for ten days, Bill." She gestured toward the living room. "My brother's still interested if you are."

Bill felt stunned by the remarks and could only wave a "No" to her and turned back down the hall. He stopped at the photograph, pushed his thumb nail into the top and ripped his image from it. It looked like a good picture of Marge, alone.

"Tell your mother I left a message for her on the bulletin board," he said as he let the screen door slam behind him.

As he left he could only think of unimportant things like how it was a good thing they didn't rod the old Ford because he would sure do a burnout if he could. All he wanted was to get as far away from a relationship that only needed a flush handle to make it complete. He quickly reached the city limits and turned down an old county road. It turned into another and then another. As he drove, the scared, sick feeling left him. It wasn't as though he didn't know he would be alone again. It was just the way it happened. There were things about how relationships have changed he couldn't deal with. But, until he could execute the plans pushing into his mind he knew he had to be alone.

He was now in the rolling hills and valleys of Amish Country. He'd felt really comfortable here after retiring from the Fire Department in St Paul Minnesota. As he came over a small rise, he saw a figure at the side of the road. It was Moses Yocum, the first Amish man he met since coming to Augusta. Moses was the Patriarch and Bishop of the local Amish clan and they met at the feed mill when both of them were getting things. After meeting, Moses immediately began espousing the pure joy of plowing with horses rather than the sinful tractor Bill had hired to plow for him. A friendship between two seemingly different men began immediately. Both were strong men accustomed to the responsibility of leadership. A dry sense of humor was just below the surface and they enjoyed each other a little more whenever they met.

"What's that sign you're pounding on, Moses?"

Moses had been trying to get a For Sale sign into the road bed in front of a small farm. The base course on the shoulder had packed down over the years and the sign teetered and fell when he stopped pounding on it. He stepped over to the car and leaned in the passenger window, broad brimmed hat, long beard and all.

"Aye, William! I wondered who was out here burning up our good Amish roads with one of these sinful contraptions."

Bill couldn't help laughing. "They're not all bad, you know."

"Well, at least you got a nice old one instead of one of those sinful vulgarities some folks have when they stop to stare at us sensible people."

"I've noticed that hasn't stopped you from riding in a newer truck or van on occasion," Bill teased.

"True enough, William. It's no sin to ride on rubber tires if one has a need, but you'll never get me to drive one. When the steel wheel was left behind for the rubber tire it was a short drive downhill to sin."

Bill sensed the seriousness of what Moses was telling him and didn't tease anymore. He had noticed a large new machine shed on the farm and changed the subject.

"Why are you trying to sell this farm?" he asked.

"Aye William. It is a sad story. A woman widowed just after her sons moved west to join another clan. She can not keep the place by herself."

There was something about this small farm that interested Bill. If there was going to be a natural disaster in the near future he knew a small farm in a protected valley would be just the place to make a "last stand." He wanted to know more about it.

"Why don't you hop in Moses and we can talk more about it on the way home."

"Oh, I think not William. I have to get this sign up, somehow. And then, my boy is coming back with the buggy. He just went home for the milking."

"Well," said Bill, "I may be interested in the farm. I'd like to find a small place outside of town."

"Umm," Moses pursed his lips and nodded. "Then, you can give me a ride home. I live just up the hill, you know."

Bill didn't know, but guessed Moses' farm was up in the flatland area. He leaned over and pulled the handle, opening the door. Moses picked up his hammer and the sign and carefully got in. He smelled of hard work, sweat and a lot of time spent in the barn.

It was a short drive, as Bill had guessed. They talked for a few minutes about the farm, how the young men had left the area for other clans with farms and young women to marry.

"It's a shame we don't have anyone to farm it now that our young men have moved on. We'd like to keep it in the clan, but I've known you for some time and if you want to live there I will offer it to you."

In a split second Bill made his decision. "Thank you, Moses. It is a place I would like to have."

Moses solemnly offered his hand and Bill took it. They spoke for a few more minutes and Moses said he would offer Bill the same price he would offer an Amish man if there was one to buy it. He named a day and time and asked Bill to meet him to look at the place. Moses needed time to go over with his wife and tell the widow the farm was to be sold. Bill agreed and offered his hand to accept the price. Then, Moses reached out the window and pushed down on the door handle. He got out as carefully as he had gotten in and took only his hammer. "You can keep the sign, William. Good bye, for now." He closed the door, turned and walked up to his house.

Bill pulled ahead and around the semi circle driveway which led him back to the road. His mind was picking up speed faster than his old car. "What just happened?" was a good question to begin with. "Well, this afternoon I broke up with a woman I was beginning to love…but, it was OK because I didn't want to have an affair with her daughter, or her son! Especially her son! I then bought a small farm in case a volcano happens out West and kills everyone in the whole world. I guess that sums it up. I'm sure glad I don't have to go home and explain this!"

Chapter 4
The Last Big Surprise

At the appointed time, Bill pulled into the semi circle drive of the farm he was buying. He had chosen to drive the old 34 again because it was the only thing he owned that was older than he and right now the stress he felt made him feel older than he was.

Moses was waiting beside his buggy as he came to a stop. Bill got out and waved to him. He walked up to him and the men exchanged hellos.

"This is my wife," said Moses, gesturing toward the buggy. A woman looking as short and heavy as Moses leaned forward, nodded and quickly retreated back inside. Bill had heard the local Amish women were not well educated and only spoke a type of Germanic Language so he was not surprised she didn't speak.

"She will go inside the house and wait with the widow till we are finished looking around." Said Moses.

"All right."

"Let us start with the barn." Said Moses and began walking toward it. He gestured toward the land, "as you can see the farm is small, about 35 acres. The soil is good, but you can't make much of a living from a small farm. It's no wonder poor Ezra died. What with the hard work and the alcohol sickness."

"What? How did he get anything to drink in Amish country?"

"He told me he was trying to make a good Beet Wine."

"Who would buy Beet Wine?"

"Apparently no one, and he didn't have the heart to pour it out, so…Well, here we are at the barn." It was a "Pole" type building and Moses said he and the other families built it two years ago after the old barn burned down in a thunder storm. The horses were taken outside and apparently Ezra went back inside to save their harness, or something.

"As you can see, it's a big barn. Really too big for this farm. But, this is what we learned to build. Normally we build a traditional post and beam type, but this style costs less and goes up with greater ease. So we built it this way."

They pushed the sliding doors open to the cool darkness within. Bill could see the poles were set closer together than a commercial builder would have set them. It looked much stronger than it needed to be.

"This was the first pole barn we built," said Moses, "so it has only the sliding doors and one passage way facing the house. We decided to wait on installing any windows until we were sure what would be needed. We sunk a well and put in a standup hand pump."

"I see that," said Bill. "My grandfather had a pump like that. It should never need any kind of repair."

"No, it shouldn't. The water table is high hereabouts and you should never run out of water.

"That's good news. I see someone cut a lot of firewood and stacked it inside the wall there."

"Before the young men left for the West I had them do that, replied Moses. I didn't want the widow going cold over the winter. There should be a good three years supply here and a lot more beside the house there."

Bill looked around the inside of the barn. The well and the firewood were a blessing he hadn't expected. If he had to build a survival shelter these two things would be indispensable.

The dirt floor looked like it was pretty rough and there was no smell of animals ever having been housed in the barn. This building was better than he had hoped for.

"Let us go inside," said Moses interrupting Bill's thoughts.

"All right." The men pushed the sliding doors together and turned to the house. It was an old farm house; No frills and of course, no paint or electricity. It was a small two story with a porch on two sides and something about it made Bill wish he could know the story of everyone who had lived in it and what had become of them.

They mounted the sturdy steps and when on the porch Moses stomped his feet to remove the barn dust, or just to announce the arrival of the men-folk. They walked in the back door and entered the kitchen. Bill had never been in an Amish home before and didn't know what to expect beyond wood stoves and no electricity.

In the kitchen was the wood fired cook stove he expected as well as a table and chairs. The kitchen was neat and clean and everything seemed to be thoughtfully placed. It was too warm, but someone had fired the stove and made coffee. Moses led the way into the dining room.

The two women stood up when they entered. Bill was totally unprepared for what he found. The widow was taller than Moses' wife, slender and despite the plain blue dress, beautiful.

"We'll sit down," said Moses and he pulled out a chair.

"Um, yes," mumbled Bill as he pulled out the chair and kicked it trying to sit down before it was out, pulled it out further and fell into it. He hoped no one noticed his clumsiness.

"I haven't felt like this since High School and I hope I'm not talking out loud," he said to himself.

"William, this is Miriam." That was the only introduction given.

"I believe we will have coffee now."

Miriam reached for the old metal coffee pot and began pouring. When finished she slid a cup to Bill first. He reached for it afraid to touch her, but she withdrew her hands first. He thanked her and stole a glance as he pulled the cup to himself. Her eyes were green, and very sad. When the others received their coffee Bill tasted his, not knowing if he were sipping it or pouring it down his chin.

"So, William," said Moses. "We have agreed on a price, but haven't decided on how to complete our agreement."

"Oh, ah, yes," said Bill, "uh, well, I was, uh, thinking of paying by check and."

"Good," interrupted Moses. "I will get the papers out of the buggy. You will drive me to your bank and we will sign the papers there. Then we will come back here and have a nice lunch."

"Fine." Said Bill. Then he thought; "maybe she'll serve Beet Wine," again hoping he was not thinking out loud.

"May I speak?" he heard someone ask in broken English. It was the first time Bill had heard Miriam speak. As startled as he was he quickly said yes for fear Moses might tell her not to.

"In the Bible we are taught that a woman shall leave her home and the two shall live as one. I left my parents home and this is the only other home I have ever known. My sons are so far away and I do not know where I will go. Perhaps someone will take me in when I have no home."

"Oh, no," exclaimed Bill. "I don't want your house, uh, er, your home. "I only need the barn. You see I want to do experiments in intensive, small, raised bed gardens grown in minimal light and temperature control. I have a lot of things to design and build, and, and I don't want to take your home from you. Please say you will stay." He hoped he didn't sound like he had totally lost his mind.

Miriam covered her face with her hands, but couldn't conceal she was weeping.

"So, it is settled. We will leave now and be back soon," declared Moses. The men got up and left to go to town.

The time spent on the bank transaction was uneventful as Moses had been doing the land sales for his clan for a long time. The banker looked strangely at Bill for a moment, but then got down to business.

The papers were signed and notarized and the check written in a matter of minutes. A little small talk followed and after the obligatory handshakes they left.

Back at the farm the lunch was all ready prepared and the four of them ate quietly, if not quickly. When they finished, Moses prayed the "Thanks" as he had done the "Before" meal Blessing. Bill expressed his thanks to all and said he would be out again soon to start his experiments in the barn. He turned to Miriam and asked if he could stop occasionally to see how she was doing.

"You may come to do your experiments and we will discuss calling later." said Moses. Miriam looked down, modestly.

They got up from the table and walked outside. Moses walked Bill to the car as his wife got into the buggy.

Bill got into the old 34 and Moses leaned in the window. He offered Bill his hand and said, "It will be good to tell the Elders the farm is sold and the widow cared for. Good bye for now, William." Then he turned and walked to his buggy.

Bill started the old 34 and idled it around the driveway to the barn. "Well", he thought, "I've got my survival shelter. And I've met an incredible woman. Fifteen days ago I would have said an idea like this would be crazy and today I'm into it lock, stock and barrel. I have no intention of explaining this to anyone!"

Chapter 5
PREPARING TO SURVIVE

Becky had taken Kiia to the beach for the afternoon so Bill went directly to his closet sized office to plan his family's survival, if need be. He was now confident he could sell the property and recoup his investment if it wasn't needed, but what he learned on the campout bothered him too badly not to pursue a plan of action. He pulled a legal pad from the desk and started making lists.

First, the barn; It will need a floor if people are to live in it for an extended period of time and be healthy. How will I heat it and keep plants, animals and family warm?

Insulating it to keep it warm; Commercial insulation is everywhere and I can employ some of the older Amish men to install it.

Clean air will be difficult if volcanic ash fills the air; No one will be able to breathe that.

Food sources; we'll have to be totally self sufficient. At first there will be no outside sources anywhere. We'll have to store as much dried and concentrated stuff as possible and grow what we can.

Lights for growing; There may not be any electricity. How will I power the "grow lights" to insure fresh vegetables? Will a low voltage system work?

Water; No problem if the well is as deep and dependable as Moses thinks it is. Since we will have a hand pump I don't think we will need to worry about a second well.

Privacy/Secrecy; if this thing really happens I can't let my plans be known. If anyone even suspects this might be a safe haven there will be a panic and no way to defend my family.

Labor; there will be a number of things I can't do for myself. All basic construction can be done with help from Moses and the men he recommends.

Electricity; Having electricity run in to a load center with several attached receptacles to power a saw and drill…Add a switch for alternative power; ei a gas generator; no, I don't want to hoard gasoline.

Bill heard the back door open and slam as only a kid could do. Becky's voice followed. "Hey Dad, we're home!"

"I'm in my office. Be right down."

As he stepped from his office he received a crash-hug around a leg from Kiia. Bill leaned down and picked him up for a Grandpa-hug. "So, a bare bottom boy all covered with sand," he said with a laugh. Kiia only laughed back and began to babble about the day at the lake.

"Careful, Dad, he's covered with sand and if he didn't pee in the lake you could be in for a surprise."

"It wouldn't be the first time. I'll put him on his potty. You start the bath and I'll start the grill. Burgers for supper tonight." He put Kiia on his little potty while the boy went on and on. "Man," thought Bill, "this kid has got to be destined for radio or television." Becky came in to start the bath.

Back in the kitchen, he took hamburgers, baked beans and corn on the cob from the freezer. He looked at the frozen food and wondered how long it would be this easy to put together a summer meal. He went outside and started the grill.

After they had eaten and Kiia played himself to sleep, Bill sat down and tried to relax. He reached for his newspaper, but none of the headlines were important enough to take his mind away from his plans.

"So, Dad, you've been busy lately."

Bill was startled. He was afraid she might have guessed something, but dismissed the thought right away.

"Yes, I have been. You know, ever since I got hurt and forced into early retirement, I've been content to take it easy. But, I'm too young for this easy living and I am thinking about starting a small business.

"What kind?"

"I'm thinking about some sort of delivery business. I've got my pickup and that would keep the investment down."

"What kind of delivery?"

"Oh, nothing heavy." In this small town there are a lot of people who need things delivered or taken away. And, the Amish always need someone with a truck to help with things."

"I think you would like something like that."

"How is your Distance Education Degree coming?" Bill changed the subject. He knew it was slow work because of "little boy interruptions."

"It's OK. Learning computer operations via the computer isn't the easiest."

"Uh-huh. I'll be able to take Kiia along, occasionally," Bill thought that Miriam would love to meet him, a little at a time. And, he continued to himself, until he learns to talk well I will be able to continue my never ending adventure in private.

"Oh, say," he went on, "I'm thinking about selling the RV to that guy who lives over by the feed mill."

"Dad?" Becky protested. "We need the RV for family get-togethers. Kiia loves to go camping in it."

"I know, honey. But, you saw how crowded we were at the lake and I have my eye on a longer one. You know, another six to eight feet in length would mean another bed in there."

"But, would it be as easy to drive?"

"Hey, before your old Dad made Chief I had to drive every type of fire truck known to man: both in town and out! If it's got wheels I can drive it and teach you to drive it. Just keep in mind, if you can get the front bumper through the rest of the vehicle will make it too!"

"Well, OK. Can we look at the new one before you get it?"

"OK." But, tonight I'm going to turn in early. No camper or job searches for a little while." He felt surprisingly relaxed now that he had some plans made and had a little room to move without having to tell Becky what was going on. He slept well that night for the first time since he discovered the threat of a life ending catastrophe.

He rose early the next morning and fixed a quick breakfast. He filled a large water bottle and left the house. His pickup was kept behind the garage while he was away. He grabbed his "traveling-tool box" just inside the garage and put it on the floor inside the truck. It started and he eased his way past the house and out onto the street. The town was still asleep as he drove out to Amish Country and in a matter of minutes he was turning into his farm's driveway.

He was surprised to see Miriam outside and sweeping her porch. She looked up, startled. Then she recognized Bill. He waved from the truck, but she looked down at her work and pretended not to notice. "What a dummy," he thought. "You don't just wave to an Amish woman. At least, I don't think I should. Man! I have been out of the He and She thing for so long I'm not sure what to do. Better put that on the list of things to talk to Moses about."

He parked the truck and started for the passageway, but remembered the barn had no windows or electric lights and turned toward the front with its big sliding doors. They opened easily and let in enough light for him to measure the inside. When he got his tape measure, pencil and paper from the truck he made his first note; get some locks. "I guess I'm not as trusting as the Amish," he thought.

It didn't take long to measure the rectangular building and note the location of the well pump and doors.

"I'll get a price on insulation for the ceiling as well as the walls," he thought, "and then see if someone wants to bid a concrete floor and the electrical service.

He looked for Miriam as he drove out, but she was no where to be seen. "I'll stop by the Farm Supply store first to get a price on insulation. Maybe I'll get a hat to tip when I see Miriam next…that is if Amish men tip their hats to women…They should have a lot of shell corn and various legume seeds there too. I read once where most of the third world poor people eat nothing but rice and legumes…I'd better put in an order for some galvanized garbage cans too…mice and rats can't get into them."

The ideas were flowing too fast all of a sudden and when he got to the Farm Supply store he stopped in the lot to make more notes. "I'll need all that fire wood, but some of the large wood fired furnaces are built to run on electricity to flow the heat and I can't count on electricity. And I don't like the cost of those kinds of heaters.

Inside, he passed through the tool section and saw a wire feed welder on sale. He had learned to weld while a Fire Fighter and a tool like that would be necessary in the building stage of things.

Someone had left a flat cart in the isle so he loaded the welder onto it. As he cruised the store looking for ideas he found the galvanized garbage cans. There were ten 50 gallon cans and he loaded them next to the welder. Later, in the garden section he looked at grow lights. He wasn't satisfied with their size as he was planning on four foot by eight foot raised bed gardens, on rollers. He made a note of the email address on the lights so he could contact them that night."

Bill walked to the building materials center and explained what he needed for insulation and wall board.

The clerk entered the dimensions into his computer and had the estimate in a minute. "Take this to the checkout and after you pay for it they will give you directions on how to pick it up." Bill thanked him and said he would let him know when and if he needed to start.

"What are you going to do with all them garbage cans, Sir?"

The question stopped Bill for a moment. "Oh, I guess I'll use them like a lot of other people do and throw away most of the things I buy." He turned away before another question could be asked and made up his first important rule; multiple purchases must be made at multiple places to keep from arousing undue suspicion! Except for the insulation and wallboard he paid for his purchases and headed toward an electrician's shop he knew of.

Chapter 6
A Hands On Approach

Driving back to the farm the enormity of the project was just beginning to settle in on him. The electrician wanted a blue print for anything done and Bill wasn't in the mood to hire an architect. It took a little talking, but the electrician said he would establish a load center in the barn and additional wiring could be done after an architect had been contracted to design a proper plan. Once the load center is in, Bill thought, a licensed handy man can complete what little else needs to be done.

As he pulled into the farm he saw Miriam in her garden. She looked up, recognized Bill's pickup, and continued her work. Bill smiled and nodded as he drove past the house to the barn. There will be about a million trips, he thought; I hope she will warm up to me fast.

He unloaded the cans, the welder and what felt like a ton of odds and ends of things. Seeing Miriam reminded him that Moses would know some young men who could help convert the barn into a green house and living quarters.

It wasn't quite lunch time when he finished and decided to run up to the Yocum farm.

It was a quick drive up the hill where Moses was outside the barn working on his buggy. He set his tools aside when he saw the truck pull in.

"So William, you have a sturdy looking truck too."

"Yes, I have. In fact, I have what feels like a fleet of vehicles each time my insurance bill comes in."

"We insure nothing more than what the bank requires us to. A sturdy truck like this could be a blessing to many."

"Yes," said Bill. "And I offer myself and my truck if I can be of help to you."

"Thank you," replied Moses. "Can I be of service to you at this time?"

Bill was surprised by the offer even though he knew he needed help. He pulled the insulation estimate from his pocket and showed it to Moses. They talked about it and the possibility of putting a concrete floor and heating in the barn.

"The problem with you English is…" began Moses.

"English?" asked Bill.

"Pardon me. The people of our faith speak a type of Germanic Language and the men only speak English to communicate with our English speaking neighbors. Hence, you are known as English."

Bill just nodded as he felt he was learning about his neighbors and knew it was a privilege to be trusted by them.

"As I was saying; the problem with you English is that you think we Amish have no knowledge or skills because of the difference in our education."

"We are schooled till pubescence but have highly refined skills in things spiritual and in farm operation. Now, take this estimate from the Farm Supply building center. We buy a lot there and this is not the low price that is offered to us. The electrician is someone familiar to us as he removes the load centers from our homes. We believe electricity is not in our best interests, so he frees us from it.

"Now, about this idea of a concrete floor, we have schooled ourselves in reinforced concrete foundations and a floor shouldn't be difficult to build. You were right to dismiss the newer wood furnaces as they operate on electricity. We are not unfamiliar with large mass fire places which heat up fast and radiate for hours. There is much for us to talk about."

"I have a problem with labor too, Moses. I haven't had time yet to hire anyone and would be interested in hiring Amish labor."

"A wise idea, William. We are familiar with all aspects of farming; though not the experimental type of farming you are planning. But, we will adapt. I have two young men in mind. They are finished with the summer planting and will have a few weeks before cultivation and harvest.

"How much money should I offer them, Moses, and when will they wish to be paid?"

"It is our custom to offer labor for free, in the name of God. I believe your cause is noble and just."

"But, there must be things they need money for. Maybe I could offer gifts or cash from time to time."

"William; I am the Bishop and I cannot permit anything into our community that would lead to sin. I will tell you if money or gifts will be appropriate. Do you understand?"

"Yes," said Bill, a little chagrined. Moses could convey more with a stern look or tone of voice than anyone Bill had ever known. I wonder what kind of Firefighter he would have been, he thought.

Moses picked up his wooden tool box and put it in his buggy. "I do not carry a timepiece, but it is now lunch time. Go eat and fuel the pickup. We will go to meet the men I told you about. Amos has a piece of equipment that he wishes to lend to Michael and a pickup will be needed. After that we will go to the Farm Supply Store to get better estimates. Bring your checkbook."

Bill agreed and got into his pickup. There was something about the way Moses used the term "checkbook" that made Bill realize his hands would make money available long before he would actually build anything with them.

Bill drove back into Augusta and stopped at the Quick-Stop. He fueled the truck and checked the oil and tire pressure as he wasn't sure what Moses had in mind. He went in to pay and decided to have his lunch too. He found himself wondering how much longer he would be able to go anywhere and buy what he needed. Back in the truck, he drove to a small park and ate.

A feeling of melancholy came over him again as he thought about the possibility of the lake blowing its top and the incredible loss of life everywhere. He forced himself to finish his sandwich and fruit and walked to the trash barrel with the waste.

He saved half the water bottle in case the equipment to be moved turned out to be a bigger job than he thought. He got back in the truck and drove out to Amish Country.

Moses was waiting by the buggy, with his arms folded when Bill pulled up. He opened the door and got in.

"Your timepiece is almost as good as my instincts, William."

"Thank you," said Bill, not bothering to mention he'd forgotten to wear his watch that day. "Where to?"

"Out the driveway and to the North. First driveway to the west."

It was a short distance even if one walked it. They pulled into a small farm and up to a traditional looking Amish house; no paint or sign of electricity. A tall lanky man walked out and Moses opened his door and stepped out.

"It's on the north side of the barn, William," said Moses and proceeded to talk to the farmer. Bill pulled around the drive and backed up to the north side of the barn. He stepped out, pulled the seat back forward and fished out a worn pair of leather gloves. He wasn't worried about anyone knowing his hands weren't as calloused as the two farmers, but he wasn't about to apologize for being a little more safety-conscious than most other men.

The equipment to be moved was a home-made drag for keeping a driveway level. It obviously couldn't be dragged to another farm, but looked easy enough to lift into the pickup. Moses walked up.

"William, this is Amos. Amos, you pick up that end and slide it into the bed. William, you take that end." And, leaving no time to question his authority he gave a quick one, two, three, and the men picked up the drag and slid it into the pickup bed.

Amos bounded over the side and sat on the drag as if he thought it would fall out. Bill shook his head and moved to the cab with Moses.

"Where to next?" he asked as they started down the driveway.

"Back to the south and then east into the driveway we passed to get here."

Bill drove back to the farm that bordered his own, but was up on the flats rather than in the small valley he was beginning to like best. This farm was almost a carbon-copy of the others and a young Amish man strode out as they pulled in. Moses stepped out when Bill stopped.

"Amos will show you where to put the drag," he said.

Bill looked back though the window and Amos pointed to a place between the barn and another out building. Bill backed up to the place and Amos was out in a flash. They dropped the end gate and Amos pulled the drag to the edge. The two men pulled it out and put it down with a thud. Amos turned toward the bed and Bill got in the cab and pulled down to where Moses was standing with the other man. He got in the cab and motioned back to where they picked up Amos. They drove over to leave Amos at his farm.

"That was Michael," said Moses.

"Great," thought Bill. "Aside from Moses, no one around here has a last name, or talks."

"I told them about your experiment in growing food in less than ideal conditions and they said they would help."

"Thank you," said Bill as he pulled into Amos's driveway. Amos bounded out of the truck's bed and strode toward the barn without looking back.

Taking that for a "good-bye," Bill turned around and Moses gestured back to Bill's new farm.

Miriam was washing the outsides of her windows as they pulled in. The thought of a friendly face, albeit quiet one, made him smile.

"Let's check your measurements before we go to town, William." They opened the barn and Moses re-measured.

"I prefer metric to SAE," he muttered. "I think you should consider insulating the whole building even if you don't intend to use it all," he added.

"All right," replied Bill. "I'd like to talk about how I can heat this large building too. I would like to have hot water heat in the concrete floor and the large-mass fire place to radiate additional heat. I think that will give me an even heat source no matter what the weather. I've drawn up something a little like what I have in mind. A belt driven off an electric motor would move the hot water. And if we put an additional pipe inside the chimney beside the flue we could heat additional air which could be driven into the interior when the temperature dropped below zero Fahrenheit. If the electricity failed, the water and air pump could easily be turned by a hand crank."

Moses looked intently at the sketch and Bill could tell he was interested.

"Our homes are drafty in the winter time William and I have often wished for an idea to keep the floors warmer. I've never thought of this. If you fired your stove and then spent some time on the hand pump you could have a constant source of heat day and night. I like this. Let's go to town and price out what we need."

As they pulled out of the drive, ideas flowed from both men, like water.

By the time they reached town they'd decided to "floor" only three quarters of the barn or eight-tenths and leave a dirt floor for a couple of animals so there could be some fertilizer for the raised bed gardens. Bill hadn't planned on any animals, but if Moses wanted some he would play along. Besides, hay for the animals will help insulate the walls when it got desperately cold, which he was afraid it would be when the sun couldn't get through the volcanic ash to heat the earth.

As they drove into the parking lot, Moses said he had a lot of used brass pipe from homes the Amish had razed and he would sell it cheap.

"Today, we will order the insulation, some more brass pipe and elbows, and the rebar to strengthen the floor. We will order ready mixed concrete trucked in when the time is right.

Once inside the store Bill was impressed with how well Moses made his way around. The clerks seemed to know him and there was no doubt they respected him. In less than an hour the estimates for the insulation and floor were completed.

Moses asked for delivery to the fire number of Bill's farm without telling them it wasn't his own. Bill didn't recognize the clerk so he said, "Oh, if you have ten fifty gallon galvanized garbage cans, put those on the truck too." The clerk made a note and Bill was glad for no questions. Moses didn't seem to notice as he was all ready looking at hand-pumps. They ordered what they thought they would need and went to the check out counter.

There was a time a total like this one would have dropped Bill on the spot, but now he was caught up in his project. He was going to save his family, come hell or high water.

It was late in the afternoon when Bill brought Moses back to his farm. Moses got out immediately as both of them had the feeling they had made and talked out every idea they could think of. Moses looked back into the truck.

"Ten more fifty-gallon garbage cans, William?"

Bill laughed out loud. "I'll try to explain that to you some other time, Moses." The old man turned and walked toward his home.

"The boys will be there in the morning to unload and get started," he called back. "They'll need those new gloves you bought, too."

Bill laughed out loud again. He didn't think Moses had seen him pick up a small case of gloves.

Chapter 7
A Good Start

Bill rose early, packed a lunch and headed for the farm. As he pulled in he noticed smoke from the chimney and hoped Miriam was making coffee. He pulled up to the barn just as a horse and buggy rolled up. Amos was driving with Moses in front. When they had stopped, Michael jumped out of the back. Amos then turned the horse to the fence line along the road and tied it there so it could get a little more used to the sight and sound of motor vehicles.

Moses and Michael went into the barn with the sketches and estimates while Bill waited outside. He was determined to converse with the Amish Men and this seemed to be a good chance to speak with Amos as he walked back to the barn.

"That's a nice horse, Amos. It looks young and strong."

"It lost a ball going over a fence." He replied as he strode past Bill into the barn.

Bill stood there for a moment. Well, it was a start, he thought. Maybe I should let them decide what to talk about.

Then he turned and walked into the barn. The two young men were looking at the sketches while Moses finished his conversations with them. He reshuffled the papers when Bill walked up.

"William, you have asked for my help in this project of yours; a plan to grow plants inside with minimal light and heat. So, here is what I propose.

We'll convert eight-tenths of the barn to a concrete floor leaving the back two-tenths for a few feed animals which will provide manure for compost. Two cows should do."

"Or a small herd of goats. Manure for the plant beds and meat and milk to sell for a profit," added Michael.

It was the first time Michael had spoken. His voice was quiet and confident. Bill liked him immediately.

"Or a small herd of goats," agreed Moses. "Now, if you want to heat with a large-mass fireplace we should put that in the middle of this part of the building. Then you can set your so called grow lights is such a way the raised beds can be rolled around them for periods of night and day. The heated floor and the large-mass fireplace will also keep the hand pump from freezing up and you will have all the water you need. You know, William, we Amish don't farm this way. Someday you will have to explain this experiment of yours."

"I'll do that," replied Bill. "Have you checked into the brass pipe you were telling me about?"

"I know where it is and we can go get it right now. We will be back by lunch time. I told Miriam to prepare lunch with coffee for us."

Bill turned to Amos and Michael. "If the truck comes from the Farm Store, can you get it unloaded and start sorting it? Both men nodded. Great, thought Bill, we are up to at least a sentence a day. He turned and walked out to the pickup with Moses.

It was going to be a warm day, but the morning was still cool enough for Miriam to be working in her garden. Bill stopped at the pickup to watch her. She was chopping weeds and raking so the garden would be productive. He was pleased to see how graceful she looked at her work.

"What are your thoughts, William?"

Bill had decided to always be honest with Moses. "How could Ezra turn to strong drink with such a good woman to love him?"

"Love isn't always part of a good marriage," William, "and there are those among us who wonder how a man could die without his good wife coming to rescue him. Still, it will be hard on her to be so alone from now on."

Bill clenched his jaw and got in behind the wheel.

"Moses?"

Taking that as his invitation to get in, the old man opened the door and slowly let himself in.

"When I bought the farm, you said you would tell the elders the farm and the widow would be well cared for. Is she being shunned?"

"That is a harsh word, William, even for us. Let us just say she will be alone for a while."

"Moses, I want you to give her permission to speak with me. And I want to provide for her when she does things for us."

"Done," said the old man as he fished a note from the top of his bib overhauls. He handed it to Bill who opened it; salt, pepper, sugar, silverware for four people, fabric to make napkins, a table cloth and a basket to carry meals to the barn. The list was so short and simple he would have been saddened by it if he weren't elated by the prospect of being able to stop and talk to her.

He started the truck and followed the directions Moses gave as he drove. The Amish farms in this area were all quite small since they were worked with horses, not tractors or any motorized equipment. They pulled into the third farm past that of Amos and Moses directed him to stop by one of the outbuildings.

"I will go and tell them we are here," said Moses.

"I don't know why," thought Bill. This area is so flat and the farms so close together I couldn't drive anywhere without being seen. Bill waited in the truck and in a few minutes Moses returned with a man who looked older than he.

Moses leaned in the window and handed Bill a folded piece of paper. "We will load all the brass and use what we need. You'll return the rest when we are finished and you will give me this much cash."

Bill nodded, put the note in his pocket and got out. The brass pipe was neatly stacked in a small building. It had been properly cut with no jagged ends or bent pieces.

As he expected there were no introductions and the loading was done with no conversation.

47

When finished, Bill wanted to say thank you or good bye, but the man had already turned his back and was on his way to his house.

Well, thought Bill, there must not be a lot of arguments around here. He eased the truck out the driveway and out onto the road. In a matter of minutes they were back at his farm.

Amos and Michael came out of the barn when they pulled up. They had been using some old rakes they had found in the garden to smooth the dirt floor. They certainly were men who didn't like being idle.

The pipes were unloaded and put in the back of the barn so as not to be in the way when the foundation for the large-mass fire place was dug.

Bill looked at Moses and said; "I'm heading into town to check on an End Loader to dig the foundation hole, and then get the things Miriam needs."

Moses nodded.

Bill turned and got into the truck. He looked for Miriam as he left, but she was inside by then. It didn't take long to get into Augusta and he decided to stop at a Second-Hand Store he knew of.

It was a good idea because he found a couple of card table and chair sets and a larger table which came with eight chairs. The store was a gold mine of used things and had a section of new items bought from Odd-Lot Auctions, damaged merchandise and returns. By the time he left he had two twelve place settings of silverware and dishes. "We might break or lose something," he thought. "And, it won't hurt to have ready made table cloths and stuff too."

Bill had gone through the house wares section and took anything that was brightly colored. He'd seen the inside of Miriam's house and thought it could use a little brightening up. There was an isle of paper products and he over-bought there too so the used items could be burned in the cook stove to save time doing dishes. There were only two picnic baskets and to eliminate the problems that come with making the wrong choice, he took both. The clerks really seemed to appreciate him stopping by, he thought.

At the grocery store he got the salt, pepper, sugar, a three pound can of specialty coffee, some plastic forks and what ever else caught his eye. He put the groceries in the cab because the bed seemed a little full. It didn't dawn on him that he had left with a list of five items and one errand to run, which he'd forgotten, until he pulled into the driveway with a loaded truck.

He took the four bags of groceries and went to the back door. Miriam met him on the porch with a bewildered look on her face. As he looked at those green eyes he decided not to explain. Instead he asked if he could leave some of the other things on the porch. Four trips later he had all the paper goods and the table linens on the porch. He chose a brightly colored combination of paper linens, plates and cups and told Miriam he would have the table ready when she brought out the lunch.

"Yes," she said, and another great conversation was started.

Chapter 8
The Real Work Begins

Bill set up the larger table in the shade of a beautiful Oak tree. He deliberately chose the brightest, most contrasting colors of paper plates, napkins and tablecloth. Miriam arrived almost immediately with vegetarian type sandwiches on home-made bread. She poured the coffee and despite the place Bill had set for her, she hurried back to the house.

He called the three Amish men and could hear them wash up at the pump in the barn. They came out to the table and seemed hesitant to sit down after seeing all the colorful things on it. Bill sat down first and the three men followed in stunned silence. They looked long and hard at the colors.

"Well," thought Bill, "I wonder who will go blind first."

He started to eat his sandwich and the others followed. It was another quiet time that Bill tried to liven up with remarks about how good the food was and how nice the table looked.

After a few affirming grunts they "wolfed" down the food and went back to work.

It was a good idea as the truck from the Farm Supply pulled in when they were getting to the barn. Bill pulled the four corners of the table cloth together and lifted it over his shoulder. He hurried toward the house to burn it all in the stove. The three men looked back at the now empty table as if something strange had just come and gone from it.

It didn't take the driver long to off-load the small fork truck he carried on the back of the trailer. He fired it up and began unloading pallets full of insulation, sheet rock, chimney blocks and liners, concrete, a cement mixer driven by a small gasoline engine and everything Moses and Bill had thought they would need to complete the interior of the barn.

The three Amish men guided the pallets to what they hoped would be the best placement. When the trailer was empty and the sorting begun, Bill called the driver aside and asked him if he knew anyone with an end loader who could dig a foundation hole for the large-mass fireplace.

The driver said he had one and did some sub-contracting with it. A price was agreed upon and the hole was to be dug the next day. Since the fireplace would be inside and not have to suffer the extreme cold temperatures an outside unit would, the hole wouldn't have to be deep. The driver said he would bring some crushed rock for the foundation and sand to mix the concrete.

Bill went into the barn to help finish sorting out tools and material. Then three of them started nailing up the studs and Bill stapled insulation between them.

The wiring Bill had planned could be added as "on-wall" if they got around to where the breaker panel was to be added before the Electrician arrived.

The afternoon flew by with a lot of the walls insulated. When the shadows grew long, Moses announced it was milking time. Amos and Michael immediately put their tools away and began to wash up. Despite a days work they didn't seem to mind going home to do a lot more.

"We'll be back in the morning William, after milking."

"O.K.," said Bill. "I'm going to stay on a while and check things out. See you in the morning."

As the Amish men left, Bill unloaded the rest of the tables and chairs from his pickup. As he was doing so, he was surprised by the arrival of the Electrician. He walked out to the Electrician's truck and noticed scrap wiring and a used circuit box in the back.

"Hello, Mr. Thomas, I finished early and thought I would stop out with some of the used stuff we talked about."

"I see that. Let's off-load this stuff and I will show you what I want and where to start.

He grabbed what he could carry and the Electrician carried the breaker box. They dropped the equipment inside by the passage way. Bill explained that he wanted only two outlets by the load center; one 220 volts and the other 110 volts. He would order more later after he had time to contact an architect to draw up his other ideas. Of course, he had no plans to be drawn up, but he wasn't going to tell him that. Anything he would need in the future could be done alone.

"If all you want is the breaker box and two outlets, I can do that now. But, the access from the road will have to be done next week. I can get a trenching machine in, but we will have to wait till the Electric Cooperative runs the wire from the road to the box. You know you have bought land on the only underground feed in this end of the county."

The Electrician went on to tell Bill about the improvements that had been made in this area. Apparently the local Dam had just been remodeled and since it was such a small one it was made into a "Peaking Plant." The amount of water behind it wasn't enough to generate electricity twenty four hours a day. The gates were opened from six a.m. to nine a.m. and then closed until enough water built up and they were opened again from six p.m. until nine p.m. These were the peak use periods for the area.

"You're lucky, Mr. Thomas, if all other electrical generating facilities failed, this one would perform during peak times forever. It's totally computer operated and as long as there are no earthquakes to break the feeder line there is no way to lose your source."

"That's interesting," said Bill. He liked the possibility of having some "juice" for his lights he wouldn't have to generate himself.

"Let's install the breaker box. This way we will be done when the cooperative digs the trench and lays the wire. All they have to do then is connect it and go."

"Good idea. I will be finished in an half an hour."

He was true to his word and on his way. Bill finished closing up. He planned to order the grow lamps over the internet that night.

After checking in with Moses in the morning, he would make a sweep around the county to buy a number of deep service twelve volt batteries, two high output truck alternators, some DC to AC inverters and anything else he thought would help him generate electricity for his lights. The possibility of two separate three hour periods of AC electricity wouldn't keep his lights burning or batteries charged long enough to grow food for his family to eat for over a year. Or for as long as it would take for the air to clear and warm up.

He had accomplished a lot in the last few days and suddenly felt very tired. As he passed the house on his way out, he notice a lighted lamp.

"I wonder if Miriam is a reader?" he thought. "I've been too busy to open a book for a couple weeks now."

Back at home, he parked the truck and walked in through the back porch. Becky was upstairs finishing Kiia's bath.

"Dad?" She called.

"Yah, Hon," He returned her call. Sorry I'm so late tonight. I'll be up in a minute. Did you leave me anything for supper?"

"In the fridge. Young man if you don't settle down I'll pull the plug and you won't be able to play in the water when Grandpa comes up."

Bill pulled out the cold pizza and a Pepsi.

"Be up in a minute, Kiia," He called out. He sat down and had his supper before going up to play with his grandson. Once upstairs, he took a towel out of the linen closet and went into the bathroom. Kiia was more than ready to play.

"Becky," Bill asked, "I'd like to go on the internet to look for some grow lights tonight if you're not too busy. I'd like to have some for indoor plants this winter. Can you look for a source?"

"Sure, Dad, are you thinking about becoming a farmer as well as a delivery truck driver too?"

"In a small way," he laughed.

He watched Kiia play in the water for a while and then suggested a good rinse before drying and checking out some favorite books. Being read to was a favorite activity for Kiia and he was easily convinced. Especially when Grandpa did the reading.

They made their way down the hall and Bill tucked him in. The book shelf was right next to the bed and Bill knew all the right ones to pull out. They laughed and talked for a few minutes and then started to read. The boy must have been tired as it didn't take long for him to drift off. Bill was glad to have pleased his grandson so easily and quietly turned off his light to go downstairs.

"You've been late twice this week, Dad. Are you sure you aren't overdoing it just a little?"

"Nah," he replied. "I do a lot of driving around to stores asking for delivery business, and that's not hard. What little I've done has been mostly to the Amish farms and they always do the unloading. I've really started to like them a lot."

"I've heard they can be nice once you get to know them…O.K. here are the websites for grow lights. You can look at them while I check the laundry."

"Thanks Becky."

"Oh great," he muttered, "something else to plan for.

Clean cloths for seven people for more than a year." He quickly penned a note in the little book he now carried.

Chapter 9
Heating up

Bill started out for the farm early again. He had his checkbook to pay for the fireplace foundation hole and hoped the driver could finish the excavation in one day. He and the others could work on the insulation and wall board until the sand and gravel that made up the foundation fill was thrown in and watered down till it was firm enough to be built on.

He began to feel a little anxiety about the task he had set out to accomplish. He'd never attempted a building project like this before and, worse yet, never had a crew he couldn't talk too. "Well," he thought, "at least it's only a life and death situation and not a major fire!"

He slowed to turn into the drive and looked for Miriam as he knew he would forever. She was in the back with some rugs over the clothes line. She was beating them with a stick to clean the dust off them. "Make a note," he thought, "don't spend a lot of money on a vacuum cleaner.

There may not be any electricity for one."

He parked beside the barn and began to open it up. The Amish wouldn't be down for another hour so he took the time to check the supplies he was keeping out side. It wasn't the time of year to see any dew and everything was still there. He spent a few minutes moving the insulation around the interior of the barn until he heard a tired old truck engine pull up.

The excavator pulled up in an overloaded old dump truck with a Bobcat on a trailer. He jumped out of the truck and started ramping the trailer to get the earthmover off loaded. Bill came out as he finished removing the come-alongs that held the mover to the trailer.

"The Amish aren't here yet," said Bill.

"No matter. I done a lot of work for old Moses and he told me what he wants. I just dig a hole bout the size these folks want and they make any adjustments to what they think is best. I'll make it bout 5 meters square and a meter deep, drop the hole-gravel just outside the door and when you folks are done you can barrow in what you need later. O.K?"

"O.K," said Bill, wishing he had spent a little more time with the metric system.

The driver fired up the Bob and backed it off the trailer. He stopped by Bill, "You paying or him?" Bill showed him his checkbook and waved him in with it.

"Good!"

He backed into the barn about ten feet past where the hole was to be and began removing sand. He had made two passes across the width of the hole and was down a foot when Amos drove up with Moses and Michael.

They tethered the wagon pulled by a different horse by the road in such a way it would have to be close to the moving bobcat too. It was an older horse and didn't seem to be phased by vehicle traffic. Bill resisted the temptation to comment on the horse and walked quietly into the barn with Amos.

Michael had his tool belt on and was selecting the next stud. Moses watched the bob make a couple passes, nodded to the driver, and turned to get a tool belt with Amos. The four men went to work.

Bill had decided to insulate and wall the whole barn so that if he decided to keep animals during the cataclysm they would have a comfortable place to survive too. The wall to separate the living quarters from the animals would be built above the floor. The concrete would be poured later and wall and floor were planned to be stronger than needed.

The Amish men used a small rough cut hand saw rather than the table saw Bill had bought. He had forgotten their independence from electricity and they used the hand saw so well it didn't seem to waste any time. Moses helped the younger men until they had gotten so far ahead of Bill he could come back to help staple up insulation.

When the driver stopped the bob, they all stopped. Moses approved the dimensions of the hole and Michael went up to the house for a bucket and water glasses. When he returned he had a sweet cake that Miriam had baked for them.

Amos filled the bucket at the pump and brought it to the table. The five of them quickly finished off the cake and drained the entire bucket of water.

Bill, the driver and Moses made small talk about the foundation hole and how well it would support the large-mass fireplace. Michael and Amos remained silent.

The foundation boards and reinforcing bars would have to be built later so the driver agreed to dump the gravel from the truck into the middle of the hole so he could load the Bob and go.

When he had finished, the others put the insulating aside and worked on the foundation. The wooden frame was built quickly and the gravel leveled. A few wheel barrows of sand were smoothed over the gravel and it was time for lunch. Bill went up to the house.

He was about to knock when Miriam came to the screen door. She nodded in a way that told Bill to come in. He opened the door and went to pick up the paper table cloth and napkins.

"William?" came a quiet voice. "What became of the cloth I was to sew into table linens? I can't find it in what you brought."

Bill realized immediately she wasn't prepared for his sense of humor. He apologized and said the paper products were for another use.

"I'll go into town after lunch for the fabric."

"Just plain white fabric. And a spool of white thread. I have a needle left to sew with," and she gestured toward what Bill considered an antique treadle sewing machine.

"You know, it might be easier to get what you want if you were to ride in with me," he asked.

"I can't," she looked away. "I can't get away. I'll get the lunch."
She turned and hurried into the kitchen.

"Smooth move, Bill," he thought as he grabbed some paper products and hurried to the table he had set up outside the barn. The men were waiting when he finished. Amos had the water bucket filled and Michael had the water glasses. Moses looked at the table.

"Perhaps Miriam should set the table in the future?"

"Perhaps you'd like to roll some hose, Firefighter!" snapped Bill. Then realizing how sad that remark made him look, he apologized.

"I'll go get the fabric after lunch," he promised.

He stepped back as Miriam brought the lunch. She set the table, placed a short note under his plate and left for the house. The men sat down and Moses led the prayer. Bill picked up the note and looked at it. Her penmanship was business-like, in a feminine way. "Some white material for a tablecloth and napkins, Please, William." He put it in his shirt pocket knowing he would keep it with the first one.

The meal passed quickly and the prayers were heartfelt. The men made small talk on the way back into the barn. The studding dividing the barn into one large and one small room was completed and half the insulation was up. They would be ready for the wall board by late afternoon. Bill had bought the thicker type wall board with moisture barrier built in. He was aware that temperature control and condensation would be difficult to predict so a better grade was necessary.

The men talked about fasteners and material for a few more minutes and then Bill got into the pickup and headed for town.

He spent a few minutes feeling guilty for snapping at Moses, but it didn't take long for the problems involved with "saving the human race" to take over. On the earlier trip he had seen something at the second hand store and he headed there first.

Once inside the store the grins from the clerks reinforced his original thought about shopping at several different locations. He really didn't want anyone guessing what he was doing. He passed several shelves of old glass canning jars and lids and decided new ones wouldn't cost anymore, so he decided to mail order what he would need. Back in the corner was what he wanted to look at.

It was a hand cranked washing machine. By the look of it someone had ordered it new with the idea of keeping it to sell later as an antique. He opened the lid and knew he was right. It hadn't been used at all.

"Man," he thought, "if I could depend on electricity three to six hours a day I would just order a new Maytag." Then he chuckled, "this is a new Maytag, just a little bit older!"

"It's a nice old piece, isn't it?" asked the clerk.

"Yes, my grandma had one. I remember seeing it in the corner of her basement," he lied.

"It's been sitting here for a long time, and I need the space."

"Well," said Bill, "Make me a good deal and we can talk."

She looked at a card she was carrying and quoted a price. It was low enough compared to buying a new electric one so Bill countered with a lower price, just to do so. He didn't have the floor in the barn yet and didn't want to buy things he couldn't store.

She agreed to the price and when Bill asked if she would store it for a few weeks if he bought it, she agreed again. It was a small enough decision to make and despite it being too early to buy a washing machine he felt good about doing it.

He paid and left the store to enter the hardware store. There he bought matching clothes dryer; three rolls of clothesline and all the pincher clothes pins they had. He crossed back to the pickup and threw the bag into the cab.

"How about that? He thought. "My first completed solution since buying the farm. Clean clothes for everyone."

He knew of a fabric store in nearby Eau Claire and headed there. Inside he looked around and wished at least one of his women had been a seamstress so he would know what to look for. A clerk rescued him and showed him fabric suitable for a table cloth. He chose what he thought was a better than average grade and asked to have it cut. He had to describe the table sizes and the fact there would be place mats and napkins also. The clerk tried to sell him some contrasting colors, but Bill remembered white was the color of choice right now. Some white thread, a very nice set of matching scissors and a little more fabric than the clerk recommended and he was back to the truck. The pair of scissors had gold plated handles and brightly plated blades. They were nestled in red velvet and in a gift box. They were beautiful to look at and had a heavy, well balanced feel. He was sure they were of high quality and were too beautiful for an Amish man to consider buying for his wife. He also guessed they were more ornate than Miriam would ask her husband to bring home for her. He had thrown them in his cart with no more thought than; "I bet she'd like these."

On the way back he was so busy thinking about how much he was spending, he wasn't aware he had bought his first gift for Miriam.

He knocked on her door and reviewed what he had in the bag from the fabric store. When she came to the door he handed the bag to her.

"I wasn't sure how much to get, so if there is too much you can save the extra." Then, realizing he had bought her a gift, he added, "if there is something there you didn't expect, uh, just accept it and we can talk about it later." He knew he was turning red and when she started to blush too he turned and strode quickly to the barn.

In the barn the Amish had completed the studding and now there were two rooms. One room took up more than three quarters of the area and the back portion would easily house two or three cows with enough hay for at least two years.

"I want to insulate the outside walls of the animal area too," said Bill. "I know the animals can endure colder temperatures than we can, but I may need to go back and forth to the animals and I don't want a big temperature drop for my plants."

"I understand," replied Moses. "You ordered enough insulation for the entire barn, both walls and ceiling."

"You will note we have left room for a door between the rooms."

"Good. I want sheet rock on all walls and the ceilings in the back room and this big one. I don't want the animals to damage or try to eat the insulation."

"William, I think we should tape the joints to seal them and then cover the sheet rock with a waterproof primer."

"So do I. Moses."

"But don't spend a lot of time trying to feather or smooth the joints. I'm not building an expensive house here."

"Understood. I would say we will have all the sheetrock roughed in by the day after tomorrow and we will need an additional two days for a rough tape and seal. But, I think we must get the brass pipe soldered together by next week so we can complete our mid summer cultivation."

"Moses, I've been thinking about that small motorized cement mixer we bought. It will do for the large mass fireplace we will build, but I want to get the floor cement trucked in from a professional facility."

"That would be wise as it all must be down before any of it starts to dry. And now, my stomach tells me it is lunch time. I'm sure Miriam has put the lunch on the table under the oak tree."

Bill turned and quickly strode out of the barn, hoping to see her, but she had already gone back to the house. The table was set with paper products as there wasn't time for her to do any sewing yet. Bill was impressed at how much better things looked when a woman had the chance to match things up. The sandwiches and apple juice were already there and only the coffee was yet to come.

He reentered the barn to wait his turn at the pump. The only bar of soap he had bought was in hard service and would be gone before long.

"I'll get more soap tomorrow, and more towels." He said.

"Bring these towels to the table," said Moses. "Miriam will launder them for us."

Bill rushed through his hand washing and went out to the table. The men took what had now become their customary seats and Bill frowned when he saw the coffee was already poured and Miriam had returned to the house.

"Patience, William. Let us now pray."

Chapter 10
Progress Noted

Moses had been right in the amount of time he said it would take to finish the insulation and sheet rock. The men had grown accustomed to working with each other and anticipated each others needs for holding things, having the right fasteners and tools and generally helping each other get things done.

In less than two weeks the walls were up and the brass pipes were soldered together for the in-floor heating system. They had just test filled the pipes and had added some pressure from an old air pump to check for leaks when Bill stumbled over one of the marker stakes and fell. As he twisted himself to avoid falling on the pipes he landed on his left hand and arm.

As is the case in many accidents a person's eyes see stars and their mouth says things they wouldn't normally say, but Bill he remembered his good companions. Amos was closest to him and pulled him to his feet before he could roll onto any of the pipes.

"Take him outside into the sun light," came an authoritative voice that Bill recognized as Michael's.

Amos pushed and guided Bill through the brass pipes on the floor so as not to damage the work they had just completed. They walked to the table under the oak and Bill sat down. Michael knelt down on one knee, took Bill's left hand in his and as he watched it and Bill's eyes, he gently moved it around.

"I perceive there are no broken bones, William, but most assuredly you have a strain if not a sprain of the wrist. Hold your arm and wrist steady and I will go to the buggy for some medicinal herbs to make a poultice." He turned and strode quickly to the buggy.

"Michael is our healer," said Moses with obvious pride. "He is the youngest we have ever had," and then went on to tell about how quickly he had learned.

In a minute, Michael was back with an old worn leather case. He set it down to open it and revealed what looked like a primitive First Aid Kit. It had several small baby food jars filled with what looked like crushed, dried leaves. Michael opened three of them and shook a measured amount of each onto an oblong sewn bandage. He added a little water, folded it over and wrapped it around Bill's wrist.

"This poultice will draw the swelling out of the injured tissue and there is a little medication to ease the pain also. The bandage will help hold the wrist straight and you shouldn't cause any further injury. If it dries out a little before bed tonight just dampen it; and again in the morning. I am going to give you another poultice, dry, to use tomorrow night after this bandage. Keep it damp for the next day. Do no more work with this arm for at least three days and then stop using the poultice.

Do you understand?"

"Yes. Can I take an occasional aspirin too?"

"You may take whatever the English take in a case like this. Just don't take too much."

"So," boomed Moses. No great harm has been done and we must now get about our farming for a week or so. We will return when the time is right and if the concrete floor has cured we will begin building the large mass fire place."

They agreed and while Michael closed his kit, Amos closed up the barn. The pipes had held pressure without leaking so there was no more to be done till the concrete trucks started coming tomorrow. Bill watched as the three Amish Men folded themselves into their little buggy and then eased himself into his pickup. As he passed Miriam's house he wanted to stop and spend the evening with her, relaxing away the day's events. But, it wasn't time for such familiarities and he slowly turned for home.

He wasn't sure how to explain the wrist bandage and was relieved to find a note on the kitchen table stating tonight was cribbage night and Becky and Kiia would be sleeping over at a friend's house.

Bill chuckled, thinking about how he had taught his kids and their friends how to play his favorite card game and now they were the ones who made the time to play it. He made a mental note to stop for several decks of cards and a couple more cribbage boards to keep at the barn. If they had to live there for a long time he was going to make time to shuffle some cards.

He took some leftovers from the fridge, heated them and ate while listening to Kottke on acoustic guitar. "That reminds me," He thought, "I'd better find a low volt-low amp sound system or learn how to play acoustic myself."

Suddenly, the long day caught up with him. Almost on cue, his left wrist began to throb so he cleaned up quickly, located his bottle of low grade aspirin and swallowed two of them. He dampened the poultice on his wrist, grabbed the small boom box and headed up the stairs. Determined not to allow the day's worries rob him of a good night's sleep he washed up, restarted the CD and by the time "lost love and Pamela Brown" were sung about, he was asleep.

There are some nights when everything favors the kind of sleep a person would like every night. This was one of them. The temperature was in the low Seventies and a gentle breeze brought fresh air through the screened window. Bill slept deeply knowing his plans were made and being executed as best they could be.

He awoke the next morning before the alarm could spoil his sleep, rolled out and stripped the bed as he did when he was a young fire fighter. It only took a few folds and the bedding was placed over the quilt rack to be remade that night. He knew it didn't make sense to strip the bed each morning, but he enjoyed being a fire fighter so much he kept every bit of training he could. He showered and dressed quickly almost expecting an alarm to go off when he was the most unprepared.

In the kitchen he fried up a couple eggs, spilled them into a bowl of legumes and added some salsa. He'd taken a lot of ribbing in the station kitchen about liking the high protein-high fiber of the legumes with his eggs, but the high energy breakfast served him well when the fires kept him busy all day.

He threw some yogurt and sandwich fixings into his cooler, refilled his water bottle and headed for the garage. Today he would drive the 34 Coupe again since there was no need to bring tools or pick up anything from the lumber yard. Selling the camper had brought in enough money to complete the interior of the barn and he loved that old Ford too much to part with it unless it was absolutely necessary.

As he put his things on the passenger side he had a tinge of guilt about not seeing Kiia for a couple of days. There had been a real blurring of the roles of father and grandfather between him and the boy, but it was a relationship that had become important to both of them.

He eased the coupe out onto the street and noticed a red tint to the sunrise. The radio weatherman predicted rain by mid morning and Bill hoped he was right. The concrete workers would be happy to work inside if the rain started and he was sure Amos wanted some more rain for their farms. The hay Ezra had planted before he died was on its second year and would yield a good crop if the moisture was right.

"I wonder how much hay a small herd of goats would need if they were kept inside for a year or so?" he thought. Actually, he didn't even know what goats eat and made a note to learn a little more about them; Just in case Michael found some instead of a couple of cows that he thought he would need.

As he pulled into the drive, he noticed Miriam in her garden tying up her tomato plants and apparently getting ready for rain. Apparently she could read the sky just as well as the local weatherman could read his computerized reports. He parked the coupe and opened up the barn.

While waiting for the concrete contractor he checked the tarps over his own building supplies and added some weight in case the rain came with some wind.

The contractor rolled up in his beat up old flatbed truck right about then. He got out and eyed Bills coupe. After a few car compliments Bill couldn't return they entered the barn and sized up the job quickly.

"Whatcha going to do with that big hole in the center of the floor?"

"Work around it for now and I'll do something with it later," Bill replied.

"All right. Well, here's the deal. My guys and I prefer to work inside when it rains so I'll radio them to come here after they finish checking the tarps on the job we started yesterday. Then I'll have the concrete we ordered to finish over there brought here. If no one gets in the way we can have this poured today. O.K.?"

"O.K.," said Bill. "I'll be over in the garden, if you need me." He turned and walked to the garden not knowing what he would do or what he would say to Miriam. She studied his approach to the garden as he pretended not to notice her watching. The grass had grown too tall for there to be a path to the garden. It had also grown wild around the garden fence. He made a mental note to bring out his power mower and weed whip.

"Good Morning," he said at the garden gate.

"Good Morning, William."

For a woman who lived so close to God and to the land, she had an almost regal, unapproachable way about her. She was tall, slender and graceful beyond any other woman he had met. She stood in the midst of plants of all types and sizes. They owed their very existence to her planting and nurture of them.

Her touch must have been as important to them as the sun, soil and rain.

"I, uh, was, talking to the contractor, and he, uh said he wanted to work alone with his crew, and um, I uh told him I would be working here in the garden, But I should had said I would be *asking* you if I uh, could…"

"I understand, William. Something got into my garden last night and ate more than I am prepared to lose. Would thee seek out an opening in my fence and repair it?"

"Oh, sure! May I?" He pointed to the gate as if to ask permission to enter the garden. She nodded. He entered and closed the gate. It didn't take long to walk around the recently hoed garden to find a trail though the fence grass that showed the entry point.

The hole, dug under the lattice work, would allow a small rabbit to come and go easily until it grew bigger.

"I think I've found it," he called out. "And, I think I have what it will take to discourage any more shopping trips for this critter. I'll be right back."

He walked carefully toward the gate.

"I have some tight mesh left over from the concrete reinforcement and nothing will be able to dig under or chew through it."

She nodded.

He went through the gate and carefully closed it. The contractor had been joined by his two men and they were just adding some more pieces to the metal reinforcement that was necessary for a good concrete floor.

"You guys did a good job here. Why didn't you finish up and pour the floor yourself?"

"They had to go back home for summer cultivation of their crops," Bill replied.

"Amish, huh? I worked for that old Moses once. That guy could pinch a nickel till the buffalo dies."

"It is interesting, isn't it? How intelligent they are with minimal education," Bill countered.

"Yah, ya gotta love em."

"Yes, you do," Bill thought. "Especially some of them." He picked through some of the cast off pieces of mesh.

"If you don't need these pieces, I'd like to use them to plug up some holes in the garden fence."

"Yah, we're done with that stuff now. We're just waiting for the first concrete truck to git here."

"O.K., said Bill. "I've got a small table saw under one of these tarps and I'm going to pull it out later.

"No problem. Why don't you put an extension cord in through the passage way and keep the saw outside? I'll have the guys pull out that saw and set it up for you before we have coffee."

"Thank you," said Bill, "I appreciate that."

He had located his tool belt, hammer and nails. Two pieces of mesh would be enough to cover the hole and extend far enough on either side to discourage any nearby digging. He walked back to the garden and stayed outside the fence. There appeared to be only the one hole, so he forced the mesh beneath the soil and tacked it to the old lattice. He walked around to the gate.

"That should do it."

"Thank you, William"

Bill looked over the garden and the tomato plants she had tied to sticks that were too short for the job. He also saw the pole beans lying on the ground and that the squash plants were sending out 'runners.'

"You know," he said, "I could cut some stakes for a lot of these plants you've got here."

"The stakes Ezra cut...um, the stakes I had have rotted and I... "Thank you William." She looked away rather than show how she felt.

"I'll be right back," he said and strode quickly toward the barn. The saw was already out and the men were drinking their coffee. Bill selected several of the extra two by fours he had bought. He decided to rip the six footers into three pieces and the eight footers into two pieces. He figured on tying them into tripods for the pole beans and squash plants to climb on. It didn't take long to set up the saw and make enough stakes for six tripods. As he ripped the two by fours the saw seemed to screech and shriek when he hit knots that bound the blade. It was so loud he was sorry he had forgotten to wear hearing protection. He then cut a point on each stake, shut off the saw and gathered the stakes. As he walked up to the gate Miriam was looking at him with a stern expression.

"William, wouldn't it have been better to use a hand saw rather than risk falling into perdition?"

Bill had forgotten the Amish didn't approve the use of electricity.

"You're right," he said. "I usually do use a hand saw.

In fact, I prefer one."

"My God!" he thought. "I just got her to talk to me and I'm lying to her all ready."

"What will thee do with so many stakes, William?"

"Oh! I plan to make tripods for the pole beans like you have done in the past, I'm sure. And then I'd like to make them for the squash and

cucumbers to climb on. If the fruits hang the ground parasites can't dig
into them and spoil them."

"I am impressed with that idea, William. Will you show me what
you have planned?

There were many pieces of used bailer twine looped over the fence
and Bill grabbed several. He tied the top of three six foot pieces for the
pole beans, set them and then tied eight foot tripods for the squash and
cucumber plants. He set the points into the soft earth and tied one vine
to each leg.

"The squash and cucumber vines are heavier than the pole beans and
will have to be curled around the stakes and tied before they will accept
the stakes as the way they will grow. Resist the temptation to grow
more than three or four fruits per vine. They will grow sweeter and
more flavorful if the vine doesn't have to support too many."

Miriam had moved closer to watch Bill tie and set other tripods. She
was tightly holding her hoe with both hands and leaning forward on it
as if she were depending on it to keep her supported and protected by
the old ways.

"On the day thee bought Ezra's farm I wasn't sure you were a
farmer, but I knew thee had the heart of a good man. I shall go now to
prepare sandwiches for lunch" and she released the hoe so I fell into
Bill's hands.

"We shall eat on the porch so we can watch the workmen in the
barn."

Bill hoed around the plants he had staked and thinned them to three
per hill. He did the same to the other hills after he had tied the tripods
and pushed them into the ground. There were other hills of plants
which could use tripods, but he decided to wait until he could know
what she wanted.

When he looked to the house, Miriam was standing on the porch by
a small table and two stools. The food was prepared and she was
waiting patiently with her hands down at her sides.

Bill went through the gate, being careful to close it. He left the hoe
against it because he wasn't sure where she would want it. As he got to
the porch steps he saw a basin of water, a bar of home made soap and

a towel. He washed his hands, then his face, ran his fingers through his hair and rinsed his hands again. As he started around the corner of the porch he looked back to see the soap was still in the basin. He turned around to refold the towel and fish the soap out of the water and replace it on the towel. He rinsed the soap from his hands again and muttered, "Enough," while shaking the water from them.

He rounded the corner and she was still standing there. This was not the table under the oak where he and the Amish men had eaten. This was the porch of her home. Not sure of what he should do, he simply gestured to the two stools and she began to sit. He pulled his stool out so he wouldn't hit a table leg when he sat.

"In my faith the husband is the spiritual leader, uh I mean the man is the spiritual leader of the family, uh the spiritual leader. So I would like to pray in my Tradition."

"I am not familiar with other religious traditions William, but if thee lead, I will follow.

"Thank you," he said quietly, and began his prayer. It was a quiet lunch and they both tried to watch the concrete work being done in the barn. They had hardly started eating when the workers stopped for lunch themselves.

One of those mild panics which abhor silence came over Bill and he began to compliment Miriam on the lunch. After he had complimented everything on the table except the crumbs which were mostly on his side, she said;

"William, in the bag from the fabric store there was an ornate package which I didn't open."

"Oh, yes, I didn't know what you had for scissors or how sharp they may be so I when saw this package of two matching ones I thought you would like them. Please say you will accept them."

"We do not ordinarily have things which are ornate or lavish when plain things work as well and promote a modest and humble life before God. I will have to ask Bishop Yocum for his permission to accept them."

"That's a good ideal," he said. "But, first open them to see if they fit your hand and cut straight." Bill was hoping Moses would say yes if she had used them.

"I will consider that before they take me to Sunday worship," she said, guessing his intentions.

Another concrete truck rumbled in using the same tracks made by the others in the soft driveway.

"Why don't I rip the other boards to make tripods while you prepare the hills you want tied up? The concrete truck will be louder than the saw and no one will know electricity is being used."

Miriam walked to the gate so she wouldn't have to agree to an act which could lead to perdition.

The concrete truck was rumbling and the work men shouted instructions to each other. Bill pushed the wood through the saw a little faster than he would normally, but he wanted to please her. When an idea about a lattice came to him he quickly ripped enough wood to build it. He was sure that would please her too.

When finished, he gathered up the boards and hustled over to the garden. Miriam saw him coming and opened the gate. Together they made the tripods and a lattice, tied up plants, hoed and weeded until they were startled by a voice.

"Well, that's about it for us. You folks want to take a look at it before we go?"

They looked at each other and Bill said, "Let's take a look." She nodded and they walked to the barn using their inverted hoes like walking sticks. The contractor looked at them as if they were very strange to him. Looking in from the large door it was a good job. The floor was level with the hand pump base, and filled in the entire room Bill had hoped would supply food and living space. The area where the large mass fire place would be built looked like a gaping hole, but wasn't important to Bill. Miriam stared with a look of disbelief.

"It looks good," Bill said.

"Awright. Watch your mailbox. I'll need a check in ten days." He turned to his crew.

"Hey, you guys, you think we're going to leave this equipment? Get it cleaned up and back in the truck. I'm buying the first round!"

Miriam's eyes widened a little at that remark. She looked down as she shook her head. Life with Ezra had been boring, even frightening at times, but at least it had been predictable and safe. Her worship, her friends and her children had kept her busy and, at times much fulfilled. She had no time and little inclination to know of the world outside her faith. It saddened her to see her boys go west to find farms and wives to settle down with, but that was to be expected as they aged. Ezra's accidental death shook her but she didn't feel fear until the elders announced the clan could not farm her land and would sell it. In a little over a year life as she knew it changed so much and she felt so alone. Her husband was dead! Her sons rarely sent word! Her home was an island among the English and apart from her clan!

"How can any of this serve God?" She turned and brushed past Bill throwing down her hoe. Bill felt a tear on his hand as she ran to her house. He wanted to follow her, sweep her into his arms and hold her till he could crush the fear out her and replace it with his love. Instead he felt as if his feet were in the new concrete. He couldn't find the words to tell her how he felt and what his mission was in her life. The fear of a natural disaster which only he believed in, and how he alone would be the one to save those he loved was so big he could only raise his hand and rub the tear into his skin. He picked up the hoes, put them in the shelter by the garden and went home.

He had never felt so tired, so heavy. Even the car seemed unable to move as it once did.

Bill backed into his driveway and shut it off. The smell of the grill was strong as he approached the back door. Becky was turning the bratwurst and boiling a pot of corn on the cob.

"Hi, Dad," she called. "My friend Cherry is coming over with her two girls and Kiia; God, what's wrong with you? Are you sick?"

"No, no," he waved away her question. "I'm just a little tired from a tough day. I'll be alright after a good night's sleep. How are Cherry and the girls?" He tried to appear cheerful.

"They're O.K.," but what's with you? I heard you broke up with Marge."

"Oh, that was almost a month ago and the way I feel tonight has nothing to do with her, or her kids."

"So?"

"So," he drew a long breath. "It might be best if I sneak upstairs and we talk about it tomorrow. I can't describe how tired I feel right now."

"How is your heart? Do you have any shortness of breath? She asked.

"It's not my heart, at least not in that sense." He turned toward the back door before she could ask any more. A strong leader doesn't break down before anyone. In the morning, he thought, he would tell Becky about Miriam, but not about buying the farm. Then he would tell all to Miriam if she would let him.

In his room, he set the lock on the door and forced his desire for privacy on anyone who might intrude. He showered and prepared his bed in a matter of minutes, grateful for the bathroom in his room.

In his prayers he submitted himself to God as he always did.

Always one to face whatever he feared, he brought before the Lord his new found love and the fact he might have lost her, the stresses of preparing to save his family in the event of a cataclysmic disaster and the need for secrecy. How could he save everyone or even turn away anyone who discovered what he was building? The last thing he asked for was for God to take over all the worries and give him a good night's sleep. He rolled into bed and prayed fervently until sleep put an end to the day.

It was unusual for him to sleep more than eight hours, so it surprised him to see he had been down for more than twelve hours. He had slept well and the stresses that had been building in him had abated enough to be in the background again. They were nothing more than plans again and would be accomplished in good time.

Kiia had gotten up as early as his mother had feared he would on a Saturday and she was up getting him breakfast. Bill dressed, stripped his bed and folded the bedding over the quilt rack again.

"Good morning, happy family," he called as he came down the stairs and into the kitchen.

"Grandpa!" Kiia called out, nearly bouncing off his chair.

"Hey, big boy," Bill called back. "Look at that breakfast all over your face." Kiia looked back with a smile so big it almost covered the mess.

"What time did you get to bed last night?" he asked Becky.

"Late." She said in an exaggerated tone.

"Play any Cribbage?"

"No. Cherry is only interested in passive activities. You know; television and talking about any man she has seen or just heard about."

Bill laughed. "She sure is a good hearted woman, but I wish she could find what would make her happy."

"Don't we all," yawned Becky.

"Look, I said we would talk today, but why don't you let me watch Kiia while you get some sleep? I have a lot of laundry to do and I have to catch up with my share of the cleaning too. We can talk after you are rested up a little."

"I don't know. Do you think you can handle him alone?"

"Sure. We'll have some laundry basket rides and maybe even get some cloths cleaned. Then we'll do what we men folk like to do best; talk smart and act dumb!"

"My only son; sick and twisted before he gets to puberty," Becky laughed as she got up. "Thanks for taking Kiia for the rest of the morning, Dad. Cherry has been my best friend since moving here, but keeping up with her can be a chore."

"No problem." He said as he sat down with his plate of eggs. "Little Man Cub, you and grandpa are going to have a good time together." They looked at each other and laughed between bites of food.

Bill cleaned up quickly and when done joined Kiia in the den where he had been sent to get out his art supplies; crayons and coloring books. Playing with a child always intrigued Bill. Any time Kiia felt threatened by the quality of Bill's art he would snatch the crayon away and tell him to use the broken one he gave him. All morning long Bill got to play with the broken toys or anything Kiia felt had little play value. The boy kept a close hold on his sense of control and Bill always let him win or gave him praise for any accomplishment. But, when playing on a toddler's level became crushingly boring, Bill suggested reading.

This was an activity both enjoyed and Bill decided to stay with it until Kiia wanted to stop. Bill tried a new twist to reading this time. He knew Kiia recognized the books he liked on sight and Bill insisted he take only one at a time from the bookcase and return it before he could have another. Becky thought he was just trying to keep things picked up, but if she had ever watched a firefighter she would have known they always put things back in the same place so they could find them in the worst of conditions. Bill knew he would always be a firefighter at heart.

The morning flew by and suddenly Kiia announced; "My tummy hurts."

"It sounds like lunch would be in order. Do you know we didn't even have a snack?"

"No."

"Well, then, let's have some lunch. What do you say to some chocolate milk and peanut butter sandwiches?"

"Yah!" and he was up and scampering for the kitchen.

He was already on his chair when Bill got to the fridge. He reached for the milk and Becky came in looking somewhat refreshed. They made small talk and the sandwiches, and then sat down together.

"Do you feel more like talking today?" She asked.

"Yes," he said as he put down his food. "I haven't had a lot of time to think out what I have wanted to tell you, what with watching Kiia this morning. But here goes."

"You're right about Marge. I did break up with her and her whole fam-damly. I mean, there was a lot more there than I realized when I first met her. I can't see myself living like they do. So when we got back from Yellowstone I drove over and ended it. On the way back I bumped into that Amish Man, Moses Yocum."

"I know of him, and you've mentioned him before."

"Right. Within the next two days I met a woman of stunning beauty, bearing and intellect." He then wove a convincing tale of starting the delivery business and his interest in Miriam. Even though he tried not to reveal his affection for her, Becky's intuition told her that her father was already in love.

75

He went on about helping the Amish with the barn instead of revealing he had bought the farm and why he had done so.

"So, she's Amish, then?"

He looked up, startled she had guessed.

"Dad!" She protested. "They don't marry out of their clans."

"I know, I know." But, I have the strongest feelings that this will all work out. You know, when you and your brother told me about your loves, I felt a little apprehensive too. I mean, it was all so fast, but both of you were so sure it was right. And before the drug thing ended your marriage for you, I came to be sure it was the right thing for you too. I'm not jumping into anything right now. In fact, I'm taking a breather from everything for a couple of days to think."

"I figured there was more going on than just delivering things."

Bill laughed in a good natured way. "I'm not making any plans," he lied, "and I really want to spend more time with her. I think both you and Luke will like her." He was careful not to explain too much, but had a feeling her intuition was putting together a little more than he wanted her to know.

Kiia interrupted with a tantrum which signaled it was time for his afternoon nap.

"I think it is time for a little boy to go down," said Becky.

"Not to mention his mother and grandfather," said Bill. "Suddenly I feel a little beat too. Later, I think I will clean up the coupe and we can all go out for dinner if you don't have anything planned."

"Nope. We can talk a little more then."

Bill dragged himself up the stairs and was asleep as soon as he lay down. He still had some stresses to heal and sleep was the cure. After an hour or so he forced himself up and went out to the garage to clean the coupe. He kept it up well although he'd cleaned up his fire trucks more often.

Dinner was early and informal as Kiia could name more fast food restaurants than he could the colors he used or the books he wanted to have read to him. Talk was small as they saw to Kiia's needs first. Becky asked a few questions about Miriam and Bill lit up as he answered them. She was sure he had found someone to love, but was still apprehensive about whether or not the relationship could come together.

"You haven't told me about her looks and how she acts."

"Well," said Bill. "She's tall and slender. Actually taller than any of the other Amish women I've met and a little younger than your old dad here. I think she is really intelligent even though she has little formal education. When she speaks, in English that is, it's obvious her thinking is clear. And when she speaks she makes eye contact; and what eye contact! She has the most beautiful green eyes. I've never met a woman with such green eyes. I think she is the most beautiful woman I have met since your mother."

"And, how is it she isn't married?"

"She was! Her husband died in a barn fire.

In fact, it was the old barn that was replaced just before I bought the place."

"Bought the place?" If Becky had been wearing glasses she would have been looking over the top of them. "Bought what place?"

He couldn't remember a time in his life when he felt so trapped by something he'd said. His mind raced for answers as he didn't want to reveal any of the reasons for the purchase.

"Well, it started off innocently enough. I was thinking about a place to keep the old pickup, the coupe and the new camper. You know the yard we have now is really too small, and when I saw this new barn I stopped to ask about renting some space. Old Moses was there. You know, I have been friends with him for a long time."

"I know Moses," she interrupted.

"Yes, and he said the whole farm was for sale and they wouldn't be renting any of the barn. So, since the farm is so close to the city limits I thought about making homesteads out of it to sell off at a profit. And that is where I am right now; preparing some plans for making some money!"

Bill didn't raise any fools and he was sure Becky wasn't buying into the real estate idea. Revealing his love for Miriam was such a big thing he didn't feel he had the time or energy to create an elaborate deception.

"So, to keep this all short, I met someone I know I love and got a good business venture as well. Becky, I'm not as young as I used to be and ideas come to me more clearly than ever before. I really feel I found what I need in life when I met Miriam, and the farm idea just came alone with her.

Bill was right. Becky wasn't buying into the farm idea at all.

But, she knew enough of her father to realize there was more and it would be revealed in due time. She turned to Kiia and made a show of cleaning his face and then the table.

"Will we be able to meet her?"

"Oh, I think so. I'm not sure when right now, but it should be soon. I've been so busy at the farm for the last month I haven't had time to make any other plans. And, I have done some delivery work for the rest of the clan. It's much smaller than I thought it was." He felt comfortable returning to the truth.

"I know this is a lot to digest right now. It is a little more than I had hoped to reveal in one sitting. I'd hoped to have a lot more planning done for the farm before I told you about it. And I never expected to fall in love again; at least not as quickly as all this has happened. I'm sorry, Becky. I really am."

"Dad, there is nothing to be sorry for. I can't think of anything I would want for you more than loving and being loved. I'm just a little afraid of it not working out for you."

"Until we talked, it never occurred to me that it wouldn't work out one way or another. Lately I have been feeling how lonely a person could be after being widowed. Raising you kids and then being a grandfather filled my life, but now I'm feeling it may be my turn to find something special. I want this relationship with Miriam to work and I'm going to see Moses next week to see what his clan will or won't do in matters like this."

"I hope it will work out, Dad; I'm so afraid you will just get hurt over this."

"Trust in God, Becky. Everything works out for the good of those who love Him. Remember that!"

They picked things up and headed for the door, Kiia leading. It opened from the outside and in walked Marge and Beth.

"Well, Bill!"

"Hello, Marge."

"I got your message from my bulletin board."

"Yes. It's better to tell it like it is, I guess. I'm no longer in the picture on your bulletin board or in your life. I'm sorry."

"Don't be. I'm seeing someone else anyway," she said coldly. "I hear your car has been parked in some Amish farm yard. And, you've been buying strange stuff all over town."

"Men can enjoy shopping too, you know. Becky, Kiia, let's go. Goodbye Marge."

He pushed the other door open and they left without any further words. Once in the car he breathed a sigh of relief.

"I'm glad that relationship is over. I can't imagine a relationship with a woman whose daughter AND son are her worst competition!"

Becky laughed. Kiia was too busy with the toy that came with his dinner to know or care what they were laughing about. Bill started the coupe and they eased out of the parking lot. He turned toward home thinking the Amish take their Sunday worship even more seriously than most faiths and today would not be the best day for a drive by.

"I'm not sure I am ready to see anyone else today. We didn't argue or anything, But yesterday I had an overwhelming feeling of the great sadness Miriam is feeling.

Her sons moved to the west coast to find their own farms and wives and after they were settled her husband was killed in that fire. I'm not sure why the clan decided to sell the farm, but she had to see her homestead gone too. I didn't have the nerve to force her to move after seeing how sad she was. After she said this was the only home she has known since leaving her mother and father's house, I…"

"It was the right thing to do, Dad. But, I still can't figure out why you suddenly wanted a farm."

"Well," he laughed and suddenly became careful so he wouldn't reveal too much again, "I've always been interested in growing flowers and vegetables and would like to experiment in an indoor environment with the goal of having a garden center."

He hoped Becky would take the partial truth of his statement as the whole truth. He was in too much an emotional turmoil right now to try to explain the whole survival plan.

"There is a lot more to work out right now and I would like to have a little more time to think things out. Please don't tell your brother about any of this right now."

He laughed, despite his tensions and Becky did too. They pulled up too the house and Bill backed the coupe into the garage. Becky went inside to check for phone messages while Bill pushed Kiia on the swing he had put up in an old Oak tree.

He hadn't been pushing long when he felt a strange trembling in the ground. It only lasted a few seconds and he was sure Kiia didn't feel any of it. The boy was laughing and singing while he was being pushed higher and higher. It wasn't too noticeable, but it shook Bill more emotionally than he cared to experience this weekend.

Becky came out of the house and called out to Kiia.

"Hey, big boy, Cherry called and we're going over there and then to the pool for a swim." Want to come, Dad?"

"No, sweetheart. I think I'm going to spend some time making more plans. You know how a lot of things look clearer and better when they are written down and studied. You two go ahead."

"All right, if you're sure. Come on, Honey-boy, we're going to go play while Grandpa stays home and works."

Bill laughed and hugged them good-bye. Then he turned toward the house and went in to the computer. He got online and surfed to an Army-Navy surplus sight. He ordered a dozen army beds and the bedding. For a reason he didn't even think about, he ordered an additional 100 surplus Army blankets and bedding.

He found several suppliers of dried legumes and rice, dried vegetables, survival cooking equipment and utensils, dried spices and herbs and even a few cookbooks. He ordered every thing that caught his eye. If it were possible to run for your life while sitting at a computer, Bill was living proof it could be done. He had moved assets to debit cards and could spend without worry of the banks stopping him. The tremor he felt in his own back yard had so unnerved him he was now in full flight. If he saw anything he thought he could use to protect his family he bought it; and many times more than one in case it would wear out or break easily.

At one website he bought bibles, study guides and prayer books. At another he bought some art supplies with appropriate papers and sketch books. He and both his kids had the ability to draw so he got a lot of pencils, artist chalks and even a set of oils and water colors.

He didn't think to buy literature, but he did know there were a number of used bookstores in the area. If there was time he planed to get an encyclopedia and whatever would make a good read if there was more leisure time than the desperate survival activities he expected.

He had everything addressed to the farm as he knew Miriam would always be at home. She could keep things on her porch until he got there to move them into the barn. He'd had a lot of time to think of her in the last two days and he was sure he could win her heart if she would only give him a chance. He would see her the next morning and then drive up to see Moses.

He continued to surf and order anything he felt would be a necessity; first aid kits, garden utensils, seeds that he thought would provide additional food from the raised bed gardens yet to be built and even fertilizers. He ordered several 12 volt auto batteries, connections, switches and DC to AC converters so they could power the grow lights and have enough light for good living. He searched and ordered with a combination of reckless abandonment and Divine Inspiration. If he found something he wasn't sure he would need he would take the attitude of, "well, God can sort this one out," and ordered it anyway. After three hours he was exhausted and decided to work on the barn for a few days and think about anything else he might need. There was no need to try to find anything he could get locally in small quantities and not arouse suspicion. He went to the history and cleared the addresses he had visited.

Then, he went upstairs to his little office and reviewed his plans and the things he had all ready accomplished. He had started keeping a journal in order to keep his thinking clear.

It would be of little historic worth if this disaster did not happen and if it did, there would most likely be no one to read it anyway. But, Bill was a man accustomed to pre-plan and be accountable for whatever the consequences would be. So he continued with his journal for more than another two hours.

When weary of that, he looked around his office and bedroom for things he would one day move if he needed to. As he looked around he savored the memory of each item he planned to take to the barn. He wrote nothing as he enjoyed his memories, then closed the journal, turned out the light and went to bed early.

He was soundly asleep when Becky came home late with a sleeping Kiia. She put him to bed and went back downstairs to turn out the lights and close the doors. She was surprised her father had left the house is such a disarray as it wasn't like him to do so.

This next week she hoped to meet Miriam as she was sure her father loved her and would ultimately want to marry. The rest of the questions she had about what her father was up to would have to wait. She knew him to be a man of little guile or intrigue and felt it wouldn't be long before he revealed what was on his mind.

She tucked Kiia in for the night and went to her own bed. He was old enough to sleep straight through the night and she expected to do the same. Memories of Tom flooded her mind as he did every night. He was her life's choice and losing him was something a good woman would feel forever. She tried to push away his memories with prayer and after a while fell into a fitful sleep.

Bill was up and gone in the morning before Kiia and Becky stirred. His fire training still served him well when it was time to rouse from a deep slumber.

This morning he chose to stop at a local cafe for breakfast and then head out to the farm. As he drove, he remembered he had left the barn door open Friday afternoon and he was a little afraid someone driving by might have gone in for a look, or worse yet, stopped to vandalize or steal. Either way, it would have been something he could not afford.

As he pulled into the driveway he saw the buggy Moses and the two Amish men drove when they came to work. He didn't see them as he drove up so he parked and hurried to the barn.

The three men were inside and walking about on the new concrete looking for flaws or imperfections. Bill thought it had dried well and would not be a problem over the long run. The three Amish looked up and only Moses said hello. The two youngest were walking around the perimeter looking for problems and talking softly as they did.

"It looks like a good job, William."

"Yes," Bill replied. "They worked pretty hard last Friday. I think you know them."

"I do. The owner can be a little insolent and disrespectful, but if I deal firmly with him he will do the job."

Bill smiled and nodded. He'd seen how Moses has ordered things his clan needed and how he had insisted on the best prices or he wouldn't buy at all. The people he dealt with all respected him and didn't joke around.

They had walked around the barn and were now standing at the hole in the center where the Amish would build the large mass fire place.

"I've asked Miriam to bring coffee to the table under the Oak Tree. After we have had our coffee and have talked, we will bring the field stone to the barn to build the fireplace. Let us see if she saw you drive in."

The walked to the passageway which looked out to the Oak and the table had the coffee pot and cups on it.

"Good," said Moses. He turned and said something to Michael and Amos in their language and then walked out to have coffee. Bill followed, which was not his custom. He was accustomed to being a leader, but Moses had a strong personality also.

They sat down and after a second of uncomfortable silence Bill picked up the coffee pot and poured two steaming cups. They brought up their cups and smelled the coffee with deep breaths before taking small sips. Bill had long believed the two of them to be of the same pattern of man, only cut from different cloths. But, he was sure he didn't want to be in a confrontational situation with him.

"She makes good coffee, William."

A ripple of discomfort splashed through Bill. He wanted to tell Moses about what happened last Friday when Miriam appeared to be so hurt, but merely agreed with Moses and hoped the old man would continue.

"We brought the buggy to get Miriam for worship yesterday. Then we spent the day with our clan and she spoke little with me and my wife, or anyone. That is unusual for her, but I think I have an understanding. What is your understanding, William?"

Even a strong man has to let go a heavy burden at times and Bill was no exception. He explained his desire to help Miriam with her garden and that he had shown her what was being done to the barn.

He spoke of how lonely he felt she was and that he only wanted to spend time with her and do things for her. He stopped short of talking about love and his feelings about her.

After an awkward silence, Moses drank deeply of his coffee and put the cup down firmly.

"You are right about her loneliness. It is an emotion both of you carries as a burden. It is a heavy one and drains the soul of peace. I have known her all my life and you for a little over two years. Two years is not a long time in some situations, but in your case I have come to know you to be a good man. I wish I had many like you in my clan, but it grows smaller each year and I have no one like you for Miriam. It is a sadness for me to have one of my own sad and lonely without a way for me to help. However, be that as it may, it has come to my attention you have given her an impressive gift."

A stab of fear went through Bill. He had forgotten the warning Moses gave him about gifts and any kind or remuneration.

"The gift you gave her is considered more than a casual act in our world. It is an offer of further caring and support and is taken very seriously by a woman."

Bill took a drink and swallowed what felt like the driest coffee he had ever tasted. He put the cup down, not knowing what to say.

"I am the leader of my clan and its Bishop. What I am about to say is my decision in this matter. I have no one for her to marry and it is time for her, and you I might add, to remarry. It is not our custom to marry out of our faith, but as I said, I have no one for her.

"So," he removed a small piece of paper from his shirt pocket, folded it in half and slid it across the table.

"Here is some information about Miriam you will need to take to the people at your county government. In two weeks you will give to me what you English call a marriage license. Then, in two weeks I will celebrate your marriage for you. I will not shun her. Not now or forever. But, if I do not receive the papers from you in two weeks I will send her away and you will never see her again. Of course, she will return your gift at that time."

Bill was stunned, but slowly reached for the paper and put it in his pocket. He hadn't been aware his feelings for Miriam had been so obvious. As he had grown to love her he had also feared their faiths would tear them apart. To have the secrets of his soul revealed and fulfilled left him with a "heady" feeling.

He looked at Moses with a smile that also showed a sense of chagrin at having the old man find him out. Life without her had become unthinkable even though he didn't know how he would be able to keep her.

"Thank you, Moses. You are a wise man."

"Wisdom is a gift from God," he replied. "It came with my natural sternness. If we hurry we should be able to haul two loads of field stone to the barn by lunch.

The old man got up from the table and turned toward the barn. Bill followed in silence.

Inside, Michael and Amos had leveled the gravel in the hole, added some water and had stepped the mixture into a firm foundation. Moses looked at their work and gave an approving nod.

"We will now bring the field stone," he said.

The young men stepped out of the hole and the four of them walked to the truck. Moses slid into the front seat with Bill and the other two sat in the bed facing the tailgate. It was a short, quiet drive up the hill. At the first field Bill was struck by the thought that all the stones found while plowing or cultivating had been stacked together and not just thrown around the perimeter of the field. It took little time to load the truck and Bill felt much younger and stronger since knowing he was free to love again.

"Someday," he thought, "I'm going to have to tell Moses he was wrong. We'll get three truck loads of stone before lunch, not two!" It took very little time to get the three loads and lunch was on the table when they finished. Miriam had returned to the house after leaving a short list of items wanted for the next few days' lunches. Bill read it aloud and then put it in his shirt pocket as he always did.

Moses prayed the blessing, as he always did and the men ate quickly, in silence. At such a small table there was no need to ask to have something passed. This time Bill didn't mind and he was sure the two younger men knew nothing about what he and Moses had discussed.

They hauled five more loads after lunch and then Bill suggested they quit as he had to run into town to refuel the truck. They looked at what they had hauled down that day. Moses said they would need at least ten more loads and that could be done the next day, weather permitting.

They moved the cement mixer into the barn and began a concrete-stone foundation. It would be slow work to fill the large hole, but it would go quicker once they reached floor level and began the fireplace and chimney inserts.

There was enough scrap copper pipe left over to encircle the fire place to provide hot water for the floor and enough clay tiles for the two chimneys Bill wanted. With the ten loads of rock they would bring down tomorrow they would have a weeks worth of back breaking work.

In the morning, Moses and Amos stayed at the barn while Bill and Michael began the first of their trips. Bill excused himself at lunch to run an errand that he only described as "very important."

Once at the courthouse he went to the register's office and requested the forms for a marriage license. The information Moses had given him was adequate for him to complete all of them. Knowing how much work he had to do this week he told the clerk he would get the blood tests and signatures later and return the forms next week. He laughed to himself when he thought it would be best to tell his kids first before they saw the notice in the papers.

Of all the things he had kept secret over the last six weeks this was the one secret he was afraid to announce as the approval of his two kids was very important to him. But, he thought, that was something to worry about later as he had to get back to the farm. The others had finished lunch and were back at work. Bill separated the forms Moses would have to have Miriam fill out into one envelope and put it in the buggy. His forms he put under the seat of the truck.

As he backed out of the truck Michael walked up with a small basket. "This is your sandwich and a covered cup of cool tea."

"Thank you," said Bill, surprised at the ease in which Michael spoke to him. "I'll put it in the truck and eat it when we get to the next field."

They both got into the cab and Bill started driving up the hill to the flatland farms. Both he and Michael had become comfortable with each other's company over the past few weeks. Amos was always standoffish and despite the high regard he felt for him, Moses often retreated behind his role as Bishop and leader of his clan. But, once alone, Michael was open and friendly.

"You know, I am not completely unfamiliar with vehicles which ride on rubber tires."

"Oh?" Asked Bill hoping he wouldn't say anything that would end the conversation.

"Yes. One spring there was an English who stayed with us. He had a pickup truck too and one night when the elders went to sleep we went out into the newly plowed field for a ride. We would ride on the front and when he stopped suddenly we would see who could fly the farthest. Amos won, but broke his arm. I set it, but we were caught and had to re-plow the field.

"I can't imagine why," Bill tried to look surprised.

"The English was sent away as soon as he had hauled enough of the rocks to the piles we are now removing. By fall, the corn was high and we would then throw rotten tomatoes at passing cars and run back into the corn to keep from being caught. But, we were caught again."

"I haven't met a kid yet that hasn't tried some kind of stunt thinking he wouldn't ever get caught." Bill smiled. "I tried a few things myself."

"We are a strict people and I soon settled down."

"I've been told the Amish men wear a beard when they marry so the unmarried women can tell the single men from the married."

"That is correct, William. We don't shave our faces after we marry."

"How long have you been married?"

"I married Ruth when I was seventeen and she was sixteen. We have three year old twins, Anna and Mary, and my wife is pregnant again."

"Congratulations. Anna and Mary are the names of the mother and grandmother of Jesus."

"Aye. You know your Bible, William?"

"Like most Americans, uh English," he corrected himself, "I only know a little and should spend more time with it. I think I may have some more time for it in the future," But he didn't want to say anymore.

Michael gestured to the driveway at a different farm and Bill pulled in. The younger man hopped out and after a moment's conversation with another Amish man returned.

"This way," he pointed. "Eli says he farms as much rock as he does crops and he's happy to part with them. The field we are going to is lying fallow this summer so we don't have to worry about damaging his crop.

Bill turned off the short driveway into the field. The field stones covered an area at least ten feet wide along the entire length of the field.

"My God!" exclaimed Bill.

"I trust you are praying, William."

"I am," he said as they jumped out of the truck and set to work. A sense of urgency overtook them in this field. There were more rocks than they needed, but if they took them all Eli could expand his field the next time he planted. It would be a small, but welcome increase in his income.

They worked quickly, and of course, quietly to fill the pickup several times before finishing. The old truck creaked and groaned at every bump in the road. The rear springs were at total capacity, but luckily didn't break. They pulled up to the Barn with the last load just as Moses and Amos came out. Moses studied the larger than needed pile of field stone and the overloaded pickup.

"I see you met Eli," he noted.

"I guess! We decided to clean out the whole field. Moses," he added, "There are traces of rare minerals in a few of these stones. I've thrown them in that small pile there."

"Mineral like this?" asked Moses as he pulled a stone from the pickup.

"Yes."

He squinted at it for a moment.

"Gold," he said. A mineral you English prize greatly."

"I thought so," said Bill. "I think we should separate out these stones and return them to Eli when we are finished."

"A kind and honest thought, William. Let's store these in the back of the barn until we know how many we have."

"All right." Bill and Michael began unloading the truck while Moses and Amos piled the "gold stones" in the barn. When they returned, the four of them made short work of unloading the pickup.

"We will look at the rest of them as we build with the fireplace," said Moses. "Now, it is time for chores." Moses led the younger men to the buggy and found the envelope from the Register of Deeds William had left for him.

"Perhaps we should start a little later tomorrow." Bill called out as Moses studied the envelope.

"The sun rises at the same time for the rested and the weary," he said and got into the buggy. Michael got in the back and Amos drove.

Bill watched them move slowly out of the driveway and onto the road. Then he turned to close up the barn. He hoped he didn't look as tired as he felt. He rolled the door closed and since he hadn't installed any locks, he turned to leave. As he got into his truck he looked over to the house. It wasn't dark enough for lights yet so he couldn't see if Miriam was doing anything. He hadn't seen her all day and he ached to see her more than his body did because of the stones.

He wanted to go up to the house and hold her. He wanted to hold her and kiss her and make her feel his love without saying a word. He wanted to lay with her that night and speak of love without using words. He wanted many things, but right now he knew he had better get home before he got so tired he would fall asleep. Since the wedding was set for a Sunday, four weeks away, he decided to court her in the terms of her people. He started the truck and eased away from the farm.

At home, Becky had started dinner and Bill slipped inside for a shower before spending time with her and Kiia. He came down to the kitchen in less than a half an hour, refreshed by his shower.

"Dad," said Becky, "you look exhausted. You have been working way too hard lately. I thought you were going to slow down."

"I am. I am!" He knew he was lying again, but added; "After this week, things will slow down a lot. Today, I just had to move a lot of things around. I've got some big news for desert tonight. When do we eat?"

"Well, you can call Kiia to the table right now. We're having his favorite; sliced and diced wieners, refried beans and I was going to serve chocolate cake for desert, but…"

"We'll have your desert first," laughed Bill. "Then mine. I'm sure we will enjoy both."

He left the room to get Kiia. Becky felt he looked happy, and maybe a little younger than he had for quite some time. She was grateful for that as she was more and more aware of the years he had been caring for his two kids alone. If he had found love again she was going to support him.

Bill and Kiia came into the room with a rattle, clatter and enough laughter to brighten any family. Kiia was babbling away as Bill got him into his high chair. He took one hand and when Becky brought his plate and took the other they had a quick prayer and Kiia began to eat. Bill and Becky filled their plates and sat down quickly.

They ate quietly for a moment and then Bill spoke. As most men do, he tried to build a good case for what he wanted to do. If fact, he talked all around it and finally Becky interrupted.

"So, you want to marry this, this Miriam?"

"Yes," he replied. "How did you know?"

She replied with a blank look.

"All right, all right. I may have been explaining it a little too much without actually telling you what I want to do." He put his fork down and Kiia stopped eating too.

You are aware I have been alone since your mother died and I don't want anyone to think I am being disrespectful by wanting to love again.

"Dad, I've been alone myself since Tom left."

"I know, I know. I'm sorry. But, as you are aware I have been friends with Moses Yocum and his Amish Clan since we moved here more than two years ago." He didn't want to admit he'd only recently met Miriam, but he felt sure he couldn't be wrong about the feelings they had for each other.

"As Bishop and leader of his clan, Moses has granted permission for us to marry and has stated he would preside at the ceremony and we could then have the marriage blessed in a Church after that. That is something I want. "The important thing is I will be accepted by the clan and Miriam won't be shunned as one who has married out."

"When are you planning to get married and will we get to know Miriam before the wedding date?" asked Becky.

"Yes. The Amish don't believe in long engagements when the couple seems right for each other and they sure don't believe in divorce either. So, I think you will meet her soon, but I'm not sure Luke and Sarah will get here on time so they will meet her the weekend of the wedding."

"And the weekend of the wedding will be?"

"In about three weeks, give or take…"

"Dad!" Becky exploded causing Kiia to drop a whole handful of refried beans.

"Becky, it is all right. Her side of the family is putting on the wedding and all they are going to worry about is whether they are wearing clean work clothes. You won't have to go out and buy anything and we aren't going to invite anyone other than immediate family." He quickly added; "And that means we don't tell anyone, and I mean, WE DON'T TELL ANYONE. Even and especially our best friends! Have I made myself clear about the privacy angle?"

"Well, I know you don't like my friend, Cherry, but she has been my best friend since we moved here."

"I know," he interrupted. "But, I am marrying a strongly religious woman from a very religious clan. I don't think they will understand the sexual adventures and misadventures of your best friend. She doesn't have to be there and I don't want to have to try to explain her ways to those who live in an opposite manner."

"Besides," he added, I don't think she will be comfortable in a church setting twice in one day.

"Well, she's not Rahab the Harlot, you know," she spat back at him.

They both laughed when they realized how they had taken the conversation to an extreme of seriousness. Kiia, who had been watching the conversation by looking back and forth laughed too, but had no idea what was said.

They ate quietly for a few minutes as Kiia talked and showed off what he felt were choice pieces of wiener. He was a good eater and a healthy boy.

"I'd better call Luke right after we eat," said Bill. Do you think he would be my best man? I mean, I would like that, but it is something you don't often ask your oldest son to do."

Becky laughed in spite of her mixed emotions. "Yes, I think you had better call. I'm sure he is expecting to hear from you."

"Hmmm. It sounds like you have been talking to him about this already."

"Well, you have been too busy to call so I did. And he should know what is going on in our lives too."

Bill smiled and laughed to himself. This wouldn't be easy to explain and avoiding it any longer would only make it more difficult.

"Let's pick up the kitchen and then I will call."

"That is a good idea because they are expecting you to call. Sometime soon, I mean."

"I hope you haven't gotten them all stirred up about my plans."

"Of course not," Becky replied with a forced look of innocence.

Bill picked up quickly and left the kitchen. He sat down with the phone and punched in the speed dial for Luke. Sarah answered and when Bill spoke she immediately began teasing him about taking so long to call.

They had been wondering if they would ever get an invitation. Bill was suddenly grateful for Becky's calls because he didn't have to start from the beginning. After a few minutes of good natured kidding Sarah asked if Bill wanted to talk to Luke. He said he did and then she asked what color she should wear. He was going to say wear something in a light to dark blue, but smiled and said they would talk about it later.

When Luke got on the phone they traded information about work and home and then Luke broke the ice.

"I hear you are in pretty deep with someone of the female persuasion."

Bill laughed. "After what I went through with my last foray into relationships I guess that is a fair description. Actually I discovered I really am in love with a woman I have known for some time, but never looked at her in that way. He went on to describe Miriam in ways that only someone in love could.

He ended with; "She has the most incredible green eyes and sometimes when we look at each other it is as if we are thinking; is this the one, Lord? Is the one you saved for me?"

They talked for over a half an hour about the similarities in their relationships and the feelings they both experienced in the beginning. Luke interrupted to tell his dad he remembered being asked if he was sure when he announced his desire to marry Sarah.

"I have to ask the same question to you now, Dad."

"I remember that night and the answer you gave me, Luke. My answer is the same. Yes, I'm sure. But, I think I'm a little more scared than you were at that time."

They laughed and talked for a little longer. Luke thought the thirty day notice was a little short for a wedding ceremony.

But he said they would make it to Augusta whatever the date. Bill said he would call again as soon as he was sure of the date, time and church. When he hung up he was glad Luke didn't question the church location because he hadn't asked the local preacher for a wedding date yet and didn't want Luke to fear the wedding wouldn't take place in a Church. Before he would forget, he called the church to talk about the possibility of a shared service. Bill wanted to have the blessing of his church on his marriage.

His pastor sounded open to the idea, but asked Bill for a letter outlining his intentions and he would then contact the local Bishop. They talked about merging people of such diverse religions and lifestyles. The pastor had been interested in the Amish since coming to Augusta and said he was looking forward to meeting some of them. They said their goodbyes after agreeing on a day to meet in the future. Bill was happy about the way things were coming together. He now found himself thinking more about his marriage than about saving the world.

Becky had finished clearing the supper dishes and had gone into the living room with Kiia for some family time. Bill joined them. He spent a few minutes bringing Becky up to date and then got down on the floor to play with Kiia for a while. As always, he let the boy choose what to play and then let him win.

After an hour or so Kiia tired enough for his mother to take him up for a bath. He was a high energy boy, but tired in mid evening and was easily persuaded to call it a night.

Bill booted the computer and began surfing the net with the idea of finding something that would make life in the "survival mode" a little more interesting and a lot more possible.

A Discount Office Supply Website caught his eye and he checked out some sale priced notebooks and accessories. The prices were low and he ordered a wireless notebook, printer, some flash drives and even a satellite dish because if everything went to hell in a hand basket he wouldn't be able to depend on dial up or cable. No earthquakes or eruptions should disturb the movements and functioning of existing satellites he reasoned. Of course, he had no intention of using the internet as he didn't want anyone to know where they were struggling for survival in a time of mass hysteria and less that good judgment.

Without giving a good deal of thought to it, he ordered a case of ten reams of paper and no additional ink cartridges. This lack of foresight would cause no end of difficulties later when they were trapped inside the barn while the earth struggled to repair itself.

He heard Becky coming down the stairs and quickly closed the site and deleted the history. He still wasn't ready to reveal what he was really concerned about. Becky turned on the TV and when she chose what Bill considered one of the more moronic sitcoms he said his goodnights and went upstairs. He sat at his desk and pulled his notes out of the drawer. He noted the purchase of the computer and then reviewed the entries he'd made so far. Not knowing what he would actually need for his family to survive for two or more years he had to accept his plans as being adequate.

For the next two weeks he set goals to finish the large mass fireplace and complete the raised garden beds. After that, he would not need the help of the Amish men and would wire the low voltage lights on his own.

He planned to test the circuits and time the electrical draw to see how long the lights would stay on before the batteries would need charging. Keeping the lights lit would be very important as they would need more electricity to start them then it would take to keep them on. He didn't know how to figure the startup energy as opposed to the continuous use energy so he just planned to keep them on twenty four hours a day. The raised garden beds will be built on wheels so they could be rolled under the lights for eight to ten hours and rolled away for a night time level of light while another bed would be rolled into place for a daylight period.

So much of what he was planning was untested and there was so much left to be planned he accepted his ideas as workable and went on to whatever else entered his mind. He grew weary of his speculations after a while and turned his thoughts to Miriam and what he had left to complete if they were to marry in a little over three weeks. He jotted some thoughts to use in the letter to the pastor and local Bishop, and then some more to ask Moses about.

The hour grew late and he wasn't sure he was doing more planning than fantasizing so he turned off his lights and went to bed. The thought of an arranged marriage wasn't the norm for most Americans, but Bill felt comfortable with what he had done. He and Miriam would be good together, he felt. After a while he realized he was keeping himself awake with fantasies so he re-prayed his night devotions. Sleep came and in the morning he arose refreshed.

Since Becky and Kiia usually slept in he went directly to the computer. "If I am going to survive a natural disaster," he thought, "have I ordered enough provisions?

Any more than two years and I'm not sure I would want to survive anyway." He called up his list of items ordered and ran down it.

Furniture; two tables and ten chairs; twelve military beds; Twelve mattresses with a hundred each sheets and blankets; twelve pillows and pillow cases.

Kitchen; two each twelve place table settings of dishes and silverware. Half dozen boxes of assorted crystal serving bowls, actual number of bowls unknown.

Food; none, yet. He'd ordered some vegetable and herb/spice seeds the Garden Catalogue offered, but no boxed or convenience foods to be cooked. His plans were for them to eat legumes and rice as staples and whatever they could grow would have to do. The farm supply company accepted his order for fifty pound sacks of ten different kinds of beans and four kinds of rice. When offered free freight if he'd order a whole semi load Bill did so. If that overfilled his fifty galvanized garbage cans he'd just have to find a way to keep the rest from rotting or being eaten by mice and rats. As an after thought Bill ordered another twenty large galvanized garbage cans along with a dozen galvanized five gallon pails with tight fitting covers.

Tools; they had the construction tools they'd used to finish the interior of the barn and Bill had gotten some brooms, mops and cleaning soap for the floor. He'd gotten some hand tools for the plant beds after they had been sown and two watering cans as there would be no water pressure for hoses and sprayers. They would keep the two flat shovels he had bought for the Amish to mix concrete for the large mass fireplace.

Furniture; Two sets of tables, and chairs to seat 12 people. No living room furniture as there would not be a room like that. He would have to check into camp type chairs later.

Clothing; He didn't pick up any winter clothing for the kids and decided he would wait for the women to pick things up.

Books; He'd ordered the bibles and the art supplies, but how much would be enough? There was an old school blackboard at one of the second hand stores and it was free if a person bought two pails of chalk so he made a note to stop back and pick it up. If he could find a good encyclopedia he would get it, but nothing for the computer now. He planned to keep it and the satellite dish hidden until after the initial disaster had abated enough to reveal their position. There was no one he wanted to Email. He didn't want to risk being discovered when they wouldn't be able to defend themselves against fear crazed people who had no plans for survival.

Bill checked the time and seeing it was late saved his work and headed for the door. He arrived at the farm on time to see Moses, Amos, and Michael entering the barn. They were already pouring cement to build the base for the fireplace. Since the fireplace was going to be a lot heavier than the usually small house type they had leveled the bottom of the hole and filled it with highway base course. After tamping it down by walking on it they had started to fill the hole with rocks and concrete. They were near the floor level when Bill walked in.

Chapter 11

The Heart of The Hearth

Moses looked up to greet him. "We came early today because of the amount of time it will take to build the large mass fireplace.

"I understand. It'll go a little faster if you let me mix the concrete in the motorized unit, rather than by hand. May I?"

"You may."

Bill went outside and moved the mixer close to the sand pile. He mixed the loads a little richer on concrete than was called for, normally. He was going to avoid cracking between the stones at all cost. Amos continued mixing by hand and informed Bill he too was mixing "rich" to avoid cracking later. Moses intently chose and placed stones while Michael hauled them in. Re-enforcement rods were cut and fit as needed and the work progressed so well they were at floor level in less than two hours.

They stopped long enough to bring in heavy wooden forms to shape the twelve inches of the fireplace that sat at floor level.

A steel firebox and an assortment of firebrick were brought to the site. The copper pipe that would be soldiered into a cage around three sides and the top of the firebox were measured and cut. Michael proved to be very good at this and soon had a cage to fit the dimensions of the fire box with one layer of firebrick around it. Water would be forced through this cage of pipes and when heated would be forced through the pipes in the concrete floor. The combination of the heated concrete floor and the radiant large mass fireplace would keep the barn comfortable in a long cold winter. Or, so Bill hoped.

Moses wanted to build the fire place in one day without any of the concrete getting completely dry before the next batch was mixed and stones set. This way the whole mass would be one piece instead of several layers of dried upon dried concrete.

"Let us begin, again," said Moses.

They put their backs into it and moved a lot of stone and mixed a lot of concrete. When the forms were filled to twelve inches about the floor, Moses checked for level while Michael walked around the forms looking at the chalk lines he had made after they had built it.

"The lines are visible so the base is square," he said.

Moses acknowledged the news with a nod and said, "Let's move the chimney blocks and liners in so we are ready when this level begins to set up. I don't want to waste any time."

The Amish began to haul in the blocks and liners while Bill brought in more fire brick to line the steel firebox.

Bill had purchased an extra large fire box because he had always liked the old pictures of people having a stew pot boiling over the fire and a fire brick ledge to bake bread on after the fire died down. Little did he know there would be very little meat available after the cataclysm happpened. Then, the beginning of cataclysm announced its impending arrival.

For about ten seconds the ground shook! It was an unmistakable earthquake type of shake. All four men stepped back and forth like drunks hoping to stay on their feet. When it was over they were all upright and staring at each other with bewildered eyes.

"An earthquake." said Bill, confirming what each of them didn't want to believe.

"I've heard of such things in our oral traditions," replied Moses, "but it was generations ago that it happened." Amos and Michael nodded agreement and seemed relieved that Moses could explain what happened.

Bill was sick at heart to feel his worst fears were being announced by the quake. He didn't want to say anymore than he had to. Finishing the barn was too important to reveal his plans or bury his head in the sand and stop here. The wood for the next tier of forms was outside and he said he would bring them in if the others would check the fire place to see if it was still square.

As he stepped outside the barn he was surprised to see the cement contractor drive into his yard at breakneck speed. He was hanging out his window yelling obscenities and demanding to know what happened. He skidded to a stop and jumped out of his truck. He faced Bill and shouted out the same question like a broken record.

"What da hell happened? What da hell happened?" and would have continued if Bill hadn't interrupted him.

"It was probably just a little tremor…"

"That was not 'just a little tremor," what da hell just happened? I was on my way to install a septic tank and toilet and I was on the road and off the road and on again. What da hell just happened?

Bill questioned the man about the job he had been on the way to and he began to slow down a little. It was better to get the man and his helper back on the road again without them guessing what was being built in the barn. But, there was no getting them back on the road again.

"I ain't leaving here till I'm sure it's safe to go home," he shouted, and repeated himself again and again.

Bill held up his hands to force a word in edgewise. "You were going to install a septic tank and toilet?" he repeated till he got a "Ya" out of him.

"You know, you could install that stuff here where you are safe and then get more to install later."

Somehow the logic of that made sense and the contractor began to nod his head and repeat "Ya, Ya, I could do that."

"I'll write you a check when you are done. Come into the barn and I will show you where I want the toilet set." The contractor followed Bill like a scared puppy.

Inside, Bill made a mark on the new concrete floor and told the contractor not to stray from the mark because of the heat pipes buried in the floor. He explained the exterior drain pipe should be buried an extra foot or so below the normal four feet and he wanted the unused and scrap Styrofoam cut up and laid over it. If it got really cold this winter Bill didn't want the sewer to freeze up.

They went outside to find the contractor's helper regaining his senses and getting out of the truck. The contractor told him to off load the Bobcat and septic tank and he would show him where to dig. He grabbed the tools to cut a hole in the floor and said he would bring in the power auger later.

"I can do this," he mumbled to himself, "I can do this."

Bill left the two terrified men to regain their senses and install the toilet. Inside the Amish has already started to add more concrete and stones. Moses had sent Michael to Miriam's home and then to the homes of the rest of his clan to determine if there had been any damage or injuries. He would be back in an hour with a report of no major damage to structures or furniture, but a lot of broken dishes and windows.

"We'll finish here before returning home, Michael," said Moses.

The four of them worked quickly filling the area around the firebox and water-pipe cage. This was where the heat would be made and as much recovered as possible. When they covered the firebox they didn't need to build any more forms and just added stones and concrete around the chimney flue until they got to the ceiling and then to the roof top. One of the flues was to take the hot exhaust from the fire box up and outside and the other, which ran down beside and against it was to heat incoming air. This would give Bill four ways to reclaim heat from one fire; radiant heat from the fire and the large mass fireplace, heated air from the outside and the water that was heated and run through the pipes in the floor. In the event of a long cold winter he and his family should stay warm.

All six of the men worked at a pace none could sustain without the bad scare they had just received from the tremor.

In the corner of the barn, concrete was broken up and a hole dug for the toilet. In the middle concrete was mixed and poured and stones filled in to build the heat source. Out side the hole was dug and the septic tank lowered into its place. Pipes were connected and Styrofoam broken up and laid over everything to prevent subsequent freezing. All six men worked as hard on their jobs as they did at trying to understand how the earth quake could have happened and what it meant. Maybe what it meant could be forgotten or overcome by concentrating on their work. It was a vicious circle which in the end produced a result that would be invaluable to the survival of Bill and his family. It was good they were all so busy and didn't notice only Bill had a determined look on his face which was different from the look of fear in the eyes of the others. He alone knew the real reason for rebuilding the barn.

"Ya, I think that will do it for us." said the contractor. He had come up behind the others as they were walking around the fireplace checking their work. His eyes didn't show the fear they had when he had started the installation of the toilet and septic tank.

"Hey, how the hell are you going to get any water over to the crapper?"

"Oh!" said Bill. "I'll have to get back to you after we get the plans drawn up. What do I owe you for today?"

"I'll bill ya. This has been a hell of a day and I'm going home to forget it ever happened."

"All right," said Bill as he watched the two men walk to their truck. They double checked the Bobcat to make sure it was secure on the trailer, and then drove away. Bill turned to the Amish.

"It appears to be level and square, William. We will leave now. I am sure there will be extra work to go with our usual chores."

"I understand, Moses. Can I bring up my truck tomorrow. I'm sure there will be things to get for repairs"

"That will be a Godsend, William. We will start repairs right after chores."

Bill watched as the Amish walked to their buggy and left. He wondered if he would ever have the quiet confident faith these men seemed to have. They didn't look back or wave. They just got in their buggy and faced the life that lay before them.

Bill made a quick walk around the day's projects and marveled at how much they had accomplished. The fireplace and chimney were magnificent to look at and an overwhelming contrast to the lonely and necessary little toilet in the corner.

"Yes," he thought, "I'll worry about getting the water to it later."

He walked out of the barn and closed it. As he walked to his truck he saw Miriam in her garden. He ached to go to her and hold her. He wanted to kiss her and tell her everything would be all right. His plans were going well and she would always be safe with him. As he approached the garden he stopped. They had no chaperone and closeness would not be acceptable to her way of life and courtship.

She looked up at him and her eyes said the same.

"We accomplished a lot today despite the tremor. Tomorrow I will be back to help the men of your clan make repairs."

"Thee looks weary."

Suddenly Bill felt the very essence of her observation. Every muscle in his body felt weary and he turned to go. But, he stopped and faced her.

"God grant you restful slumber tonight, Miriam and may his angels hold you tight in their embrace."

He walked quickly to his truck and drove away. He looked back to see her in the beautiful sunset, alone in her garden, watching him. He forced himself to drive away and his speed increased. He cursed himself when he realized he had forgotten his cell phone. He was suddenly sure Becky had tried to contact him without any success.

When he got home, his suspicions were confirmed. Becky heard the truck as he pulled onto the driveway and was on his case as he walked to the kitchen door.

"You know, I could probably get a hold of you easier if you thought about carrying your cell phone with you!"

"Yes," said Bill. "Hey! You break all this glass?"

"No! Where have you been? Do you have any idea what happened this afternoon?"

"No," he lied. "I was up in Amish country all day. You know how quiet it is up there. What happened here?" He tried to keep a straight face.

"Only the first earthquake in the history of Augusta, that's all! Do you mean to tell me you didn't know we had an earthquake?"

"Well, I felt a tremor while I was working, but it sure didn't feel like an earthquake." It didn't seem like enough to stop working."

"Men!" Becky muttered. "Well it did seem to create a lot of work around here," she continued. "And, I could sure use some help around here right now! Honestly, Dad, you could spend a little more time around home, you know. You do have a grandson who would like to see more of his grandfather.

We spent all afternoon at Cherry's house cleaning up the mess there. She was in a panic all afternoon about this thing. I just don't know."

Bill kept silent and let her run on until she ran out of energy. He grabbed a broom and began to sweep up the glass in the patio area. Only the older windows that hadn't been replaced earlier when they bought the house were broken. The newer ones had held. He was glad of that. In fact, he was pretty happy the house had shown itself to be as strong as he thought it was when he bought it.

"So, Cherry was pretty shook up over this thing?"

"Oh, now don't try to make fun of her feelings. I know you don't like her and you think she isn't very smart, but she is my best friend. And she is good to me and Kiia."

"All right, all right," said Bill. "I'm too tired myself to argue about anything or anyone. I'm glad she is a good friend to you. I'll get the old screens from the garage so we can keep the bugs out tonight and I'll get new windows tomorrow. Did you and Kiia have supper yet?"

"Yes." If you would get home at a decent hour you could eat with us."

"I know, Becky, but, you have to understand how important it is to get this farm ready. It just may make a lot of things easy for us in the future."

"That's all well and good Dad, but Kiia is beginning to wonder if he still has a grandpa. You haven't spent a lot of time with him lately."

"I know, I know. I feel bad about that. I'm just glad he has a super mom in his life. I'm going to slow down in a couple weeks. You know, just before Miriam and I get married. After that I will be around a lot more. I promise.

Now, this isn't a big mess and I can get the screens up soon. So let me get this done and we can all get to bed at a reasonable time tonight.

"All right," she said," resigned to her father's wishes. "I'll make a sandwich for you and then I'm going to bed too."

"Oh," Bill said, rubbing is fore head, "I have to leave right away in the morning to get some glass for us. I'm sure everyone else will be needing some to repair their own damage. There can't be enough around here for everyone." When she didn't reply, he turned toward the garage.

It didn't take long to sweep up the glass and install the old style screens in place of the windows. The dark kept him from a detailed clean up as he couldn't see well enough to look for shards.

Becky had left him a nice sandwich so he grabbed a soda to go with it and headed upstairs. The laptop was in sleep mode, but it didn't take long to get it to his "goals" page. Checking off the large mass fireplace gave him a real sense of satisfaction. So did having the toilet in as he hadn't known how he was going to get that done. The disposal of waste water from washing clothes was going to be easy now. Just use it to flush the toilet!

Tomorrow he would pick up the washer, the portable cloths line device and whatever there would be room for in the pickup. Glass for the Amish community would be the priority for now though. It had been a big day and suddenly whatever could or needed to be done tonight had little importance. Bill shut off the computer and stretched out on his bed. He had no time to undress as sleep overcame him immediately.

Chapter 12
Faith explored

Bill rose early that morning and got ready to leave as quickly as he could. He left a note for Becky and Kiia trying to explain how important it was to complete the next few days of work. Signing it with love only made him feel how lonely they were when he was gone during the quake.

He drove straight to the Amish farms and saw Moses leaving his barn. The old man looked up when he heard the truck approach and walked to the passenger window. He leaned in.

"Good Morning, William, I knew you would be early today."

Bill laughed. "But not early enough to be ahead of you."

"True enough," replied Moses. "I have a list of needed things inside along with my papers, er, ah, checkbook. I will be right back."

Bill resisted the temptation to turn on the radio and enjoyed looking over the farm. True to his word, in a moment Moses came down the path to get in the truck. The engine fired up and they were on their way to the farm supply store.

"I have little hope of getting any glass, William. We can not be the only people who suffered in the incident yesterday.

"Well," said Bill, "one should always be positive."

"I believe God will reward me in my endeavors, William. But, always there will be the lesser and greater among us."

Bill agreed and went on to comment about the how he admired his faith and that of the other Amish he had met.

"Faith," Commented Moses. "It can be seen in action, but can not be judged as real or not. It can be felt by one who seeks it and yet, range from weak to all consuming and back to weak again. It is a mysterious gift from God. Are you as much a man of faith as I think you to be, William?"

Bill was a little surprised by the direct question.

"I try to be," replied Bill as he turned into the Farm Store parking lot. His heart sank as he saw a line of customers extending out of the store and at least a block long.

"But, right now," he continued, "I don't have much faith in our chances of getting *any* glass today."

Moses let out a grunt that sounded as close to a laugh as anything Bill had heard from him in the whole time he had known him. Bill turned the truck toward the highway and they drove away. As they approached the four corners where they would turn toward Amish country or toward Augusta, Bill made a quick decision.

"How about we stop at one of the local diners for some coffee and maybe even a plate of cakes and eggs?"

"I have no money for such extravagances. But, if you will pay, there might be a need for the glory of God to be made present there. Yes, I will stop."

They pulled up into the parking lot and the local Café was a sorry site. Most of windows were out, but the glass door was still up and the electric sign said the place was open. Bill walked in ahead of Moses and took the cleanest booth. Both men slide into it and looked at the menu.

"Be with you in a moment, Gents," came a voice from the kitchen.

The voice had a familiar sound to it, but before Bill could grab Moses and head for the door, Marge came out of the kitchen. He'd forgotten she worked here.

"Hiya, Gents. Well," she started, "if it isn't the old lonesome stranger?

How are you doin' and throw in a couple good reasons too."

"I've been fine, busy, hungry and not necessarily in that order. I'd like the breakfast special."

"What about Little Boy Blue here?"

"I will have what he is having and my clothing is the same color as yours so a remark like that is not needed."

"Yah, the color is the same, but have you ever seen it worn this way," and she gave her hips a shake.

"My wife has an outfit just like that, only she wears hers under her dress." Moses replied dryly.

Marge exploded with a laugh. She quickly spun around and ran for the kitchen. Bill saw her push her false teeth back in her mouth as she entered the kitchen. He turned toward Moses and tried to apologize.

"There is no need to apologize, William. You could not have known such a thing would happen. I do sense a great need for the presence of God to be brought into a place like this, however."

Bill agreed and tried to make small talk while they waited for their food. It didn't take long as they were the only ones in the diner. In a few minutes the cook came out with a tray and unloaded it before them.

"Here's your breakfast. Don't know what you said to Marge. She's still in the can. I think she pissed her pants."

Bill looked at Moses, wishing his flesh could crawl him out to the truck again. Then, it happened.

There was what felt like a vibration and then it felt like something picked up the diner and slammed it back down hard.

The quake didn't last as long as the one yesterday, but it was more severe. The rest of the windows popped out and it sounded like every dish in the place dropped and broke. There'd be no lunch served here today.

Bill fished a ten dollar bill out of his pocket and threw it on the table. Of all the places to die, this was not his choice. They struggled out of the booth together.

Moses stopped to help the cook to his feet. Bill grabbed his arm.

"He's O.K. Let's get back to the farm. Besides, the way he smells he'll be in the restroom and on Marge's lap before we get to the pickup."

"An unpleasant way to leave the lesser of our brethren, William. I will be right behind you."

They raced through the broken glass door without having to open it. As they opened the pickup doors Bill cell's phone began to ring. He started the engine first and started driving toward the barn. He held the phone to his ear.

"Dad?" A stern female voice filled his ear.

"I know, Becky, it was the same here and I didn't cause it. Are you and Kiia all right?"

"Yes, and I know you didn't cause it. I just want to know what is going on. You get back home. Right now!"

"I have Moses with me and I have to leave him with his people. Then I will come straight home."

"Dad. What's going on? I think you know and I want you to tell me now!"

"Honey, all I know is this quake stuff is really rare here in Wisconsin and we can talk more when I get home. I'm driving too fast to try to talk on the phone at the same time. I love you and I'll be home soon. Bye."

He hung up on her and concentrated on giving Moses the fastest ride home he had ever experienced.

"William, we will stop at your farm first. I saw no other buildings down and I think that will be the case on all of our farms too." Bill marveled at his control in this situation. He slowed the truck and turned onto the road leading to Amish country.

"William; you were expecting someone?"

Bill was surprised to look toward his farm and see two semi-trucks parked by his barn. Miriam was standing on her porch and appeared relieved to see his truck pull in. He stopped by the house and he and Moses got out at the same time.

"William; I will see to my clanswomen. You see to the trucks."

"Yes Sir", he replied. He hadn't been second in command at an emergency in a long time, but the old ways of respect came back. He strode over to the trucks. The drivers were talking together and both looked as though they had taken the quake well. They had a fork truck on the ground and the barn's doors open.

"Hi," said Bill as he approached them.

Both men returned his greeting with a little small talk about the recent quakes also. Then they offered their bills of lading. Bill took a quick look at the amount of legumes and rice totaled in the one and signed as having received the load. The other was an assortment of his other orders; grow lights, the computer and hardware, a satellite dish, 20 galvanized cans, 500 drum sized plastic bags, 1000 blankets...

"A thousand blankets," exclaimed Bill. "I ordered only 100!"

"Lemme see," said the driver as he grabbed the bill of lading. "Oh, yah. It says here bedding is sold in sets of ten, so if you ordered a hundred blankets, sheets or mattress covers, take it by ten and what you see is what you get. OK?"

"OK," I don't have a loading dock so we will have to use whatever ramps you have on the trucks.

The driver that brought the fork truck had ramps and Bill made a deal with him to help unload the other truck after the first was empty. They opened the truck with the legumes and rice first.

Bill was a little disappointed that the pallets weren't stacked to the top of the trailer, but the driver told him the bottom bags on the pallets would split if there was too much weight on them. Taking him at his word, Bill showed him where to put the food pallets in the barn.

There were a number of things that could be taken off the other trailer by hand and a two wheel hand cart. Bill elected to help here and let the other driver work alone. He wanted to get the 20 galvanized cans with the other 50 and the drum sized plastic bags in as soon as they could. The bags would be put into the cans and the legumes, rice and grains divided accordingly. That way, if rats or mice became a problem they would not be able to get into foodstuffs he couldn't afford to lose.

An Amish wagon came into the yard as the unloading began. Amos was driving and when he stopped, Michael and a man Bill didn't know got out the back. Michael went over to talk to Moses and the other two looked over the trucks. They talked quietly and gestured toward the trucks as if they were looking at adult sized toys. Moses walked up with Michael.

"Miriam is well and looks forward to your company in these uncertain times. I told her your preparations have been successful and she will be given to you in marriage on the last Sunday of September. She has asked for permission to start a period of modified fasting and prayer till then. I approved modest fasting and as much prayer as she wished."

"Thank you," Moses. "I will begin a modest fast to go with my prayers too." Turning to Michael, he asked if the other members of the clan were well. Moses answered for him and said all was well.

"It would appear you are in need of our help, William."

"Ever since I bought this farm I have been indebted to you, Moses. Yes, I would like some help getting the trucks unloaded and the bags of feed into the galvanized cans."

"I have to find the marking pens so we can label the contents as we dump the bags."

"Michael has an inventory in his mind of what you already have and he will find what you need. The rest of us will begin filling the cans when you tell us where you want them placed."

Bill gestured to the back wall which separated the animal space from where his family would live. Moses said something in their language to Amos and the other man, whom Bill decided to refer to as "the other guy" until someone introduced him. The three Amish men lined some cans against the wall and Bill found the box of plastic drum bags for them. As soon as the bags were in the cans the Amish began opening the feed bags and filling them. They kept different species together and soon were installing covers. Moses had the other guy make crude ladders and they laid them on the rows of full cans so the next can filled with the same seeds could be put on top.

The lids on the bottom row crushed down a little, but made a better seal against rodents. It was good the Amish started filling the galvanized cans as the truckers brought in things so fast the barn began to fill up.

As one pallet was empted, picked up and stacked with the fire wood, another could be brought in and placed there. But, too quickly, the floor was so full the fork lift was used to place lighter pallets on top of the seed bags. The driver was careful and nothing was torn or lost. In an hour, both trucks were unloaded. Bill approved the deliveries and gave the one driver fifty dollars for using his fork truck.

Back inside he began sorting and organizing the things he'd bought for survival reasons. The Amish continued to pour seed (legumes, grains and rice) into the large galvanized cans. They used his cordless electric drill to attach fasteners to the wall and pass rope through them to hold the cans to the wall. Anything as heavy as a filled fifty gallon can would kill someone if it fell on them.

Bill took the boxed satellite dish and hid it in the animal side and then put the computer into a can which he labeled "food for thought." That can he hid behind others filled with seed. He didn't want anything used that might lead people to them when they couldn't help others or defend themselves. His was to be "a family of God," not a vigilante or guerilla group.

"We have completed the task of filling the galvanized cans, William." Moses fixed his eyes on Bill and then scanned the contents of the barn. "It would seem you have an abundance of feed grains, seeds and, and whatever else you have gotten today."

"Yes," said Bill absently. "Take the extra bags of whatever you want. I have a little more ordered and ten more cans also. I hope I have ordered enough. There is so much more coming I hope I have room for it all."

"I will accept your offer, William. But, I think I would like to keep everything here in the new cans you have ordered. That way everything will be safe until we need it." Moses looked around the barn again making mental notes of what he saw.

"Oh," Bill blurted out. "Can I see Miriam later on? I want to explain what I'm doing out here in her barn."

"In keeping with our clan's traditions I have asked another woman to move in with her so she would not be alone. Your wedding will be in a little over two weeks. You may see her then and forever."

At that moment there was a tremor strong enough not to go unnoticed. Bill looked around the barn to see if anything had been shaken loose from its place. Every thing stayed put.

It's going to happen sooner than I had feared," he murmured to himself. "Moses, I think I will go into town to pick up some things and call my daughter to see how things are with her. I should be back to unload in a couple of hours and then be on my way home."

"I believe it would be best if my clan spend the next two days in prayer and fasting. We will not be available until Monday. I suggest the same for you.

"Fasting and prayer are a part of my Traditions also."

The two men nodded and turned away. They closed the barn and left in their respective vehicles.

Bill went to the farm store for more fifty gallon galvanized cans and then to the second hand store where he picked up the washing machine, cloths line and everything else he had put away in the last two weeks.

Back at the barn he unloaded quickly keeping an eye out for Miriam. Just as he drove away he saw her with another woman from her clan as they were picking fresh vegetables for their dinner. He remembered Moses' admonition about waiting to see her till their wedding day and went straight home.

Becky met him at the door with Kiia beside her. "Well, it happened again and you were some where else, as usual."

Bill squatted down in front of Kiia to make better eye contact with the boy. Kiia wasn't sure if he should react to his grandfather in the same way his mother was. In a few seconds the little boy that he was won out over any big people problems. He plunged into his grandfather's arms laughing and talking without being understood.

"Well, we sure have your mother scared, Kiia," he said to trusting eyes which didn't yet understand. "If she'll call your Uncle Luke on the speaker phone, your grandfather will try to explain." He picked up the boy and walked in. Becky moved out of the way and then closed the door. They went into the living room to use the desk phone. Bill put Kiia on the floor near the desk and gave him a toy to play with. He wanted some quiet play time with the boy before he talked on the phone.

Luke answered the phone after Becky dialed and they all shouted out their greetings. They were all together over the miles when Bill asked;

"Things get a little bumpy at your end of the country lately?

"Big time!" replied Luke. The TV says there are quakes all over the world and some of them are really bad. I don't think we got anything as bad as some of the other countries."

"I'm sorry things are worse for others," said Bill, "But I really think they will get much worse for everybody."

"I'd like to have the governments of all the countries get together and give us some answers," replied Luke. "And, by the way, why do you think it will be much worse?"

"Do you remember the day we went fishing on our vacation, the first day out when we went to the far side of the lake?"

"Yes," said Luke. "The water seemed a little shallower than I remember as a kid, and a lot warmer."

"Right," said Bill. He went on to explain his conversation with the Ranger and the geological maps he saw on his office wall, the differences in the lake maps from fifteen years ago and this summer and the fact that the world seemingly restarted itself a number of times. The loss of the dinosaurs, the ice age and the great flood told about in the Bible seemed to point to the possibility of another cataclysm.

"That can't be true!" said Becky. "By now, the government would know and would have told us what to do!"

"Not necessarily so," interrupted Luke. "My guess is they do know, but don't have a clue about what to do."

"I agree with you Luke." said Bill. "I think that right now they have more people running around in circles looking for hiding places than they have actually knowing what to do and how to do it."

"This can't be," exclaimed Becky.

The men continued to talk, ignoring Becky's outburst. They talked abut geologic theories, tides, ocean temperatures and anything they thought was pertinent. Then Bill interrupted.

"At this time," he said, "there are two very important things for the three of us to agree on right now. Number one; since we are going to get together in two weeks we must talk then, because I have some plans.

And, number two; it is very important none of us say anything about our meeting or my plans to anyone. Can we agree on that?"

"Sure," said Luke.

Becky was silent. Bill knew her fear of something this big would lead her to talk to other young mothers in hopes of saving their children. Still, it was important that no one find out about the farm. The barn that once seemed so big was way too small to house any extra desperate souls.

"Becky?"

"What?"

"Becky, you must agree to keep dad's plans a secret."

"Well, what if we could help others?"

"Becky! What if we can't help others? It's too big a problem for us to help the whole country. And, what if I'm wrong? You wouldn't want the whole town laughing at us, would you?"

"All right," she said with a giggle. "This whole thing is preposterous, anyway. I don't want anyone to know we are thinking this way."

"Way to go, Becky."

"Yes," said Bill.

She got up and picked up Kiia. "It's getting past Kiia's bed time so we're going up. Tell Sarah we look forward to seeing her and the kids in two weeks."

"Will do, Becky. Sleep well and don't spend any time worrying about any of this, OK?" Luke was more worried about his sister than he was about his dad's speculations about a big earth quake and volcano.

"I won't," she said as she started up the stairs with Kiia. "Say goodbye to Uncle Luke and Grandpa, son."

The boy turned, on the stairs. "Bye. Don't forget to come up for prayers, Grandpa." The two of them went up for his bath.

"Hey, before you go, Luke," said Bill as he picked up the phone to speak privately to him. "Do you know the dates of your flights?"

Luke told him they would come in Saturday afternoon and would have to leave by Tuesday morning. He was a key player in a big project, he said. Bill encouraged him to bring some keepsakes this trip as they couldn't be sure when or if they would get another chance to get into the barn with what they value.

Luke laughed and when he realized his father's seriousness said he would find a few things. They promised to try to calm the women and bring a few family things to the barn.

After hanging up the phone, Bill went up stairs with a sense of having done the right thing in telling his kids of his fears. He felt even better when he prayed with his grandson and watched him pray and play himself to sleep. Becky had gone into her own bedroom after Bill came up. He wanted to spend time with her, but she had shut off her light and Bill respected her need for privacy.

He went into his own room and booted his laptop. While waiting he reviewed the notes he had made on paper. The trucks today had delivered the amount of dried beans and rice he felt would last a little more than two years and they could raise other veggies with the gardens he was going to build.

Any more than two years he figured they wouldn't have to worry as there probably wouldn't be much of a chance to survive anyway.

There were enough tools for minor repairs and raised bed gardening. Anything more ambitious than that would have to be provided by the military after things thawed out; provided the government made adequate plans and executed them well enough to survive. Privacy wouldn't be as possible as any of them would like, but at least they would have twelve individual beds, mattresses and pillows and for some reason twelve times a hundred blankets, pillow cases, mattress pads and sheets. How the Army chose to sell some things in sets of a hundred and pillows individually was something he didn't want to spend time figuring out. He was just glad he didn't end up with twelve hundred beds.

He reviewed the computer notes into the night. Most of what he ordered had found its way cross country to the same terminal and then onto the trucks he unloaded this afternoon. Whatever had come and whatever else was on order would have to suffice for however long they would have to survive their ordeal. His mind was so full and so tired he couldn't think of anything else they needed. He reasoned he had never had to build and live a survival type of life and turned his computer off.

Sleep came quickly because of his fatigue and the tremors that night felt like a rocking motion which didn't fully awaken him. In the morning, Kiia came bounding into room full of little boy energy. He was elated to find his grandfather home after nearly a month of him being up and gone to work so early.

They laughed and talked abut whatever the boy thought of, but mostly, Bill looked at his grandson and marveled at how much the boy had grown in four weeks. Becky walked past the bedroom and said she was going to the kitchen just in case there might be a hungry man or two wanting breakfast.

"Oh, Becky," called Bill. "I'd like a light breakfast, lunch and dinner today and tomorrow because I want a modified fast to go with a lot of praying this weekend. I feel there is a lot to be prayed for and understood right now."

"That's an understatement."

"I'd like your help in fasting and prayer for the weekend. We'll go to church today and tomorrow. But, mostly lets stay together to pray and meditate."

"All right. I'll call Cherry and tell her we are staying home for the weekend," she replied, glad to have her dad home and available for a change.

Bill stayed with Kiia for a few minutes and they roughhoused and tickled. The boy laughed easily and had fun whenever he was with his grandfather. Soon the smell of coffee floated upstairs and Bill sent Kiia downstairs so he could shower, shave and plan their day.

He got downstairs just as Kiia was finishing his breakfast. Becky fried an egg apiece and split one piece of toast between them. Bill looked at his plate and realized fasting wasn't going to be much fun. Thankfully, fluids are a part of a modified fast so he downed a couple cups of coffee with his breakfast and then cleaned up. He asked Becky and Kiia to come outside with him to walk around their lot. They picked up downed twigs and limbs and walked and talked. Silence was reserved for their prayers. Their talked revolved around Bill's coming marriage, Becky's late mom and family in general. The weekend passed without another quake and Monday morning found them all relaxed. They had a big breakfast together.

It took a lot of convincing to get Becky and Kiia to let him go back out to the farm, but he promised them he would explain all on his marriage weekend. When he arrived at the farm he was the only one at the barn. Apparently Moses and his clan had a slow start to the week also. He went inside to straighten up the things he had gotten on Friday.

He knew he wanted to keep his grow lights lit with the batteries and inverters so he spent a few minutes figuring how many batteries it would take to power a bank of lights. Four batteries would power a bank of two eight foot lights. The batteries would last more than six hours he hoped so he planned to charge them every four hours.

The twelve volt white lights would be on continuously and charging the batteries wouldn't hurt them. He and Luke would just have to work four hours and sleep four hours just like sailors did when onboard ship. If they alternated shifts each would get enough sleep and enjoy the benefits of exercise as they pedal-powered the generator, which Bill had yet to design.

He dug the three wheel bicycle out from behind a pile of boxes and rolled it over to the large mass fireplace. The pump needed to move the heating liquid around the firebox and back out through the concrete floor would need a belt from the bicycle. A tensioner pulley and an alternator would complete circuit. The other rear wheel would need a pulley and belt to drive the fan that would draw air down the second chimney flu and through a water bath to provide clean, breathable air. He had an idea of how to do everything he wanted to complete. He hoped he was right.

He plugged the small wire feed welder into the load center and did the welding there.

When he had his components built he connected them together and added the belts. He resisted the temptation to jump on his now stationary bicycle and test its action because he wanted to have the wires from the alternator to the inverters installed and then to the batteries and from there to the lights. He didn't want to "pedal-up" some electricity until he had somewhere for it to go.

He connected up three sets of batteries to feed the three sets of grow lights. A four way switch between the alternator and the sets of batteries would make it possible to charge the sets individually or all three together. He installed a gage on the handle bars and ran the wires into the back of the alternator so he could find out how fast to pedal the "bike" to get the amount of electricity he needed to charge the batteries. If he pedaled too slowly the lights would go out. Too fast and the regulator in the alternator would stop excessive energy and his pedaling effort would be wasted.

Bill wired carefully as he wanted to save as much extra wire and connectors as possible. He used components that could be found on cars or trucks and was sure they would last as long in this application as they would in hard driving.

When he connected the lights to the inverter they glowed well. Bill got on the bicycle and began to pedal until his gage showed he was making fourteen to eighteen volts. The lights were now as bright as they were designed to be. He wanted to test the "pedal power" for a while, but he had to hook up the belt power for the air intake too.

His thinking proved correct again and the bicycle to air blower fan was aligned well enough to add the belt and adjust its tension. He resisted a test run until he had more time to test the alternator circuit also. He was startled by the sound of boots behind him.

"William, mind thee that I walk into your barn?"

"Of course not," said Bill, recognizing Michael's voice. He remembered the medical attention Michael had given him and added, "you will always be welcome here."

"A comforting invitation," he replied and stepped in.

"In the future, you don't need to ask to enter the barn, Michael."

"May you and your invitation live a long life William. I accept." He walked over to see what Bill was working on. It didn't take long for Bill to explain how the three wheel bicycle would be used to move heat from the fire place and generate electricity for the batteries which would keep the grow lights on.

"I see thee has removed the rubber tires from thy bicycle and replaced them with steel pulleys. You must know, then, that we do not have rubber tires because we feel the invention of rubber tires would lead our people away from the simple live lived for God."

"Yes," lied Bill. He knew little of their beliefs, but didn't want to go into a long discussion of the ratio of pulley size to the amount of revolutions needed to be pedaled to get work done.

"And this bicycle looks like a good form of exercise, although our people have little need for exercise because of the way we live and work. Still, I'm sure it might be a good thing someday."

"Yes," said Bill not knowing where this conversation was going. A ruckus just outside the barn caught his attention and he motioned to Michael to accompany him to the door of the barn. They stepped outside and met Amos walking up the driveway with five young goats in tow.

"It has occurred to us to gift you and your new bride-to-be with the start of a herd of goats; you now have one old billy goat of good breeding, one very young male and three females."

"Goats?"

"Yes, goats."

"Michael?" "What will I do with a herd of goats?"

"William, they will give you manure for your gardens, milk and cheese for your table and even an occasional meal."

"Michael, how will I take care of a herd of goats?"

"Thee will learn, William."

Bill looked blankly at Michael, then at the goats and finally to Amos. A strange sound, almost like a laugh came from Amos whose face Bill had thought would break if he ever showed an emotion.

"Michael, what do they eat?"

"Thee will learn, William, they will eat just about anything. Though if thee allows them to, thee will find their meat to taste suspiciously like the manure you will get for your gardens."

Bill looked at him blankly, then at the goats and finally to Amos again. He thought, "that sumbitch Amos is laughing at me!"

"Michael?" "How do goats, live?"

"Thee will learn, William."

"Michael! I have learned enough in a short period of time. Now, I need some details."

"Of Course, William." Michael was plainly smiling now. "Amos and I are prepared to build a small pen on the sunny side of the barn and then cut a small opening in the wall. The animals will go out and come in as needed. You have enough hay and feed grains for years and enough water at the pump. Your wife-to-be can do the rest. They need little care to thrive."

"Oh," lied Bill. "That's what I thought. Go ahead. Take anything you need and yell if you need help." He bent over to pick up a usable board that had been left out and the old male goat butted him behind the knee and sent him tumbling. He jumped to his feet and resisted the desire to smack the little beast along side the head. "It's better I don't lose my image of a peaceful man," he thought.

Amos was as red as a beet and in what looked like a highly controlled full-body convulsion.

"Amos," bellowed Bill, "if you don't learn how to laugh out loud you will blow your stack some day." He threw the board down for the Amish to pick up. Instead, they hustled off to tie up the goats and came back for the wood later.

Bill went into the barn and began to run the wires for the grow lights and the cables to raise and lower them to the height of the soon to be growing plants.

Again, he knew what he wanted to do and not having any plans to work from wasn't an issue. He strung the wires in an open fashion instead of running them through metal or plastic pipes. His reasoning was any future repairs would be easy to spot and make if the wires were out in the open. There are times when the safety of hiding wires was necessary to protect them from accidental damage.

But, Bill wanted the wires visible so everyone would realize how important it would be to exercise care in their day to day survival.

The sudden, loud bleating of the goats interrupted his work and he walked outside to see what was going on. Amos and Michael had finished building the pen and were watching the goat's antics. As Bill approached them the ground began to tremble again. For a few seconds it became necessary for men and animals to open their stance and concentrate on remaining standing. They all stumbled around for a moment and then the trembler passed. Both men and animals looked at each other as if to verify the other's well being.

"These are strange occurrences," said Michael, looking at Bill for some sort of explanation.

At that moment the woman who was staying with Miriam came running out of the back porch with Miriam behind her. The poor woman was crying in terror and Miriam had to catch her and hold her till the fear passed. Apparently both women had been upstairs at the treadle sewing machine and the poor woman ran out with the fabric towing the contents of the bobbin and thread spool still attached. Bill wanted to make a joke about them not getting lost if they just follow the thread back inside. But, he didn't because these tremblers were getting on his nerves too.

Miriam looked up at Bill just before the women went back inside. They gazed at each other for only a moment and Bill felt they had whispered "I love you" to each other. Soon, he vowed, we will never be separated again.

He looked back to find Michael and Amos staring at him.

"Michael, I want a flap made of metal cut to cover the doorway the goats will use to go in and out. Build one for the passage way door because it has a window. Then push dirt up against the foundation of the barn. I want no part of the barn's wood exposed to the elements. Tomorrow we will build the raised beds and then get them planted. I want you to bring the seeds and cuttings for the medicinal plants you were talking about some time ago."

"Thee seems to have a knowledge about these strange occurrences, William."

Bill looked at him intently. He wanted to explain so much to him, but knew he couldn't. His cell phone rang and saved him from what he felt would have been a mistake. It was Becky so Bill raised the phone and an open hand as if to ask for some more time before he would explain.

He pushed talk as he turned to go back into the barn. Becky's stern use of "Dad" was as much a question and as a command. Bill could hear she was at Cherry's house because her friend was always upset and afraid of everything.

"Yah, Hon, its me. You and Kiia O.K.? Yah, no problems here. Listen, I want you to call your brother and tell him I need him here a week before the wedding and two weeks afterwards. Tell him I will explain after he gets here. Can you do that for me?"

"Yes. But, Dad we really need to see more of you when things like this happen."

"I know, Hon. I'll be around a lot more just before the wedding and then a little while afterwards. Listen. I have some things for you to pick up with my truck tomorrow. I will bring Kiia with me to the farm so you can do this."

"Yes," she sighed. "You do remember he is a little boy and there isn't a lot he can do on a farm?"

"I know. But I got some goats here now…"

"Oh great! He can go out to a farm and be eaten by a herd of goats."

"Actually," Bill laughed, "I have three females and two billy goats. They will be in a new pen that Michael and Amos are building." The sound of them cutting a door for the goats could be heard. "Hey, did you ever think your old dad would go from a Fire Chief to a goat-roper?"

"Honestly, Dad, I'm about to go screaming over the hill and you're talking about career changes. All right. You can take Kiia to the farm and I will pick up your list of things. But, you know how I hate driving that old truck of yours!"

"You won't have to use the truck till mid to late morning. I have an idea for something special and will surprise you later. And, Becky? It's going to be all right soon. I promise."

"I hope you're right, Dad. Try to be home soon."

"I will be, Hon. Love you."

"Love you too, Dad."

Bill put the phone in his pocket and quickly finished pulling the wires for the grow lights. He installed a heavy screw eye for each of the three sets of lights and hung a light duty rope block and tackle. These would be used to raise and lower the lights. He was sure his plants would grow well if the lights could be moved and kept no more than three inches above them. Any more than that and they would grow spindly reaching for what they thought was sunlight.

Michael came up to look at what he was doing. "The metal door is in place and works well," he said.

"Tomorrow we should make another wooden gate just outside the door to the back room. You won't want them pushing through the door into this room and eating your new plants or feed grains.

"That's a good idea, Michael. Can you do that tomorrow morning while I finish mounting the grow lights?"

"Of course."

"Oh, wait a minute. I have just thought of something I have to do first thing tomorrow. If you put up the gate before I get here, can you start the raised bed platforms next? I'll help you finish them when I get out here. We've got to get something planted and growing soon or we'll be out of luck the way things are going."

Michael gave him a curious look and then nodded.

"All right! Now, I have to get into town to get something started that I will finish tomorrow. Actually, I'm going to get a new truck. I'll explain that later."

Michael gave him a weak smile as he nodded. Bill looked back at him as he left and chuckled as he wondered if Michael thought him a little crazy.

The old truck fired up and ran smoothly into town. It's a good thing old trucks don't know when they are being taken in to be replaced, he thought.

The first dealership he came to had a half a dozen trucks lined up and he stopped to look at the one that caught his eye. It was a four-door model, automatic transmission and four wheel drive. The color looked like something Becky would like.

"Yo, Bill."

He looked up to see Andy, the man he bought his present truck from.

"Looking to replace that old rust bucket I sold you? You've had it so long I'm almost sorry I sold it to you! Thought I'd never see you again."

"Yes," laughed Bill. "I want to take advantage of your 'instant financing' before it goes away. Do you think you can have me driving home tonight in this one?"

"If your credit is still as good as I think it is you can drive two home if you know how. Let's go inside and fill out the paperwork."

The ground interrupted them as it shook. Both men grabbed at the truck to keep their balance. It was a mild shock, but it lasted longer than any one before it. It plainly bothered Andy more than it did Bill.

Andy muttered. "When the hell will someone get these things figured out."

"Sooner or later, they will," Bill answered, "One way or another."

Andy shot him a questioning look. But, car sales had been in the cellar for the past few weeks so he said nothing.

"Hey, how is this old building holding up in these shaky times?"

"Shaky times! That's an understatement!" They walked into the building through the garage. People were pushing tool boxes back into place and picking up parts and display items. "My grandpa built this place back during World War Two and he said it would take a direct hit from a low flying bomber. I believe he was right. There is a basement under this place with walls twice as thick as they need to be. The glass hasn't even popped out or cracked up here. Go figure."

They took seats at Andy's desk and discussed the truck Bill liked. It didn't take long as Bill agreed to all the terms.

When a man is sure he won't have to make any payments because of a coming cataclysm, the price of a new truck just doesn't make much difference. The credit check went smoothly, Bill signed the papers, Andy handed him the paperwork and they exchanged keys. They walked back out to the lot together.

"You know, Andy, I've heard you've got a couple of nice old cars in the basement here. I need a place to store my 34 Coupe for the winter, or until this ground shaking stops. Have you got a little room for a fair price?"

"I've got more than a couple old classics," Andy replied. "I don't usually let anyone go down there, but I've always liked your 34. There's space for it if you want."

They exchanged thanks and made plans to meet in the morning. Bill started up the new truck and drove out of the lot. He marveled at how nice it was compared to his old one. It held the road well, despite another mild shake. He felt the earth was warning him again to take seriously his plans to protect Luke and Becky and their children.

He backed the truck into his garage as was his custom. It filled up most of the remaining room beside the old 34 Coupe. There was a coating of dust on it from the repeated shaking of the garage. Bill hoped the old building would hold up for another few weeks.

Becky came out of the house on her way to the grill. She had brats and veggies for supper.

"You're home at a decent hour, for a change." She called out to him.

"I ran out of things to do," he joked. "You won't have to park your car outside this winter. I've found a place to store the old 34. Sound good?"

"Does it ever! It doesn't take long to get tired of scraping frost off the windows and sweeping snow off on the other days."

"I agree. I also bought a new truck. Do you want to see it?"

"Sure. Let me put the food on the grill and get Kiia first."

Bill walked back to the garage and opened the door. He searched out the owner's manual and started to page through it. He figured he would know just about everything about running it, but when he got to the sound system he was baffled. "Damned electronic stuff," he thought.

Becky rushed out after a charging Kiia. He was on his way to see his grandpa and nothing was going to get in his way.

"Nice color."

"I thought you would like it," he replied, "and it's got an automatic transmission and air conditioning!"

"I like it already," Becky said as she hopped up into the driver's seat.

Bill picked up Kiia and put him in the back seat. Between he and his mother they looked over everything inside the pickup. Kiia tested all the convenience doors with repeated slamming until he got the word from his Mom and Grandfather not to do so.

"You'll have to program the radio and show me how to use the CD player later. In the morning you can follow me back to the dealership where I will store the old 34. Then drop me off at the farm and I will get a list of things I want you to pick up for me. If anyone asks just tell them

I am planning a party in the near future. And remember, no one needs to know what kind of party I'm planning. I don't want anybody, anywhere finding out about my plans. O.K?"

"O.K." she agreed, although she looked a little nervous.

"Hey," he lied, "There were only two tremors today and both of them were a lot less than what we've had in the past. Right?"

"Right," she agreed and showed a smile. "I think Kiia and I will enjoy this new truck. Won't we Kiia?"

Kiia always agreed with his Mom and Grandfather when it didn't require picking up toys or going to bed early.

"Why don't you two check on the food while I close up the garage."

"Come on, hungry boy and help your mother get supper ready." Kiia jumped out of the truck into his mother's arms and they went over to the grill.

Bill closed up the truck and then the garage. He walked into the house to help get the table set for supper.

"I want to call Luke tonight. My wedding is less than two weeks from now and I want him here on time. It would sure be good if he and Sarah and the kids could stay for a couple weeks. I want him to help me set up some things."

"I'm sure he will try, Dad, but two more weeks vacation is tough to get for him right now."

"Yes," and he thought two weeks could be tough to survive if that magma deposit decides to blow. "We will just have to wait and see."

He set the table and marveled at how easy it had become for he and his family to cook over coals or an open fire since they started camping several years ago.

Food preparation had become a way for them to set aside growing pains and problems over the years. Everyone just pitched in for meal time and afterwards it just seemed easier to get along with each other.

Becky started putting the food on the table as soon as Bill had everything in place. Kiia came out of hiding when it was time to eat without helping. The meal was fun for him with all the attention directed to him by his Mom and Grandfather. It was a rare moment for all of them what with the reoccurring tremors.

"Hey, big boy, what do you say we clean up and call your Aunt and Uncle in California tonight?" said Bill.

Kiia laughed and babbled his approval because everything he did with his Grandpa was all right with him. They finished up and went into the living room where Bill dialed the number and put the phone on speaker. The conversation was easy with kids heard on both ends. Luke easily promised to try for more time off, but was evasive about whether it could actually happen.

Tremors and earthquakes were discussed and compared. News of strange occurrences in both America and the rest of world were described. This shifting of the earth's plates was occurring everywhere and there were no explanations from any government. Bill was more and more sure he knew why. The women talked about their kids and life in general and promised to talk more when they got together at the wedding. They both laughed, nervously, about what to wear and how to react to the strangers they would meet. The call lasted more than an hour and ended only when Rachael and Kiia fell asleep and their mothers wanted them put to bed.

Bill tried again to get a commitment from Luke to stay for a couple weeks but Luke was just as firm in his refusal. He was young and involved in a career building activity at work and wanted to see things through. He did promise to get back to Augusta six weeks after his Dad's wedding. They said their goodbyes knowing they had said and accomplished the most they could under the circumstances.

Bill carried Kiia up the stairs and put him to bed. As he pulled off his shoes and jeans the boy turned onto his side without any fight. He accepted sleep as if he had never done any different. Bill looked at his peaceful countenance and marveled at the beauty and wonder only a gift from God could have. At any step in his life, Bill was ready to try to keep him there without any need for growing up. But, the boy was in a growth spurt and had become quite a handful to Becky when it was time to carry him a distance. So, grow up he would and those who would love him had better be prepared to accept the changes. Then, as if to rock him to sleep, the earth trembled; a long slow tremble. Becky came running up the stairs and into the bedroom.

She faced Bill with wide, terrified eyes. Both of them hoped Kiia would sleep through it as they weren't sure they could explain why he was awakened.

"Fix this, Dad! Please?"

Chapter 13
Deal With It

"Fix this Dad," rang in his mind all night. Bill slept fitfully and woke wishing he could sleep for another four hours. Ever since he realized the enormity of the problem he had been working on a "fix" for it. Why couldn't Becky realize there was no fix in the way she wanted it. There was no fix. No repair. There was only his hope that a small farm and barn in central Wisconsin would protect his family and they in turn would want to survive. That is the one issue he had not come to terms with. Would they want survive a cataclysmic event? Not many people had his spirit of adventure, his desire to overcome adversity till success was his.

But, in this case, what was success? Live in a confined area for who knows how long and then come out to find everyone else dead? An entire way of life lost? Where would he find husbands and wives for Becky and his grandchildren? What would be the quality of their lives? He had a nice start on a sour stomach when he pulled himself out of bed. He had a quick prayer and headed for the shower.

Becky was already in the kitchen when he got down. She'd pulled out all the stops and prepared a breakfast for a bigger family than she had, whether she had done so deliberately or was still lost in her fears wasn't known.

"Man! That smells good and looks like enough to feed a small army."

"Help yourself. I've got to get Kiia up and dressed."

Bill surveyed the table. It looked like eighteen fried eggs, one loaf of bread toasted, one pound of bacon fried along with every sausage patty from the freezer. If that wasn't enough for one man, a little boy and his mother who probably wouldn't eat anything, anyway, there was twelve cups of coffee, and a gallon each of orange and grape juice.

"This is not going to be pretty," he thought. Quickly he grabbed some containers and prepared some breakfasts for the freezer. He prepared plates for Kiia and Becky, even though she would pick at it and then begin the cleanup. He wolfed down more than he would have normally, and greeted the others as they came down.

Kiia was his usually happy self and got as much food on his face as he did in it. Becky picked and then announced cleanup. She looked at what was left on the table and then glanced at her father with an incredulous expression. Bill laughed to himself as it would be more fun to have her find the food in the freezer later and decided not to explain.

Kiia cleaned up easily and was more than happy to head for adventures in a new truck. Bill had Becky get behind the wheel and he got Kiia buckled in the back. They went over the new items and Becky started the engine.

It was bigger than the old truck, but she knew she could handle it. Bill gave her directions and soon they dropped the old Coupe off at the dealership and were on the way to the farm.

Becky had driven slowly, with more caution than was necessary and stopped in the driveway. Moses has just arrived with his wife who apparently was going to spend the day with Miriam. Bill was glad to stop and introduce Becky and Kiia to his bride-to-be. Since Moses was there he took the initiative to leave the truck and walk up, close to Miriam. He completed the introductions as best he could.

Becky and she appeared to have good first impressions of each other. Then, Miriam has eyes for Kiia alone. It was like seeing one of her sons young again. A bond was made immediately between the new family-to-be. It didn't go unnoticed by Moses.

"Becky and Kiia will go into town for me today so I can work on the raised plant beds. I want something planted and growing this week." He handed Becky a list.

"I believe," said Moses, "that Miriam has a list also. We will begin work and after the stores open you will drive your family and Miriam into town to purchase what is on both lists.

Bill looked surprised and when he glanced at Miriam she looked stunned, then pleased.

"There is work to do," said Moses and he turned toward the barn.

Michael, Amos and the other guy were already in the barn and had gathered the material to build the beds.

Bill gave them instructions as to the proposed size and let them build as they wanted to. He got out the spade and wheelbarrow to begin preparing the potting soil.

"I have experience in preparing soil." It was Michael.

"All right," said Bill. "Let's move a half dozen bags each of moss, coarse sand and fertilizer and do the mixing outside."

Michael led the way to an area he said had once been a hog pen. The soil there would be rich in organic material and would be a good basis to build potting soil. Bill sent Michael back for another wheel barrow load of bags and he pulled the cement mixer to the spot.

He checked the gas and oil and started it up. With the spade he dug up some soil and started it tumbling while he opened the bags to add what he felt would make the best mix of soil. The ratio of soil to compost would be decided with each load mixed. The soil seemed to break down to a smooth mixture when he added two spades each of moss and sand and one of granulated fertilizer. When it mixed for a moment Bill shut it down and put his hand in for a sample. He squeezed a handful which clumped well and then broke apart just as quickly. It looked "just right" to him.

Moses walked up and asked if he could check the soil. He clumped a handful and watched it come apart. He rubbed some between his palms and nodded his approval. Michael came up with the full wheelbarrow and did the same.

"How many of these raised beds did you want to have built, William?"

"Moses, I think six will be enough. I want to have at least six half-barrels for tomato plants and some strawberries. Any extra soil we prepare can be kept on the dirt floor in the animal area in case we need to add some more this winter."

"Yes. It is now time for you to take the women into town. I believe they have their lists prepared," replied Moses.

Bill looked over at the truck. Becky and Kiia were already there along with Miriam and Moses' wife. Miriam's companion was just entering the house.

"Man," thought Bill, "I wish I could have gotten my Fire Battalion to respond as quickly to work details." Instead he tried to make Moses comfortable by saying they would be back around noon.

"Mrs. Yocum knows when I will be ready for my lunch," he replied and went back into the barn to supervise the building of the raised beds.

Bill thought it interesting Mrs. Yocum didn't need a clock to know when her husband was hungry. He walked to the truck and Becky gave him a "dry" look.

"You might need these," she said as she handed him the keys."

"Oh, thank you. You and Kiia get in behind me." He walked around to open the doors for the other two women. Both Miriam and Mrs. Yocum got right in as the truck was significantly easier to enter than the smaller buggies they were used to. Becky buckled Kiia in and began to buckle herself. Bill pulled out Miriam's seat belt.

"William! Thee must tie me to this new mechanical buggy?"

"Oh, no! It is a matter of safety. Seat belts will protect us in the event we have an accident. Which, of course won't happen anyway."

"All of my sons have fallen from the buggy and not been hurt," Said Mrs. Yocum in a sour tone.

"Mother Yocum! William, show me this matter of safety."

Bill pulled the seat belt out again and stopped as he pulled it across her. He wanted so badly to pull her to himself and kiss her. He just might have if he hadn't noticed Kiia's interested look. Instead, he explained the seat belt set up and finished buckling it. Stepping around the back door he reached for the rear belt, but changed his mind when he made eye contact with Mrs. Yocum.

"Oh, fall out of the buggy," he thought and closed both doors on the passenger side. He got in behind the wheel, buckled up and started the engine. As he pulled out of the driveway he glanced at the Amish women. Miriam had both feet planted on the floor and both hands gripped the arm rests. She had one of those smiles that people get when they are off on a great adventure but are scared to death. In the back, Mrs. Yocum looked like she believed she was on a path straight to Hell.

"So, Becky, have you ladies compared lists so you can tell me where to go first. You know, something like synchronized lists?

"Yes."

"Good. Because I haven't got the slightest idea where I am going. Although," he added to Miriam, "it is a lovely day for a drive, isn't it?"

"I've never been on a drive before."

"Are we there yet," came from the back seat in a tone that suggested it would have been better not to have left home. It wasn't Kiia.

"Well, Dad I think we can get your list from the Farm Supply Store and Miriam's list can be gotten in their grocery section. I don't usually shop there, but I've heard they have as nice a selection as any supermarket."

"All right," said Bill, regaining some of his memory. "The Farm Store is just down the road. We will come back after lunch to get the things I have listed from the second hand store." He pulled into the parking lot of the store and found a space near the front door. Remembering that the two Amish women probably didn't know how to open their doors he came right around and opened them. Mrs. Yocum shot right out as if she had been saved from a fate worse than death.

"William! I am still tied to this thing!" Miriam looked quite frightened.

"I'm sorry, Miriam. Just push this button…" and he finished showing her how to unbuckle. He helped her out of the truck in a way that had to feel like a loving hug to her. Their eyes met for an instant, and then she moved quickly to accompany Mrs. Yocum and the others into the store.

Bill closed up the truck and walked to the grocery section of the Farm Store. Becky and Kiia were waiting inside the door with the Amish Women.

"Dad, your list is all hardware type stuff and ours is all food."

"Hmmm, Should I take the hardware list and leave you and Kiia to help the women-folk? We could meet at the check out isles in about an hour."

"We will need time to see the Women's things and kitchen things too." Said Mrs. Yocum. "You have a timepiece Rebecca?" and not waiting for a reply added, "Good. We will meet by the big number seven over there in two hours." She gestured toward a cart as she walked to the grocery section. "You drive Rebecca." Mrs. Yocum was definitely the Bishop's wife.

Bill grabbed a different cart and headed toward the landscaping section. It was late in the summer and there were limited supplies in almost everything he wanted.

But, some of the items were on sale at sizeable markdowns. The first thing he saw was some replacement grow lights in the size he might need so he grabbed all of them. There were only three wooden half-barrels left so he took one pick-ticket and wrote three on it. The other two pick-tickets he took from the display and hid so no one would be able to check out with one of his half-barrels.

There was a wooden thing called a Strawberry Pyramid" that stood about five feet tall and actually had seeds and soil with it. Imaging a bowl of strawberries in the middle of an ice age made sense so he put a pick-ticket with the others. He traveled up and down the isles making impulse purchases.

The shrubs were picked over and not of any great interest to him, but he noticed two small boxes on a shelf. They were Blue Berry sets and he was especially fond of Blue Berries. He made his way to the livestock supply area and got pick-tickets for sacks of barley, oats and shell corn. His list was filled and the cart was filled with his impulse purchases. There was a customer service counter in the live stock area so he checked out there. The delivery fee was reasonable so he had them deliver everything except the Blue Berry sets. He didn't want to take a chance of them being crushed. The clerk offered his thanks and a receipt and Bill turned to find the women.

He didn't have to look far as they came walking up to him. He hadn't watched the time and it too had caught up with him.

"Dad?" Said a stern Becky.

"William," said Miriam in a sweet voice. "Blue Berries. I haven't grown Blue Berries since I was a child."

Bill went weak in the knees and speechless. Then he noticed the full cart and Mrs. Yocum carrying a new rolling pin in one hand and a cast iron skillet in the other.

"Well, if someone would carry these two plants I will push the cart to the big number seven and we will be on our way home in a jiffy." He led the way to the grocery checkout and then to the truck.

The truck was loaded and before they could get in to drive away the ground started to trembled.

"Hold on to the truck," called Bill.

They all staggered to the bed and grabbed hold. The earth shook for almost fifteen seconds. It was enough for all of them to question whether or not it would ever end.

Becky had already picked up Kiia and she held him on the bed of the truck assisted by Bill. Miriam and Mrs. Yocum clutched each other and the other side of the truck. The screams of other people in the parking lot scared Kiia more than the trembler and he was whining. Bill picked him up with a hug and a big smile.

"It's all over now honey-boy. It didn't hurt and it was even a little bit fun, wasn't it?" Bill chuckled and even got a smile out of the boy. "Everybody into the truck. Next stop will be the farm." No one needed seatbelt instructions this time!

As they pulled into the driveway Moses and Michael came walking up to them. Mrs. Yocum swung down from the back seat and opened the end gate. She removed her purchases and walked to the buggy.

"Mr. Yocum, I will not be leaving the farm ever again!"

Moses replied to her in their language and helped her into the buggy. He must have asked for something because she handed him a book and an envelope from inside. Moses walked back to Bill and Miriam.

"Your paperwork is correct, William. I will now perform the wedding as I will not be down the hill for some time to come. William, you stand here; Miriam here; Michael stand at William's right and Rebecca at Miriam's left. You may hold your son."

Moses started and for a few minutes time stood still for Bill and Miriam. Their love crowded out any of the issues or fears that only moments before had frightened everyone.

"We will now sign the papers," came Moses voice from outside their world. He was still in charge. "William, you will sign here; Miriam, here; Michael here as first witness and Rebecca here as second witness. Do the same on this second sheet of paper." They followed his instructions and he folded them up when they had finished.

"I will use this copy for our records first and then send it along to the proper authorities. William you may present this copy to your pastor and celebrate as you wish in your own faith." He looked at them for a moment, then added, "Thank you for all you have done for us William and for all that you will do in the future. May God be with you and your family."

"And also with you," they murmured.

He turned and walked to the buggy. To the others, he suddenly looked very old. He pulled himself into the buggy and drove away without looking back.

They watched the buggy leave the yard and turn up the hill. Bill and Miriam caught each others eyes and gazed at each other.

When they realized they weren't alone Miriam said she would make a lunch for Bill and the others. Becky asked if she could help and the women went into the house with Kiia. Bill and Michael joined the other guy in the barn. Nine raised beds had been completed, to Bill's surprise. But, judging from the amount of sawdust around the table saw, the other guy was no stranger to the use of electric tools.

"Let's begin filling them with the soil until lunch is ready," said Bill. They went outside to the soil Michael had prepared. Bill stopped long enough to right the table that had been tipped over by the trembler. They had two spades, two wheel barrows and two buckets. When they were filled the men went back to the beds and the two Amish men lifted the wheel barrows and dumped them. Bill dumped the buckets and smoothed the soil when the beds were filled. Lunch was late, but that was good because the men wanted to finish the work. And they did.

Miriam and Becky brought out the table linens and then the food. The table was set and loaded with a nourishing lunch. Bill led the prayers this time. It was a cordial, but quiet lunch as it usually was.

"William," said Michael, "we will leave now and won't be back unless there comes a pressing need. Of course, you and Miriam will always be welcome visitors."

"I understand, replied Bill. "You and your family will always be welcome here too. I'll always be grateful to all of you for the tremendous amount of work you have done here. I couldn't have done all this without you.

The men got up and walked to the buggy. The Amish got in and drove out of the yard and up the hill. Only Michael looked back and waved.

The delivery truck from the Farm Store pulled into the driveway and up to the barn. Bill and the driver unloaded it and the driver left.

"Let's get the rest of the things out of the pickup Becky and you and Kiia can head for home."

"All right." She said in a quiet voice. She hadn't slept in a house without a man somewhere in it for five years.

"Here's the rest of that list of things I need from the second hand store. Pick up the stuff and anything else you may want when it is convenient and bring it all out in a couple days." He couldn't remember a time in his adult life when he didn't have a car or truck to drive whenever he wanted it.

It took little time to unload the pickup and they both buckled Kiia into his seat. Becky drove the truck out the drive to the road. She looked back to her father and his new bride, arms around each other. There was a sense of peace in seeing them this way and she wished that peace was hers too. They both smiled and waved. She returned the wave and drove away.

Chapter 14

The Beginning of the Beginning

They moved together in an embrace as they watched the truck move away. Bill was struck with the silence of the farm. Most of the people who have lived their lives in cities are unprepared for the lack of noise. Bill felt that now, acutely. He turned to his new bride and they held each other, gazing into each other's eyes. He bent to kiss her and bumped her bonnet. She loosened its straps and he pushed it back and off her hair. He gazed into those beautiful green eyes until their lips met and their eyes saw nothing. It was a long kiss that gradually led to sensing what their arms and hands touched; how her breasts felt against his heart; their stomachs and thighs pressed together. It ended for a moment to enjoy love's embrace. His lips brushed her cheek and the once again gazed into each others eyes.

"Show me where we will live together as husband and wife."

"Oh William," she said with mock sadness. "This is the farm. There are animals to tend to and chores to do before love can prevail."

"Ummm," he said with real sadness. Looking around, he said, "Well, let's start with the barn and go from there. You know, I've heard some pretty exciting stories about barns and the smell of hay."

"Have thee?" she smiled as they walked with arms around each other. "Perhaps thee could first tell me about my barn. I have been much afraid about all that has transpired since thee has entered my life."

"Making you afraid was never on my mind." They entered the barn holding each other close. Bill looked around, noting the smells of the new soil and sawdust. "Let's check on the goats and then we can sit and talk about all this."

Miriam agreed and they cautiously opened the door to the animal's portion of the barn. The Amish men had built a solid enclosure around the door so the goats couldn't rush past them into the living quarters for his family. It was no matter now as they were outside the barn in the pen. There were so many hay bails in the barn there was more room for them to move outside. The water and grain pans were full enough and, of course, there was enough hay for the next five years.

They quietly closed the door so as not to cause the goats to rush back into the barn. Bill set up two chairs and they sat facing each other. He sat with his knees outside hers and held her hands in his, resting on her lap. He started with his first marriage and how it led him to take his kids camping and how that trip brought them to the campout earlier this year. It surprised him to experience again the fears he felt when he first realized the possibility of the cataclysm he now accepted as coming.

They held each other's hands as he spoke and many times he stopped as he needed her love and closeness to make sense of his dialogue. He would fondle her hands and sometimes gaze into her eyes in silence, and then go on. She listened intently as he poured out his heart to her. After all, it was his heart she really wanted.

After a long talk, he stopped for a short time and then asked about Ezra and her life on the farm. She didn't talk much about Ezra other than to say he was a hard man who made too much beet wine and that he had been severe with her and their sons. The sons had left home young and went far away. When she became silent Bill spoke.

"Why don't we take some time and plant something right now. I know just what you will like."

He pulled the two Blueberry sets from the things they had bought that morning. Miriam smiled shyly at his intent to please her. She began to open the two boxes as Bill went out with the wheelbarrow to get the soil. It didn't take long to do and it had for them the importance of doing something together for the first time. When finished, the two plants looked vulnerable in their new situation as they began to seek nourishment.

Miriam rested her head on Bills shoulder as her hand sought his. They looked at the plants for a moment.

"William, would thee draw some water for my bath, please."

They walked to the house in each other's embrace. Earlier Miriam had filled two large buckets and had set them on the wood stove. A fire was always kept in the kitchen stove and the water was now hot. Bill carried them to a small tub under the stairs and added a little cold water until Miriam said it was the right temperature. He looked at her and then the tub. It took a split second for him to regain his senses.

"You know, I think I will wash up out in the barn."

"This time only, William."

He walked quietly out of the house and then ran like a wild man to the barn. He slammed the pump handle up and down till a new bucket was filled with so much water he spilled it on his clothing. A short, but frantic period of rummaging in the back produced a bar of soap and a towel. The water was cold out of the well, but he didn't notice as he completed his bath. Instead of pouring the water down the new toilet he threw it out the door and lost his grip on the bucket and had to run out into the yard to retrieve it. Miriam watched from the upstairs window as he ran out and back in the nude.

She pulled the quilt off the bed, folded it and then she slipped under the sheet. As she waited, she couldn't help wondering about the bathing habits of the man she had just married. In the barn Bill was tearing through supplies to find something clean to wear back to the house. He found the only article of clothing he had bought for the farm. He pulled it on and stepped into his shoes.

She heard him come running up to the house, then walk quietly in. He saw she was out of the bath, but which room was hers?

"William?" came a call from upstairs and he was there in a moment. Both of them were far more nervous than they thought they would be, but when Miriam saw her husband resplendent in his new bib overhauls, complete with tags, she started to laugh. Realizing how he must have looked caused both of them to laugh away their tensions.

When she reached out to him, Bill could see she was bare-breasted and the bibs were off and not used again that night.

The night came and the morning followed with two made one. There had been little sleep and much love. Love is not for the young alone. Sexual satisfaction had been achieved, but the seed for the need of love had been planted and was already flourishing.

They stirred to a slumbering awareness and Bill rubbed her back, pulling her close.

"Oh William, is it a sin in your culture to want to lie in bed when one is well enough to be out working?"

He rolled up on top of her wrapping her in his arms and legs, kissing her and wanting to touch every inch of her. He was empty and sore, but far from being satisfied. He wanted so much more.

"No?" he replied and continued kissing. She turned away and began to giggle. Her joy was so great Bill couldn't help laughing too. He rolled back and forth with her and stopped with her on top so she had to bring her knees up and outside his and he could touch more of her.

"William," she moaned. "I can't anymore."

He rolled her back beside himself and kissed her again.

"Let's find the bathroom and then we can get some rest. Will you bathe with me?

"Oh William I have never done…Yes, I will. And I know where the bathroom is."

He pulled her to the edge of the bed and lifted her up. As he carried her to the stairs she protested.

"William, I am naked."

Oh, I didn't notice."

"Yes, thee did! Put me down. I have to get my robe." She patted him and pushed past to her closet. "It is not uncommon for a men to be so bold, but a good woman must remember her modesty." She came out of their room and stopped to study him before descending to the bathroom. Bill followed and she waited for him to draw a bucket of water for the toilet tank. The pipes and wiring had been removed in keeping with Amish traditions. He filled the tank and went outside to get some wood for the stove. Behind the wood pile it still felt as good to pee outside as it did when he was a boy. He fired the stove and began filling buckets for their bath. Miriam had finished in the bath room and had filled another bucket for him to pour into the tank. He did so an then went back to the kitchen.

"The fire did not go out last night so the one bucket we left on the stove is still hot. That and one of the other buckets will provide a nice warm bath, William."

He carried them to the bathroom and emptied them into the small tub. Miriam swished the water to mix it and stepped back to wonder if two adults would fit into such a small tub. Bill slipped her robe down and kissed her long and hard on the nape. She responded by pushing back against him. He put one foot on the tub as she turned to explore him. He stepped into the tub and sat 'Indian fashion,'

"Put one foot on either side of me and sit here," Bill gestured between his legs. Arousal won over modesty and she quickly joined her husband in their bath. Bill leaned her back against the slanted portion of the tub, kissed her breasts and began washing her. She could do nothing but close her eyes and submit to joys she had never felt before.

"Eat your heart out, Ezra." thought Bill.

Love may not belong to the young alone, but the necessary energy does and they both were forced to finish and go back up to sleep. They walked up the stairs with arms around each other. Bill carried her robe.

They entered the bed from the same side.

"I have never been so naked in my life, William" she said with a yawn. He kissed her and they fell asleep before passion could keep them awake.

Their sleep was sound, but hunger awoke them at noon. It had been a full day since they had last eaten. They spent several minutes gazing into each others eyes. Then Bill pushed the covers down to expose her breasts. He fondled her and when her nipples began to rise he kissed and suckled them. She stirred and he pushed the blanket off her so he could rise up on one arm and look at her. A lifetime of shyness and modesty succumbed to his passion.

"Oh William," she half moaned. "I must be up and about my duties as a wife."

For reasons he couldn't fathom he sat up and pulled her up and out of their bed. She crossed the room and selected a dress from the closet. She had it on and was out the bedroom door before he felt they were anywhere near finished with their lovemaking. He dressed in the cloths he had worn the day before and joined her downstairs.

She was just carrying a bucket of water to the toilet so he went into the kitchen. The room was hot, and so was the water he had left on the stove. They would have a good bath later. Miriam came back into the kitchen and began to pump water into the bucket again. She was tall and so thin, but Bill could see she was used to hard work.

He took the bucket and asked; "Can we eat outside this afternoon? I mean, I haven't seen the rest of the farm yet."

She looked at him curiously for an instant. "Yes, I will prepare a basket. Would you like to eat by a little spring behind the bluff?"

"Yes," he called back and poured the water into the toilet tank. "Why would anyone take the water pipes and electrical wiring out of their house?" he muttered.

Miriam lined a basket with cloth napkins and had utensils, butter and meat from a cooler in it and a tin for carrying drinking water. Bill filled the tin and refilled the bucket and put it on the stove. He'd lived the Amish life for little more than a day and was already used to pumping water.

Miriam closed the basket and Bill picked it up and carried both it and the tin out through the back porch. It had been warm in the kitchen, but neither of them realized it was a very warm day. The sun was high and it was about one o'clock. They crossed the yard to the garden so they could pick some vegetables. A couple each of cucumbers, carrots, tomatoes and some leaf lettuce and they went out the front gate again. As they went around the back corner of the garden Bill scared up a wild rabbit.

"Oh, my." Exclaimed Miriam. "This fall he will be just the right size for stew. We will have to set out some snares."

"Uh-huh," agreed Bill without any intention of becoming the new Daniel Boone. They walked around the 'bluff' behind the garden and the barn. It was a large sand-stone outcrop which stood about 50 feet high and two hundred feet wide on the West-Northwest side of the barn and garden. The winter winds would be forced around the barn so it should be easy to heat.

They walked around the bluff along the side of the hay field. Ezra had not planted anything else before he died.

The man who had made the last cutting and bailing also cut the grass beside the hay field. It was an easy walk to where the spring was. Three small apple trees provided some shade at the spring. Bill spread out the blanket and Miriam set the basket where she wanted it and brought out the bread to slice. They were both so hungry eating ruled out any conversation for a few moments. Then they apologized for eating so fast and not talking.

"What did you have growing over there?" Bill asked.

"Oh, that was the strawberry patch. Between the rabbits and Ezra's need to make strawberry wine with his beet wine we didn't get any to eat and those last two years I…"

He touched her hand and said, "Let's walk over there to look at it." When they got there it looked like a sizeable patch that was well cared for some time ago. The plants had propagated themselves so they were no longer in orderly rows.

"Wait here, while I walk around to see if there are any late berries." He walked around for a few minutes and found only two. Back with her he pulled out the stem and put one in his lips and bent to kiss her with it. It was a gesture of love she was unfamiliar with and pulled back. Seeing the hurt look in his eyes she pressed her lips to his and took the berry. Bill put the other one in his mouth and bowed his head to touch her while they ate.

"Sweet," he murmured.

"Yes."

She reached her arm up and around his neck and pulled him into a kiss. It was a long kiss. The kind no lover ever wants to end.

The hot sun made the end come anyway and they walked back to the shade of the three apple trees. Bill opened the blanket pulled her close looking for that last kiss. Their lips met and it was still there. He caressed her back and their breath came fast. He began to loosen the top buttons and she pulled back.

"William! We are not in our home!"

He found her lips again and continued to kiss her and rub her bare back. Because of the heat, neither had worn underwear after getting up. She pulled back again as he opened her dress off her shoulders.

"Oh, William, what kind of woman must thee take me to be?"

Ezra had not been a lover and she still had a girl's shyness and fear of open, outgoing love, even with a husband. Bill looked into her eyes and she saw he was now afraid of having hurt her. Suddenly she sought that kiss she wanted to have forever and slowly lowered her arms so the plain blue dress slipped to the ground. She found the kiss and began to pull his bibs down to press her bare breasts to his heart. They pulled and pushed them to the ground and he lowered her to the blanket. They went where only the truest and purest love could take anyone.

They awakened a short time afterward and looked at each other. They discovered the beginning of a sun burn and picked up their things and started slowly for home. Inside they bathed together again and then rubbed a home made lotion into each other's skin. Upstairs they went and slipped into bed from the same side where sleep took them away again.

Morning came as it must, but this day declared an urgency that invaded everything; even love. A trembler lasting more than a few seconds shook their bed.

"Oh, William, will this never end?"

"Miriam! Our love and faith will last beyond these things. You must believe me and walk with me through all things to come. Will you?"

Her eyes searched his and finding a confidence behind his own fears she pressed herself to him trying to be one with him and feel his faith and confidence.

The earth shook again and this time they could hear things dropping in the rest of the house. Bill waited till it stopped and got out of bed, pulling her with him. He embraced her fearing he would never get enough of her.

"William," she said in a parental manner, "are the English always this naked?"

"Oh," he replied in mock seriousness, "something chronic."

"Thy smile betrays thy truth, William"

He squeezed her hand and went down stairs to pump the water for the toilet. Two days an Amish and he was already exploring their work ethic.

"William? Thee aren't going to the wood pile naked?"

Bill grabbed an old straw hat from its peg, put it on his head and replied in the negative. He walked naked to the wood pile and peed behind it. As he gathered an armful of wood he thought this firewood ritual could become very uncomfortable when the weather turns cold. He put the wood in the wood box beside the stove and opened the firebox door to throw in a couple sticks. Miriam came up behind him.

"William! Thee did go to the wood pile naked. What will the others think I have married? A wild man?"

He straightened up and turned toward her to protest because he was wearing a hat. She gasped and snatched it off his head and pushed past him to throw it into the fire.

"It was Ezra's," she said quietly. "And I have no life now but with thee."

He reached to hold her and she struggled just long enough to let her robe slip to the floor. She pressed against him.

"William, in all my life I have never felt so naughty and so loved."

A noise outside halted their love play. They looked through the kitchen window as a buggy pulled into the yard.

"It is the Bishop! William?" Getting an early start means starting before breakfast, not starting before getting dressed!"

He blocked her path to her robe and told her he could dress faster than she anytime. A determined look crossed her face and she raced from the kitchen to the stairs. Bill followed closely watching her every move. He couldn't help wondering how the birth rate of this clan could be so low with wives like her.

True to his word he was dressed first, but he didn't tell her he usually won the firefighter games that involved getting the gear on. He also didn't tell her he omitted his underwear.

I'm ready. I'll wait for you on the back porch."

"Yes! Don't go without me."

He waited for her and they walked to the barn together. Michael and the other guy, whoever he was, were already inside. All Amish buggies looked the same to Bill and the Bishop was at home. The two men had finished looking at the raised beds and were now studying the two blueberry sets.

"I see you have made an early start," said Michael.

"Yes," said Bill with a smile. "We were just inside finishing our morning prayers."

Michael smiled and looked away. The other guy doubled up with laughter and tried to get behind something. Miriam looked shocked and mortified.

"I will see to the goats again," she said and then quietly groaned at catching herself in a lie. She hadn't been in the barn since earlier in the day yesterday.

"William, I have brought along some herbs and seedlings. As I recall, you said I could plant some things of medicinal value for your tests."

"Yes," said Bill. "I would really like to get all the beds planted today. With the rest of my family coming this week I won't have any extra time this weekend." Bring your things in and I will set out what I have in mind in a minute."

Miriam had come back into the room and was working the pump hard enough to put out a fire. Bill took the handle from her and when the bucket was full carried it to the goats. Miriam opened the gate and he went in to fill the first water dish. The gruff old Billy took one look at Bill bent over, lowered his head and made his charge.

"Shoo," Miriam said to him and the old Billy veered off target and ran in a small circle. Bill looked up and walked to the other dish to pour the last of the water into it. The target was too tempting and the Billy charged again. Bill was ready and swung the bucket at him and 'clanged' him a good one. The goat spun around and ran out into the pen.

"William!" Gasped Miriam.

"Oh, it's O.K. I didn't hurt the bucket too badly! Actually he had split the seam and it would never hold water again. He opened the gate for Miriam and they went back into the barn. Michael had a box of non-descript bulbs, sets and seeds inside and was looking for the right place to plant them.

"Do we have anything for breakfast?" he whispered to Miriam.

"Enough for vegetable sandwiches. Today I must bake again."

"All right. Michael, would you like something to eat before we start?"

"No, thank you." And to Miriam he said, "I have a fresh chicken and a smoked ham in my buggy."

"Thank you, we will have chicken for lunch," and left to prepare a sandwich for Bill.

"Michael, I'll get out my box of seeds and we will plan around your medicinal things." Bill walked to the back of the barn and sorted through some boxes. "Oh, by the way, when the young male goat matures and is found to be a good breeder I would appreciate you either 'fixing' that old Billy, or at the least, fixing him for dinner."

Michael laughed and said he would. He then began to place his seeds and sets in the various raised beds. It is important that some plants grow apart from others to avoid cross-pollination.

Bill brought up his box of seeds and the two men began to set out the envelops according to space needed, equal height of the plants beneath the lights and even considered the depth of root growth. The plants would be limited in depth to the bed and to the height of the grow lights. The lights had to be within three inches of the top of plants, or the seeds in the soil. This would encourage maximum growth.

Miriam came in with Bill's sandwich and looked over their plans. She silently thanked God for a husband with a heart for love and for the land.

"Your daughter and Kiia have arrived. They have asked to help me with lunch and the baking. Thee has raised a good daughter, William." They exchanged love through their eyes and she turned and went back to the house.

Their plans were complete so the two Amish men began planting while Bill ate his breakfast sandwich. They were familiar with intensive gardening and worked quickly and quietly. Michael still hadn't introduced the other guy and Bill was too stubborn to ask his name so they worked without talking.

"Look at this place!" The concrete contractor walked in without being invited in. "You guys have really been busy."

"Yes," replied Bill. "What brings you our way?"

"Well, I poured a lot of concrete here and it needs to be sealed. You know, to keep water from soaking in and to make it easy to clean."

"I'm aware of the need for sealing this floor. I just haven't had time. This is an experiment in intensive gardening that has to be started soon."

"Yah, and that's where I come in. I can have this floor sealed today and it won't interfere with your plants.

"All right. We're almost done with the planting and then you can get started."

"I'll get my stuff out of the truck." He ran out of the barn before Bill could change his mind. The tremors had really scared him and this was the only place he'd found where everyone around him wasn't as scared as he was.

Besides, hiding at home didn't make a lot of money for his company. He returned quickly with a couple buckets of sealer.

"This won't take long, but you will have to let it dry overnight. O.K.?"

"No problem," replied Bill. "We're almost done and will pick up the floor before we leave. Some things can't be moved so seal around them."

"Gotcha. I'll get the rest of my stuff and get started."

Bill chuckled and smoothed out the soil. "Let's clean up so he can seal the floor. We can water the beds and set the lights tomorrow. It's won't hurt the seeds to lay in the soil till we make it rain. I want to make sure all containers are stacked securely and braced in place so there is no tipping or spilling when there is another tremor."

With all the wood finally built into what it was planned for there was more room on the floor and organization was easy. A few pieces of scrap wood held many things on their shelves and they were ready for lunch.

They walked out of the barn to wash up in the house. Kiia came out of the back porch like a rocket and stopped to check out his Grandfather and the two men with him who were dressed in blue and wore straw hats. Bill went down on one knee and Kiia's inspection wasn't as important as a big hug. Bill picked him up and when the women came out he gave hugs to Becky and his bride. Kiia kissed them both while sharing their hugs. Becky gave Bill a look that expressed a need to talk.

"Well, Kiia, why don't you come into the kitchen and wash up with the men-folk?" and Bill carried him in as the boy agreed to go. Once inside the Amish men became animated in their treatment of the boy.

They laughed and talked with him as they showed a sense of strong manhood. Kiia loved it. The other guy gave him a pony-back ride to the table and then both men retreated behind their Amish images.

As the oldest male Bill offered a blessing before eating and they all accepted his prayer. The food was passed and then Bill addressed his daughter.

"Did you call your brother?"

"Yes, she replied coolly. "He seemed a little unconcerned about his father's behavior."

"A Christian Wedding is accepted by all Churches. When is he flying in?"

"He, Sarah and the kids will be here tomorrow and will leave Monday morning."

That wasn't the time frame Bill wanted, but it was something for him to work with. Hopefully Luke would realize the urgency of the coming cataclysm and keep his family here.

"We have to pick them up in Eau Claire at six p.m."

"I'll call to reserve a Van for tomorrow. They'll stay at the house at night and we'll all spend the days here. I'll call Pastor O'Brian to flesh out our plans for Friday."

"Stay at the house? There's phone service out here, now?"

"All right; all right." He held up his hand and said; "They can stay with you and Kiia at home. The cell phone is on the charger inside the barn. I'll start carrying it again."

Becky, her late mother and, of course, Miriam had a way of lifting their eyebrows and looking over their noses when they spoke.

Whether it was in disbelief or disgust didn't matter to most men as they liked to see the look on the faces of the women they love.

"I believe it is time for us to return to our farms." Interrupted Michael.

"Aye." Other than speaking to Kiia, this was the first audible sound the other guy had made since he started coming to the farm.

Bill closed the meal with a prayer and the men walked to the buggy. Kiia ran ahead and stopped short of the horse. The Amish were alive and open in their attention to him and promised him a hat when they returned. Kiia jumped into his Grandfather's arms as they disappeared into their buggy and drove up the hill.

"Let's check out the barn, Kiia." He chased the boy to the door warning him not to step in because the floor was now clean and sealed and in a drying period. Bill opened the passage way and leaned in just far enough to reach the cell phone. The goats came out into the pen and Kiia thought they were way more interesting than the barn. The kids stuck their heads through the iron posts and fence wires as the kid on the other side ran up to get to know them.

A delivery truck pulled up the driveway and after giving Kiia instructions to stay by the goats or go inside the house, Bill went to see what he had ordered and forgotten about. It was the additional sacks of oats and barley, galvanized cans and pails that didn't get delivered last week. Bill had it all unloaded beside the barn door till the floor dried.

The driver looked inside and Bill explained it was an experimental intensive gardening project before he asked. His secret was still safe and the driver didn't seem interested.

Miriam and Becky walked up after he left. Miriam looked at the new pails and remarked how nice they were since they needed more pails. Bill looked down, a little chagrined at the loss of a pail earlier that morning.

"I'll order more tomorrow."

"Thee expects a greater need?" Bill knew she was teasing and he was blushing.

"Let's take Becky and Kiia behind the bluff to the spring." It was Miriam's turn to blush a little. "I want to take some water to the strawberry plants so the ground will be soft and moist when we dig some up for planting in the barn." The women looked at each other and him not knowing if the other knew what his plans were.

"'I've explained all I can to both of you. If it is more than you can bear, all I ask is that you keep this a secret." Again, they looked at each other and then he turned toward the field. They followed with their faces down in sadness. Kiia ran this way and that, happy to be on the farm.

Bill tried to be happy for them and described the farm to Becky. At the spring he drew a bucket of water. Kiia wanted to carry it and just as quickly declared it too heavy for him. Bill carried it to a plant he thought he would like.

"Euwww!" Becky cried out.

Kiia was squatting over a small garter snake and the two young ones of their species were staring at each other.

"They are harmless," said Miriam as she touched Becky to reassure the boy's safety.

"Hey," called Bill. "Here's a couple ripe strawberries."

Kiia put the snake on top of a plant and commanded it to stay. It did till the boy was on his way. Bill really hoped his grandson would like strawberries and gave them to him. The boy devoured the first one with gusto and bit into the other.

"Sneaky would like this," he said and ran back to where he hoped his new friend would be. The snake was gone, but the boy had forgotten where he'd left him so he ate the rest of the berry and ran back to his Grandfather.

City-girl Becky moved to a bare spot in the patch and started a safety watch till they left. Miriam walked over to Bill to look for the best plants. She picked two and Bill tried to scuff some dirt around them to mark them for later. He watered them and went back to the spring. Sensing Becky's discomfort Miriam suggested they go back to the barn. Kiia lead the way with Bill pointing toward the path he should try to stay on.

The contractor was finished with the barn floor and was loading his tools. He gave Bill instructions to stay off it, again, and said the warm, dry day would insure it could be walked on tomorrow. He waved as he drove away and called out a good bye and said to expect a bill in a little over a week. Bill waved back and said he would pay within a week of receiving it. A cold nauseous feeling swept over him and he was afraid he wouldn't be sending a check or ever see the man again.

"Well," he loudly declared, "what do you all say about a trip into town right now?"

He looked into Miriam's eyes and asked her if she would let him buy her a 'store-bought' dress for the blessing on Saturday. She showed she was still uncomfortable leaving the farm for any reason. Bill stepped toward her and clasped her shoulders. He drew her a step toward him.

"I will love you forever, Miriam."

She looked up and said, "And I, thee. Yes."

"So, Kiia. Do you still have the keys to the truck after drinking beer with your buddies last night?"

"Huh?"

"I have the keys, Dad. They're in my purse on the front seat."

"Everybody in, then." He walked around the truck with Miriam in hand. He asked her if she would let him open the door for her whenever they went any where. She didn't understand but agreed with anything that meant he would be close to her.

As he leaned to pull the door open he brushed her cheek with his lips. She still was not comfortable with open displays of affection, but Bill felt her go weak in the knees. He helped her up into the cab and reached around her to buckle the seat belt.

"William!" she exclaimed, and then leaned toward him to whisper, "I didn't have time to wear any underwear when I was afraid it was the Bishop."

Bill looked into the back seat; "Excuse us please. I'll leave the doors open so it doesn't get too hot in the cab."

He unbuckled Miriam's belt and lifted her from the truck. They hurried into the house and he ran up the stairs behind her. She went to her dresser and found what she needed and was ready in a moment. He reached into the empty closet where he had his underwear "airing," pulled off his jeans and…

"William! We don't have time for that!"

He spun around with a bewildered look.

"Do we?" she added.

"Wha…" He caught his toe in his shorts and did a quick "underwear hustle" before catching himself and getting his dressing on the up and up. Miriam was nearly hysterical with laughter. He followed her back down the stairs and out to the truck. For some reason they were still rushing and Bill quickly buckled her in.

He was almost laughing when he raced around the truck and got in. He buckled up and started the engine.

"Thy smile betrays thee, William."

He reached for her hand to reassure her. As they pulled out of the driveway she pulled her hand away and slowly untied and removed her bonnet.

"I don't even want to know what happened," thought Becky.

Bill found a parking place in front of the Women's Wear store. A clerk watched as the four of them got out. She'd never known an Amish woman to leave her clan, but, when she saw Bill hold her close so he could press his cheek against her lovely auburn hair she knew she had a good sale coming in.

"May I help you?"

"Oh, we're just looking," replied Becky, nonchalantly.

Miriam looked bewildered.

Bill took charge. "We will need one very nice long white dress, lingerie, shoes, some casual outfits with what ever is needed, some lingerie and umm…" He dug out his credit card and showed it too her. "You figure it out." She took the card.

"Grandpa! There's a candy machine by the door," came a distress call from Kiia.

"We'll just wait over by the door," said Bill and started pushing Kiia toward his reward.

"Grandpa, look at that big ice cream cone across the street."

Bill looked back at the clerk and told her, "no Skorts" and took Kiia's hand. "We'll be across the street, if you need us."

"Don't worry. I'm in complete control," she said to Bill and shared the same message by expression to Becky and Miriam. "I'll hold the card till you return."

Bill and Kiia made a leisurely stroll across the street and spent more time studying the menu than was necessary. Kiia always chose Chocolate Chip and Bill reinforced his choice by ordering the same. They sat on a bench across from the store and proceeded to make a mess of Kiia's clean face and shirt. After about twenty minutes of trying to converse with Kiia about anything a three year old could wrap his mind around Becky came out of the store. Bill waved an acknowledgement and started to clean up the boy before starting back across the street.

Back inside the store the women were together at the desk. Miriam looked bewildered, Becky disgusted and the clerk triumphant. "

We've done just fine, Mr. Thomas. If you'd just sign here please I'll begin to bag your purchases."

Bill noticed she didn't mention the total and just pointed to the X. He didn't really want to know anyway. He just signed and returned the pen and paperwork. Becky helped to bag the clothing and he carried it all to the truck.

"Let's stop at home. I need to pick up some things for myself."

He wheeled the truck toward home. Showing Miriam where he had lived suddenly became important to him. He also wanted to look around the house for anything he would want to keep for the rest of his life.

With her beside him he felt he needed nothing else, but now with the possibility of the cataclysm so close he wanted to leave nothing behind he would miss. He backed in and then helped Miriam out.

"Let's bring all the bags in, Dad. We'll have to remove the tags and start pressing everything." She unbuckled Kiia and he ran to his sandbox.

Miriam grabbed all the bags. This was part of her new life and she wasn't going to lose any of it.

Another trembler hit knocking Kiia into the sand. Bill pressed his daughter and Bride against the truck and they stood through it. Becky pulled away and ran to Kiia who still found such things to be fun.

"Let's go inside," called Bill and pulled Miriam with him. It was a small trembler, but they all seemed to carry an ominous warning now.

Inside, they placed the bags on the dining room table when Bill suggested they all tour the house before getting to work. He noticed Becky had already removed some pictures and mementos and had them packed. She had hers' and Kiia's clothing in bags. It pleased Bill to know she was taking his fears seriously.

"Dad, why don't you start the grill while I show Miriam around?"

"Is it dinner time already?"

"It is for those of us who didn't have ice cream."

Bill blushed and went out back to the grill. He added the charcoal and started it. Then, he went in to the freezer.

At first he selected beef, but then pulled out some Bison cuts he had been keeping for a special occasion. He thought Miriam might never had tried something like that.

"While Dad is outside I want to show you around and discuss what to take. When my husband died from the drugs a short time ago I didn't know what to keep so I kept everything I thought I should. Even if I wasn't sure I cared for it. Dad is willing to walk away from all this so you will have to choose whatever you think he may want. He won't want to take some things for fear of hurting you. I've packed most of the pictures, but we should discuss and pack the things you want him to have."

Becky handed one of two boxes to Miriam and they decided to start in Bill's room. As Miriam looked around, Becky took the initiative. They went through all the drawers and the closets. Miriam could only guess and relied on her instincts. Bill kept few mementos so the boxes weren't too full when they were finished. They walked through the main floor and then into the basement. There was an old tool box in which Bill's dad kept antique wood working tools. Miriam selected it immediately and the women planned on how to get it into the truck. They decided to keep the automotive tool box in the garage too.

Bill had a bowl of broccoli, some baked beans and the Bison ready when they came up. They all set the table and said their prayers. Miriam enjoyed the Bison.

"Dad, let's load the truck tonight so we can move as much as we can before Luke and Sarah have to be picked up."

"Good idea. Miriam would you like to stay here tonight and return to the farm tomorrow?"

"I will stay with thee forever, William."

After dinner, Bill and Kiia cleaned up, hauled boxes to the truck and the women clipped tags, washed and pressed Miriam's clothing. They decided Bill should not see the white gown she would wear to have her marriage blessed. They were happy that night.

Kiia tired early so Becky took him up to bed. Miriam showed Bill her new clothing, smiling with some items and frowning with others.

"I don't know about wearing slacks, William. These things called clam diggers; do you know they actually show my ankles? And another thing, do the English women actually wear some of the skimpy underwear I now own?"

"Oh, yes, sometimes that's all they wear when alone with their husbands."

"William!?"

"There's that look again," he thought. So he added, "Every woman should have something like that, but only wear it when they are comfortable with it."

"That's what I think." She looked at him for another decision.

"Should we pick things up so we are ready to leave in the morning?" He picked up clothing as she folded it and put it in bags. Miriam kept one bag from him, but he knew the long white dress was in it and said nothing. She looked at him with that fearful look again. He took her into his arms and they stood there and rocked together silently.

"Let's go up. I'll start the shower for us."

"I've never experienced a shower." She hung her head. "Does thee ever get weary with all I haven't done or can't do?"

"Never. Let's go up now."

They slept well that night and never noticed the earth tremble again.

In the morning they were up early and Bill had the clothing in the truck. Miriam made a quick breakfast just on time as Kiia came racing down in pajamas with Becky in 'hot pursuit' with his clothing. Breakfast was fun that morning with the excitement of Luke's arrival that afternoon.

They rented the van and then drove to the farm. Bill told Becky to find a corner in the barn and then began to haul things in.

"Grandpa, you've got a potty here. Where's the shower?"

"Where are the walls?" asked Becky.

"Well, that still has to be worked out, Honey. You can use the outhouse or carry a bucket of water to the stool in the house. Miriam will show you."

"Dad," she said with a fearful look, "I don't think I'm up to a lot of this!"

"Take every experience as it comes and when the time comes we have to accept the worst, we will be able to get by."

"But, walls?"

"I'll get the walls up when the time is right. Go inside. Miriam is inside making a lunch."

"Kiia, stay with grandpa while I go up to the house."

"O.K." His mother didn't know he was squatting in the goat pen while the kids watched him with interest.

Becky walked through the porch and hesitated at the kitchen door. Miriam saw her and called to her to come in. There was a fire in the cook stove and the kitchen had to have been a stifling one hundred degrees.

"Come in," she repeated. "Let me show thee my home."

"Actually, I need to use the little girl's room first, if that's O.K?"

"Oh, yes. Let me get this for thee," and she put a pail in the kitchen sink and used the small hand pump to fill it with water. She hefted it out and took it to the bathroom. Becky followed her through the dining room and parlor to the bathroom. There were candles and oil lamps for light and everything looked old, but well cared for.

"I am lucky to have this. Not all of our homes have an indoor potty. Thee can pour the water in here when thee are finished or pour the water in the tank before starting. There is a little handle on the side for when thee are finished." She looked at Becky to see if she understood. Becky nodded and pointed at the stool.

"Oh, yes," and Miriam stepped out to close the door.

Becky was back with the bucket in a few minutes. She used the pump to refill it and carried it back to the bathroom for the next user. Miriam came down the stairs after checking to see if her home was presentable after last night's tremblers.

As they waked through her home, it was obvious Miriam was proud of the old wooden furniture that made up her way of life. There were quilts, embroidery and crocheted items everywhere. Upstairs, Becky saw an old treadle sewing machine.

"Oh," she gasped. "You have an antique sewing machine!"

"It was my mother's." said Miriam proudly.

Becky thought of her computerized machine at home and was embarrassed for calling it an antique. She explained herself and Miriam said she had seen the modern machine yesterday.

"It was a frightening thing to see when one only knows how to use one like this," Miriam replied. "Oh," she gasped. "My bread!" She turned and ran down the stairs to the kitchen. She opened the oven and the smell of fresh bread filled the room. The heat that came with the fragrant aroma didn't seem to bother her. Becky stepped to the door for a breath of air.

It was quite a morning for Becky as she followed Miriam from the kitchen to the garden and back. The term, fresh vegetables, took on a new meaning when she had to pick them, wash them and slice them appropriately. She wasn't ready to face the prospect of having to grow them also.

"If thy father has set up the table under the oak tree I will slice the ham and we will eat.

Becky looked out and saw her Dad carrying the table with Kiia helping until he declared it too heavy. Bill set it down and sent him to tell his Mother and Miriam the chairs would be ready in a moment. Off the boy ran and if Becky hadn't seen the table was ready she would never had known as the boy stopped to watch the ants in the driveway and then chased a butterfly into the garden.

Miriam put the table linens in a basket with silverware and tableware. The food went into another and she announced she was ready.

"Miriam, I think these table linens are a little advanced for Kiia. They'll look a little worse for the wear at his corner of the table."

"He is just a boy. If thee will set the table I will carry the food basket. Then I will come back in for the coffee.

"A hundred degrees and she makes coffee," Becky thought and went out to the table. She put the cloth on the table and then the matching place mats and napkins. The silverware and tableware were old and worn, but the table looked nice.

"Miriam!" Becky exclaimed. "The linens are beautiful! Did you sew them?"

"Yes, the Bishop allowed thy Father to give me fabric other than white only."

They set the food on the table and Miriam went back in for the coffee. She made it the usual way; in a pan and then poured it into an old style coffee pot to bring it to the table. Becky thought of her mother's silver service still at home, but knew Miriam couldn't accept something that expensive even if Becky could share it.

They talked easily about the farm, the weather and Luke and Sarah's visit. Miriam and Becky seemed to be getting along well for having had little time together. Kiia just bubbled and bounced his little-boy way through everything and the adults loved every minute of his presence.

"When we pick up Luke and Sarah this afternoon why don't we plan to eat out?

"Sure." Said Becky."

"Yes," agreed Miriam. "There is enough ham left and it must be eaten tonight or tomorrow at the latest. William I see we have a larger table to set out here and…"

"Oh, no, Miriam," interrupted Becky. "Out, out."

She looked at Becky and then Bill with questioning eyes.

"I was thinking we could try that steak house out on county road X a little east and north of here. If we go early we can get in and out before the kids get too bored."

"Oh, I wasn't aware of a sss-steak house out on…" and stopped because she knew she had failed to understand.

Becky was normally very tender-hearted and near tears. She had taken Miriam to her heart and felt the cultural differences between them hurt her more as they all learned to accept each other.

Bill's cell-phone rang loudly and ended the dinner-out discussion. It was Luke calling to say they had been on the plane for over an hour and would be in Minneapolis International at three o'clock. After an hour's layover they would be in Eau Claire Wisconsin by four thirty.

"Hey, Dad," he added; "I told you I'm into the biggest deal of my career and I will need to keep in touch from your place. I'm going to need your fax and internet hookup." Do you know how to use your computer?"

"Well, not as well as I use my refrigerator door, but we'll get by!" He pushed his speaker phone so everyone at the table could hear. Suddenly, Lukey was calling "Grandpa, Grandpa" in his father's cell phone which just happened to be in his ear.

Luke put the phone in his son's hands and the boy continued to yell into it. As it turned out fishing was on his mind and he wanted to catch as many as he did at Yellowstone National Park earlier in the year. Kiia announced in an equally loud voice he wanted to go with Grandpa too and a little boy battle of rules and excuses began. Bill promised to take both boys fishing if they'd quit arguing and Lukey said O.K. and goodbye and the sound of the phone bouncing its way to the floor could be heard. Muffled instructions about being careful with Dad's phone followed and then the conversation was reestablished.

Bill and Luke talked a little and when Luke saw that Sarah and Rachael were asleep the men said their good byes. Bill shut the phone and he was visibly pleased his son was coming to his wedding.

"Dad, could we go into town soon so I can clean up the house before they get here. We made some small messes getting things ready to bring out here."

Bill looked to Miriam and she said she only needed a few minutes to clean up after lunch. The women picked up while Bill and Kiia fed and watered the goats. There was a mess in one corner of the pen that suggested to Bill that one of the goats might be sick, but he decided to wait until Michael stopped by later in the week.

On the way in to town Bill stopped at the dealer where he bought his new truck and rented a Van. Miriam couldn't recall seeing such a vehicle and asked Becky what is was and how would they use it. As she walked around it she touched the handle of the sliding door and it opened.

'Rebecca!" she gasped. "I fear I have broken it!"

"No, you haven't," she laughed and went into a discussion about heat activated devices influenced by body temperature as well as physical activity and ended by saying, "maybe you should just ask Dad."

Bill came out of the dealership and walked over to the passenger side of the van. Seeing the sliding door open he pressed the keyless entry and as it closed he opened the front door by hand and offered to help Miriam into the front seat. By now she really didn't care how anything on the van worked.

Becky and Kiia followed them in the pickup. Bill parked out front of the house and, unlike her father, Becky pulled straight into the driveway. She wasn't going to attempt backing in the new truck.

They went inside and tried to get Kiia to nap till it was time to go, but most kids sense when a nap is important to their parents and he found everything else to do. The adults picked up the house and dusted everything in it. It seemed every trembler found its own source of dust and scattered it everywhere.

When it was nearly time to go Becky gave Kiia a bath and dressed him. Bill and Miriam found a nice surprise when they went into the master bedroom. Becky had gotten Bill a new pair of slacks and matching shirt for his birthday next month and had matched a dress for Miriam to them. It was a long dress, in keeping with her sense of modesty. Together, they were a little overdressed, but Becky had chosen the colors well and they were comfortable.

Bill picked up the two child-seats for Lukey and Rachael and was installing them when the others came out to the van. They stopped and looked at each other and laughed with compliments for how nicely the others were dressed.

Miriam seemed a little uncomfortable about riding in the front again so Bill asked if she would like to sit in the back seat with Kiia. There was no hiding each others joy at sitting together. Becky got into the front seat and off they went to the Chippewa Valley Airport in Eau Claire. Miriam played with Kiia and pointed out things that surprised or interested her as they went. They were at the airport in forty minutes. It was a small airport, but it was another culture shock for Miriam. With Bill at her arm she took everything well and was comforted when he said they would sleep at the farm tonight.

Becky called Kiia to the window after the plane touched down and they all watched in excitement as it taxied to the terminal. Bill and Miriam stayed at the back of the waiting area as Becky and Kiia went forward to greet her brother and his family. After deplaning, they all walked up to where Bill stood with Miriam. She looked mostly at the kids fearing Luke and Sarah might not approve of her.

But, when Luke embraced his father and Bill kept his arm around his son as he introduced him to her, Miriam relaxed immediately.

Luke liked her right away and said he was happy for his Dad. Sarah was openly happy for her father-in-law also. Lukey and Rachael weren't interested in her as long as she didn't take their grandfather from them. Kiia was happy at his cousins' shyness because he knew he already loved this new person in his grandfather's life.

It doesn't take long to get luggage in a small airport and soon they were at the van and loading.

"I thought you would bring the camper, Dad."

"Well, the camper has gone down the road to provide additional income for my big project. We'll get another one when the time is right, Wait'll you see the farm tomorrow. You'll understand then."

Miriam and Becky got into the back with Kiia in between them. Sarah took the next seat with Rachael and Lukey got the seat behind his grandfather which made it easier for him to "back seat" drive. Luke rode beside his father. Sarah turned to Miriam and asked;

"Are you comfortable in the back, Miriam?"

"Oh, yes. I am used to being in the back of the buggy."

"At least," Becky added, "this one has windows."

They had a good laugh at that and everyone seemed to relax a little. The restaurant was a thirty minute drive and when they arrived the kids were more than ready to get out. They were seated on a patio-deck and the kids ran out on the grass to play. Ordering dinner went well as they were all familiar with cuts of steak and conversation flowed while waiting for the appetizers. At one moment Bill noticed Becky staring him down and he looked at Miriam.

She was staring at her place setting and touching the silverware with her finger tips. Bill reached over with his fingertips so she wouldn't move away in fear of a public display of affection.

"This is the salad fork, dinner fork, desert fork, and on the other side the knife, steak knife, soup spoon, teaspoon, desert spoon and anything thing else they want to add."

"So many things." Who has to wash all this?"

"Oh, they pay someone to feed a machine and they all come out clean on the other end."

"Feed a machine?"

"You know, Dad," offered Luke. "It might be easier to ask to see the kitchen rather than explain it all."

"I guess so."

The dinner came, the kids were called and a prayer prayed. It was a great family gathering. The kids even behaved. Talking was easy as they headed into the house in Augusta.

Even Bill was surprised at how easy it had become for him to refer to the farm as home now. He pulled straight into the drive and parked blocking the garage, a move that surprised Luke. The women went inside the house while the men and boys looked at the new truck. Bill hastily explained to Luke the coupe was in storage until he could be sure it was safe to have it out again.

Luke was glad to see the house had withstood the tremblers well. A lot of the buildings out West had suffered greatly. Even the restaurant they had eaten at that night looked good. Then, as if to remind everyone of the reality of things, the earth shook again and this time it was more than a trembler. The kids usually rolled around and laughed, but this time struggled to stay up and wobbled their way to their parents. They all looked to Bill as if he was responsible for stopping them, or at the least, responsible for explaining them.

"I'm working on it," he tried to sound believable. "Tomorrow we will go to the farm and look at what I'm doing."

"Then, we go fishing!"

"I promise, Lukey, we will go fishing before you all go back."

Chapter 15
Last Innocence

They stayed up late that night waiting for the kids to be totally tired and ready for bed. When they were asleep the adults talked for an hour or so without asking for or making commitments about what might be coming. Bill lead the family in prayers as was his custom since the death of Luke and Sarah's mother. Then he and Miriam went to their home at the farm.

They took his new truck after moving the van out of the way and left the keys for the van with Luke. Miriam was visibly tired from the evening and snuggled into her seat.

"I like our new truck, William"

"I'm glad when I can please you. Have I told you how lovely you look tonight in your new clothes?" He reached out to hold her hand.

"Many times William. Thee pleasures me greatly," and pulled his hand tightly to her lap.

They were silent as they left the lights of the city. It was quiet and dark in the country as Bill turned onto their road and into their driveway. He felt sure Ezra had never driven his buggy with one hand and nearly laughed in his happiness. The truck couldn't be seen from the road if he parked it off the drive between the house and garden so that's what he did.

He shut off the engine and lights and disabled the interior lights. They looked at each other in the moonlight.

"Does an Amish bride pleasure her husband in his new buggy?"

"I…" she looked around the truck wondering just how they would go about it.

He pulled his slacks down and she began removing clothing with needs that matched his. Wondering how he would get across the console and shifter he thought he had found a new definition for the term, "lover's leap," when he felt her warm hands cupping him and guiding him across.

When it was time to go inside, William swung the door open.

"Climb on my back and I will carry you in."

She reached to put her arms around his neck and fairly leaped onto his back and wrapped her legs around him. He felt her press herself against his back.

"Am I not too heavy for thee, William?"

"No, in fact I was thinking about a little stroll around the neighborhood."

"William!" she hissed. "It is one thing for God to see all, but I'll not have the Bishop a witness to this!"

By the time they got to the porch they were laughing so hard Bill had to put her down. She went into the dark kitchen and lit a candle so they could see their way around. Bill touched the water pails on the stove and told her the fire had gone out, but the water was still warm enough for a bath.

"I must potty, first," she said and put an empty pail in the sink. Bill watched as she used the pump to fill it. He was really starting to like this life style until he realized he was touching the cool stove. He stepped back and went to get some kindling to get the fire going for the morning.

He went behind the wood pile to see if he'd suffered any injury from being to close to the stove, and finding none, made use of the great outdoors outhouse.

"Yes," he thought, "I'm really going to miss this when it gets cold."

He gathered some wood and went back inside. It didn't take much to rekindle the coals and he had a fire going by the time Miriam came to find him. He carried the two warm pails to the tub and poured them in.

"Would thee enter first?

Bill stepped into the tube and laid back for her. She quickly put one foot on each side of him and lay on top of him. They kissed and snuggled while he washed her back. She brought her knees up and pressed herself against him. When love had been fulfilled they rested.

"Oh, William, I am so weary."

"We've had a big day, love. Let's go up to bed," and he helped her to her feet. Bill carried the candle and they walked together up to their bed. Miriam was nearly asleep as they walked due to the stress she had felt in meeting her new family and changing her whole lifestyle.

In the bedroom, Bill blew out the candle and pulled back the covers. She slipped into the bed from his side while he hung the quilt over the window to darken the room. They slept so deeply they missed a long trembler during the night.

Although Bill had hung the quilt over the window to darken the room it was still open and the muffled sound of a cell phone ringing woke him. He found Miriam and kissed her.

"Back to reality, Love." He pulled himself out of bed and went down to the truck. Of course, he looked outside first to make sure no one was in the yard. He found the phone and saw it was Luke's cell number. He returned the call as he gathered up the clothing left from last night.

"Hey, I thought farmers were up early in the morning," came a voice that was straining to be happy.

"I'm sorry son. The city in me overslept this morning."

"You haven't seen the news on TV yet? I ran downtown to get some newspapers and it's all the same."

"Son, we don't have electricity or newspaper delivery out here."

"The magma deposit at the lake! It's in every news story you find! Forget it; I'll explain when we get out there. Becky knows the way. See you in twenty minutes."

Bill shut off the phone and made sure the truck was clean. He rushed into the kitchen as Miriam was making coffee. She was dressed in her blue clothing and bonnet.

"William! Thee must stop walking about naked. Does everyone in the city do thus?"

"Oh, yes! I've walked up behind many couples going into their homes like we did last night."

"A sight I would not like to see!"

"By the way, that was my son on the phone. They'll be here in about twenty minutes."

"Twenty minutes? And thee has made no move toward modesty?"

Bill chuckled as she stole a look at him. He turned and ran upstairs, feeling her eyes on him. The bed was made so he put the cloths in the closet and closed the door. Grabbing what he needed he ran down to the bathroom. Miriam had left a pail of water for him to bathe with.

His loud yell told her he knew the difference between hot water and cold and probably wouldn't forget to fill the pails and leave them on the stove again. He finished quickly and went to the kitchen with a man-sized appetite. Realizing the goats needed food and water he went out to the barn. Miriam was in the garden.

In the barn, the goats hadn't suffered. Their inside pen was fresh hay on all four sides and the water dishes weren't empty. Bill got some oats for the mangers keeping an eye out for the old Billy. He was still sore from Michael's quick surgical technique performed the other morning so he stayed to himself till Bill left.

Miriam was back in the kitchen washing vegetables when Bill got back. The kids pulled up and Bill went out to invite them in. It was apparent they were taken aback when they saw Miriam in her blue skirt and bonnet.

"We are having eggs and braised vegetables this morning. Would thee join us?" She was suddenly aware of the differences in their cultures.

The heat from the cook stove was stifling and added greatly to the family's discomfort.

"Yes. Can we help?" asked Sarah.

"Yes," smiled Miriam. "Everything is in the dining room. Do you remember where, Becky?"

"I do. Come on kids; we'll set the table." Suddenly, three well behaved kids went wild with the new surroundings and they filled the dining room. Sarah was a little surprised at table linens being used for

170

breakfast, but Becky assured her this was the way Miriam wanted it. The tableware was a little mismatched, but clean and serviceable.

The kids washed up in the bathroom and were excited about having someone pour cold water over their hands to rinse them. Luke called to his Dad to come over and read the newspapers. Bill said he would after checking how things were going in the kitchen.

"William," Miriam looked at him with fearful eyes, "in my way we don't read such things when at the table. We prefer the word of God instead."

"I understand." Turning to the dining room Bill called to Luke. "We'll read and discuss the news in the barn after we eat. O.K?"

Luke agreed and in minutes the table was heavy with a large hot platter of veggies, one with eggs and another with bread baked earlier. Kids who normally had to have veggies forced on them chose to eat all they could along with the eggs. When everything had been eaten they all complimented Miriam who responded with a modest blush and thanks.

"Now, it is time for the men to go to the barn and the women to teach the young to clean table."

Realizing this was not a request Bill stood up and looked to Luke to follow him to the barn. There was a lot to show him and talk about and without the kids it would be easier. They walked in through the large sliding doors and Luke was stunned.

The barn looked overly large from the outside, but inside it looked even larger because of all Bill had been able to build and store in it.

"My God! Dad! What the hell have you been doing here?" Bill took the newspapers from his hands before he dropped them.

"Look around while I check out the news."

The papers told of multiple earth quakes all over the world and dormant volcanoes that had started to reawaken. It wasn't in the United States only. All articles spoke of government studies, but no explanations for what was happening or what might take place soon. It was enough to confirm Bill's suspicions even though it made his blood run cold.

He set the newspapers on a table and began to question Luke about what he thought about the earthquakes and what they meant. Luke revealed his concerns and they ran nowhere near what Bill feared. He was sure the world governments would find a problem and solution soon and there was no reason for pessimistic planning.

Bill was surprised, even shocked by his son's indifference and spent the next hour explaining what he'd done in the barn and how he hoped it would save his family in the event of an eruption of cataclysmic proportions.

Luke spoke of his confidence in the world's governments and his skepticism in his father's fears. He stopped short of suggesting senility, but it was obvious he had no confidence in the farm being a place of safety in the event of a cataclysm.

Bill was almost frantic trying to think of ways to convince his son when the women walked in. Becky had taken the kids to the goat pen and then would take them to the garden next.

Sarah looked around the barn and recognized what it was for immediately. She was afraid for her children, but agreed with her husband that everything would work out well in the end. She was, however, very interested in the raised beds. Gardening was a major hobby for her and she missed having time and space for it in their apartment living in California.

Miriam caught Bills attention by taking his hand and asking him to explain what was planted and what his hopes were for keeping the barn a livable space in the event of disaster. They followed him around and asked polite questions. In the end, it was to no avail for Bill to press for them to return to Augusta.

Instead, Luke asked about the plans for the wedding blessing and what they all should wear. Taking that clue Bill and Miriam talked about that instead. Lukey came racing in with his cousins to remind Bill of his promise to take them all fishing.

He felt a little numbed by the lack of concern he had encountered, but suggested a county park by a local river. They would go there after making plans at the church in the afternoon and dinner that night. Everyone but he felt better by the plans.

Since it was nearly time to go see his Pastor he told them all to get ready. He and Miriam changed to some casual clothing Becky had helped pick out and they set out in the van. The Pastor was happy to see all of them and gave special attention to the records of the Amish Ceremony celebrated by the Bishop Yocum. He stated the ceremony was valid and could receive the Church's blessing that afternoon.

It met with everyone's approval and the kids informed the Pastor he was invited to go fishing after dinner that night.

He declined with a hearty laugh and invited them all to the four fish-boils that were planned for the coming Lent. Apparently he knew the fishing was slow that summer and felt the Lenten Fish-Boils held more promise of a good dinner.

On the way home Bill stopped for some picnic supplies and bait for the fishing trip. They went to a local park built beside a river where they ate and fished till dark. The Pastor was right about the fishing being poor, but the kids had a good time. They agreed to meet at the farm for lunch the next day to prepare for the Blessing. Then they went to the farm to drop off Bill and Miriam.

Inside the kitchen Miriam turned to Bill.

"William, it seems there is little room for cooking on my stove with the extra pails of water being heated."

Bill hadn't blushed so much since he was an adolescent. All he could do is look deeply into her eyes and speak of his love for her. She stepped toward him and put her hands on his chest.

"Perhaps, if thee would promise not to burn thyself on the stove, we could leave our clothing here for laundry day tomorrow." She stepped back and lifted her skirt. Bill tried not to laugh with all the joy he felt and was content to be naked before she.

He carefully took two pails of hot water from the stove while she boldly looked at him.

As he turned, so did she and wiggled her bare bottom at him and led the way to their bath. He marveled at her beauty and open love for him despite such a modest upbringing.

Bill returned to the kitchen for the other two pails of hot water and she waited as he filled the tub. Knowing she would like to lie on top he stepped in while she guided him with a warm hand.

They lay there contorted to the small area as only lovers could. Kisses were long and loving while joy was fulfilled. The loneliness of being widowed was forgotten and life was fulfilled with love play and gazing into each other's eyes. The silliest things made them laugh like innocent children. Finally exhaustion conquered their beings and they made their way to bed. She slipped in naked from his side.

"I forgot to refill the pails," Bill groaned.

Miriam pulled the covers down which made him look at her. "I'll see to the water in the morning."

Gratefully he slipped into bed and held her tightly with feelings that seemed to be newer than the first time they had made love. Sleep finally came to them and held them tighter than they had held each other. They never heard the goats bleat out a warning for the two tremblers which came that night.

They were aware of each other's awakening in the morning. Bill rolled out of bed and held the covers as Miriam moved to his side. They couldn't resist a good morning kiss before gathering their clothing.

Miriam began the preparations for their big day as Bill made his way to the barn to care for the goats and check the new plants. He noticed two coveys of quail had moved in with the goats.

They were pretty birds and Bill liked them as soon as he discovered them. He was glad the goats didn't seem to mind them.

Inside, he told Miriam about the two coveys of quail and she seemed interested. The fact there was two pair of them and they came into the barn willingly reminded her of the story of Noah's Ark. The thought interested Bill and they quietly reflected on that incident for the rest of their breakfast time.

The slamming of car doors brought their attention back to the plans for the day. Luke had driven the rental van. Becky had several things along which she wanted to store in the barn. Luke had included some of his childhood things in an effort to please his father since he was still determined to return to California on the next day.

Bill had left the barn open when he went to feed the goats so it didn't take long to move the few possessions to the storage area.

Luke took a few minutes to look around again and he complemented his father on his accomplishments. Both men were careful to avoid the issue of staying longer as opposed to returning in a few weeks.

Luke noticed there was no apple or fruit trees in the barn and asked his dad if there were any plans to have any. Remembering there were three mature apple trees behind the bluff Bill suggested they take a bucket and spades to see what they could dig up. When they got to the trees, they took a few minutes to select one small, healthy looking limb from each tree.

Then they selected three small saplings that had set roots after having been blown over during March winds.

They hurried back to the barn so the limbs and roots wouldn't dry out before they could be grafted together.

Bill dug some potting soil and filled three buckets. Luke whittled the apple limbs and the main trucks of the saplings and began grafting the saplings to grow apples. It was a good project for the father and son as it left both with a feeling of having starting something they would like to see grow well into the future.

Sarah came into the barn to announce it was time to eat and then dress for the trip to church. She was surprised at the grafting project and Bill could easily see her interest in what they had done. Her interest in gardening would make it easy for her to want to return and Bill was counting on that.

The men washed up, closed the barn and walked to the house. Lunch was satisfying to them and then the challenge of getting the kids dressed was undertaken. Bill and Miriam took their clothing to the truck as they would dress at the church. The kids were kept inside away from food, beverages and the great, but messy out-of-doors.

At the appointed time they all arrived at the church. Bill and Miriam went to separate rooms to change and met back inside the church doors. The family processed in together as music wasn't a part of Miriam's culture and the stopped before the Pastor.

As Bill turned to face Miriam he was struck again by her tremendous, natural beauty. She wore her hair down and a sheer veil that covered her shoulders and the dress. Becky had tried to get Miriam to chose a strapless gown, but to no avail.

Her sense of modesty could not accept such a thing and even though it was a sleeveless gown it did have straps.

She captivated her husband and his eyes never left her. Neither of them had any sense of time passing or vows being made.

When the Pastor made his pronouncement Luke loudly cleared his throat to stop him and then handed him the white envelope his father had prepared. They gently turned the newly blessed couple and followed them out of the church without any display of affection. Luke drove straight back to the farm where he and Becky surprised them with a beautiful cake, ice cream and a catered meal. Miriam was thrilled and had all she could do to let others serve. She kept her veil across her shoulders all afternoon.

As the afternoon became early evening it was obvious the adults had eaten all they could and the kids had grown tired of each other. Before anyone left Miriam asked Luke and Bill to move her bed and dresser to the barn. She made a commitment to follow her husband into this new lifestyle he had built for his family. The women brought her clothing and the linens and then they left for the house in Augusta.

Once alone, Bill saw to the animals while she tried to order her belongings after the move.

They met by the hearth and Bill started a small fire and they sat before it quietly. After a while they went back to the house to bathe. Bill carefully placed her dress on the dining room table to protect it and after bathing he insisted she wear it back to their bed.

Chapter 16
There Is No Escape

They awoke in the morning at six a.m. as they wanted to. After a moment of prayer they rose and got ready for the trip to the Airport in Eau Claire. At the appointed time Luke drove in with the others and Bill and Miriam got in. The trip was short and uneventful as the kids were still sleepy and the adults feared the parting.

It was easy to check in at a small airport and few people were flying that day. The luggage was accepted and sent out to the plane. Hugs and kisses were exchanged and promises to return in six weeks were made and accepted. Luke and his family boarded the commuter plane and when it lifted off Bill, Miriam, Becky and Kiia turned to leave.

Becky asked if she could use Bill's truck for the day. Bill agreed and when they got to Augusta he dropped her at home while he returned the van. Later, Becky picked up he and Miriam at the dealership and the four started toward the farm.

When they arrived at the farm, Bill went straight to the barn. He had fed and watered the animals before leaving in the morning so he just had to water the plants before helping Miriam in the house.

It had been a little over a week since he had planted them and already there were seedlings sprouting. The apple trees, blueberry plants, strawberry plants and tomatoes were doing better than expected. Bill had kept the grow lights on the electrical power rather than the battery set up he had planned. He'd used a battery charger to make sure all his batteries would hold a good charge and was saving them for whenever he would need them. He was surprised by the sound of a buggy in the yard.

Bill came out to find Michael pulling up to the barn. It appeared Amos was coming down the hill also. Bill waved and called out a hello and Michael returned the greeting in a pensive way. He walked up to the barn.

"William," he hesitated before going on, "William, some time ago thee said I would always be welcome here."

Bill smiled and nodded.

"Not only me, but mine as well," he continued. Michael's wife, Ruth and twin daughters Anna and Mary stepped down from the buggy. Ruth was heavy with their third child.

"Of course," said Bill. "Come into the barn and look around. We will go up to the house later." Miriam walked from the house to stand beside her husband. She looked at Ruth who looked directly back at her and managed a smile. It was an important gesture because it proved there was to be no shunning of Miriam.

Bill waved a welcome to Amos and turned to walk into the barn with the others.

"William, I have some more plants and sets I would like you to consider growing for me. They are medicinal and I always have little or none available during the wintertime. It would help our clan a lot if they were more available."

"Of course," said Bill. Amos came in with a box of plant seedlings and Bill pointed to a place under the lights to put them. He made two more trips with plants and then brought in what looked like Ruth's cedar chest. Amos left with his buggy and went up the hill.

"I understand Moses is aware of what my plans were when I bought the farm?"

"Yes, William. He surmised your plan shortly after the earthquakes began. He wasn't sure how you determined what was coming, but our clan believes God has favored you with knowledge others don't have. And that brings me to our plight."

"William, when you said I would always be welcome here, did that mean my family and I would be welcome to join you and yours no matter what the future holds? You may need a healer, you know," he added.

Bill had to smile at that remark. He thought for a moment and said, "Yes, you are welcome to walk with us to whatever the future holds. But, I hope I'm as wrong as anyone has ever been about what I'm afraid of. This may be all for nothing, you know."

"I realize that and hope for the better also. But, there have been too many warnings from the earth to believe a natural disaster is not about to occur." Michael's concern showed plainly as he spoke. He went on to ask William if he could assist in any future planning and work.

Bill gave Michael and Ruth an overview of what he feared would happen. If it did, and if the world was covered with volcanic dust it could cause a two year cold spell that would freeze out anything that did not get destroyed by a lack of sunlight. He explained that the possibility of a two year blackout was only an estimate and it could be shorter or longer with more or less disastrous results.

Michael said he believed the same way Bill did and Ruth agreed. Since she said she understood, Bill believed Ruth could speak English in the Germanic idiolect as did Miriam.

"The number of people the barn life could support was unknown at this time," Bill went on. His plans were for himself and Miriam, Becky and Kiia and his son and daughter-in-law with their two kids. Now that he and Miriam were married, the number was at eight. If there was to be five more, one of them an infant, considerable thought would have to be given to more supplies.

Michael agreed and said he would be available to help with additional planning immediately. He promised additional goats for meat and milk and healing care to the best of his ability. They talked a few more minutes and Michael asked if they could return home to bring another buggy full of possessions down the hill. Bill agreed, but added that there was an equally good chance nothing would be needed and life would go on as it had for centuries.

"One can always hope so," said Michael. He and his family returned to their buggy for the ride up the hill.

Bill closed the big sliding door and he and Miriam walked out the passage way. It occurred to Bill that he and Miriam must have looked a little strange to Michael and Ruth. He had on a different pair of cargo shorts and shirt and Miriam was in a new pair of jeans and a short sleeved western shirt Becky had picked out for her. Bill turned to her and without thought began to roll up her sleeves a little.

"William!" Do I not look immodest enough for one day?"

"Not unless I don't roll both sleeves." He wanted to say something about showing more arm than leg or the other way around, and decided to kiss her instead.

There are times one's lips can be used for better things than talk. He held her for as long as she would let him.

"William? Think thee we should accomplish more today? I have some plants I would like to dig up and move to the barn. Perhaps we could move my bathtub to the barn also?"

"We could," he replied. "I will need time to decide how we could plumb it first.

Say! Do you have any books to move over here?"

Miriam said all she had was her Bible, but that in the boy's room upstairs were some books on Animal Husbandry and the school books she had used to teach them how to read and do math. Bill walked her to the garden so she could choose which plants she wanted him to dig up. He went into the house and noticed he hadn't refilled the pails to warm the water for their bath that night. They were dry so he put them into two stacks and went upstairs to fill them with her Bible and the books from the boy's room. It wouldn't make much of a library, but it would have to do. He included the few toys that were kept from her sons' childhood and started for the barn.

He called to Miriam that he would be out to help her in a minute. She smiled and said her choices were made and it would not take long. In the barn he put the pails down and walked out to the garden.

Suddenly he felt himself thrown up and off his feet. There was a crashing sound so loud and fierce it hurt his ears. He felt like his ear drums were being forced inward to the point of breaking. The time had come! The earth had taken all it could from what Mankind had done to it for centuries. Its plates had made whatever adjustments they could and magma deposits around the world were released upward. The lake ended in Yellowstone with a puff of steam that was insignificant compared to the destructive power of the volcano.

Bill felt like he had been thrown down on the ground and he had the wind knocked out of him. He rolled around trying to get his breath. There was so much dust he choked as he struggled to breath. When he could get up he was still coughing because of the dust. It was so thick he could barely see and finding Miriam was the only thing on his mind.

Pulling his shirt up he covered his nose and mouth to make breathing easier. Squinting was the only way he could see and not get dust in his eyes. Turning around and around he called Miriam's name. Finally he could see the house which had been broken from its foundation and thrown off at a frightening angle. At last, he could see what direction to take to find his wife. He didn't know how long he had been down trying to breath and was afraid Miriam might be in worse shape than he.

The garden was close as he staggered along. He heard her coughing, but couldn't see her.

The gate and fence were down so he stepped on them and went to where he thought he last saw her. Her cough alerted him to where she was and he nearly tripped on her till he heard her again. The dust and dirt had nearly covered her and he grabbed her by the arms and pulled her to her feet. Coughing and gagging they struggled toward the barn. Bill could only hold his eyes open for a second to assure his route and then he stepped forward with them closed. They clung to each other fearing the loss of the greatest love of their lives.

When they reached the passage way Bill pushed the door open and when they had entered he slammed it shut. The single light at the load center continued to burn so he knew the electricity was still available. It gave an eerie glow because of the amount of dust that had been able to penetrate the building. The large overhead door had been closed earlier as well as the passageway. The door to the goat side of the barn was open and so was the small opening for the animals to go out into the pen.

"I've got to close the door to the goats, Miriam. You pump some water and put it in the tray below the pipe that will bring clean air into the barn."

She started to the pump and Bill closed the damper on the fireplace to keep any more dust from coming down the chimney. His cell phone began to ring so he answered it as he closed the door to the animal's part of the barn.

"Dad?"

"Yes. Luke, is that you?" Bill could hear hysterical crying and shrieking in the background. It was so loud he could barely hear Luke over it all.

"Dad! You were right! We ran into a ball of fire! It's all over!"

"Bill," Sarah grabbed the phone. "We love you and Miriam. Kids, say goodbye to your grandpa." Bill heard their little voices and before he could answer Luke took the phone again.

"Dad! I'm sorry I didn't believe you."

"Luke, tell the pilot to turn around and…"

"We're already spiraling down. It's too…"

The phone went dead. Bill shouted for Luke and his family. He knew in his heart there was no one to hear him on the plane, but he couldn't stop himself from calling their names. The sound of a pail being dropped into the water bath caused him to shut his phone off. Miriam was looking at him in horror.

"Oh, Miriam. We have lost our sons. And their families. Both of us!"

She clutched her ears as if to cancel out what she'd heard. The horror of what she heard took all hope of ever seeing her sons again. In her heart she'd always believed she would see them, their spouses and her grand children.

She stumbled to Bill, searching his eyes for some form of hope. How could the man she had come to love let her children die when he was the one who planned for survival?

Bill tried to hold her; to console her. She beat on his chest one minute and tried to hold him the next. She was shrieking "No," repeatedly pushing and pulling against him. There could be no consolation for her betrayal, her loss and the fear she felt about the future. Bill feared she would leave him to retreat into an inner life that wouldn't include him. Her eyes widened at the sound of Bill's cell phone. It was as if the possibility of other survivors gave her enough hope to calm herself.

"Dad? What happened?"

"Becky! Are you all right? Where are you?"

"We were on the way to the farm when something happened. The truck went off the road. I think I am at the bridge over the creek just before where we turn off."

"Is Kiia with you? Is he all right too?"

"Yes he is. Dad, I don't know if the bridge is strong enough to cross. There's a strong wind coming up. What should I do?"

"Listen to me, Becky. It's easy to get here. Stop the truck right where you are. Push that button on the dash that says 4-wheel-high. It will put the truck in four wheel drive.

Steer away from the road to the right and drive to that shallow part of the creek just before the garden. I know you can cross there. Go to 4-wheel-low if you get stuck. Do it now! There's no time to spare. Do you understand?"

"Yes." He could hear the fear in her voice, but he was encouraged by the fact she could respond to directions. Kiia was quiet and that helped both of them.

"I see the barn! I'm almost there."

"Miriam and I will come out!" Miriam pushed past Bill and ran to the passageway ahead of him. She pulled the door open as Becky drove up past the garden. Bill went to the passenger side to get Kiia out of the back seat. The boy smiled with glee and reached for his grandfather. Bill unbuckled him and Miriam reached to take him into the barn."

"I want to go get my mother! Right now!"

"What?" Bill had concentrated so much on getting Kiia out of the truck he hadn't seen Becky's friend Cherry and her two daughters.

"I want to go my mother; Right now!"

"Dad? There is time to take her and the kids back to Eau Claire, isn't there?"

Bill opened the front door and reached across Cherry to shut off the ignition. He pulled out the keys.

"I don't think there is time for an 'over and back' trip, but if Cherry wants to go see her mother she can take the truck and come back some other time." He knew he was lying, but wasn't about to risk losing his only daughter and grandson. He walked around the truck and pulled Becky out of the driver's seat and closed the door. He pushed her by the shoulders toward the passage way.

"And, just how the hell am I supposed to get home to my mother?" Cherry stepped out of the truck in a menacing manner. Her two daughters started to whine as if they feared she would leave them somewhere.

Bill continued to push Becky into the barn despite her protests. The breeze had now become a hot wind and he wasn't going to let his daughter get caught in whatever was to come. Miriam came forward and pulled her deeper into the barn to show her that Kiia had found a place to play and she should come in and see to his needs. Miriam was much stronger than she looked.

Michael came down the hill at a fast pace with Amos right behind him. They pulled into the yard almost on two wheels. Bill threw the truck keys to Cherry and told her to hurry if she wanted to see her mother soon.

He moved quickly to the first buggy and helped Ruth and the twins get out. He directed her to the passage way and Miriam ran out to guide her and the girls in.

"We only had time to get Ruth's sewing machine and our wedding bed," said Michael.

"I'll help you unload and then we must get inside. Have one of the women hold the door for us." Bill shared the weight of the bed with Amos and Michael wrestled the sewing machine in alone. They went back to the buggies to bring in three Nanny Goats and their kids that Amos had brought down from his own herd. Michael went outside to say his goodbyes to Amos. Words were few and then they embraced. Amos pushed away first and grabbed the reins to Michael's horse to lead it up to his barn. The animal's instincts led it to choose to die where it was and it dug its hooves into the soil and wouldn't be moved. Amos threw down the reins and clamored into his own buggy. He looked back and waved to Michael, then slapped the horses rump with the reins and it ran up the hill.

Bill was pulling a sheet metal covering into place when Michael came to the passage way. The two men pulled it to cover the doorway and Bill slammed the passage way door and barred it with an oak timber.

"We have to get the sheet metal cover over the goat's door to the pen. I don't want anything getting in to harm them. Then we have to set the rest of the Styrofoam sheets over the doors to keep us comfortable."

Michael agreed and went through the door into the animal's side. He leapt over the door's pen and gate and ran to the open door to the outside pen. The animals cowered inside and were no problem. As he reached outside to slide the sheet metal door into place he looked toward the sky. It was one complete rolling red and black cloud. The heat of it felt hotter than any wind he had ever experienced. If he looked any longer he would have been too terrified to complete his job. The sheet metal door fit tightly into place and he barred it with the oak timber they had cut for it. An extra piece of Styrofoam completed the enclosure and he hurried back to his family.

Bill was just putting a light and extension cord over the animal's water and feed dishes. He wanted the animals and birds to find their food no matter what the future brought. Michael filled the feed and water dishes and the two of them went back into their part of the barn and closed the door.

Bill switched all of the grow lights on and set the switches for an instant change to battery power in the event of an electrical failure. The room took on a more cheery look with more lights on. The air inside still had too much dust and he ordered someone to ride the stationary bike to recharge the batteries and draw air in through the water bath. It was his hope they could force clean air in and the old air up the chimney.

"Cherry, you ride the bike first for at least twenty minutes. Michael and I...CHERRY! I thought you went home!"

She looked at him with wide, terrified eyes.

"I don't know what this is all about, but you must promise me that you will take care of my children if something happens to me."

"I will. I'll take care of everyone here. That is what this is all about."

"Luke? Where's Luke?"

"Luke and his family will not be joining us, Becky. Neither of my sons and their families will join us. I fear no one will be joining us." Miriam put her arms around Becky, but comfort could not be given or received when horror gripped everyone. Kiia ran to his grandfather to be picked up. The others moved toward Bill also without knowing why. Everyone wanted to cry, but couldn't find release from their fears and sadness.

The temperature began to rise in the large room and Bill went to check the indoor-outdoor thermometer. He was shocked at what he saw.

"Four hundred degrees out side! How can that be?"

Michael told him about how the sky looked like it was on fire.

Bill knew instantly from his fire training that the volcano belched fire in the sky and the winds were blowing the heat ahead of the actual fire. The heat would raise combustible materials to the point of burning before the actual fire got to them. It would be a raging inferno that no wooden structure could survive. Any thing and any one exposed to heat over three hundred degrees would die instantly. Once the temperature rose to over one thousand degrees weak concrete structures would explode to powder and offer no protection. He didn't see how any plant, animal or person could survive. He wasn't sure he could protect his family anymore.

"I need to sit down. Did anyone think to bring any chairs?" Cherry looked as though she needed to lie down rather than sit so Bill ordered the beds to be set up while he wondered how to react to whatever would come next. They put the single army cots behind the large mass fire place for Becky and Kiia and for Cherry and her two daughters. Michael, Ruth and their two would sleep next to Cherry. Partitions would have to be planned later.

The women found the linens and put the sheets on the beds. Everyone worked at a pace none of them could keep up for long. They looked around constantly as if they feared someone or something would break in at the next moment and devour all of them.

The heat began to rise inside and Bill checked the thermometer again. It had risen to over five hundred degrees outside and a fierce wind could be heard.

The sand stone ridge immediately behind the barn was causing the fire storm to go over and around the barn. It would stop the 'blow torch' affect of the fire and also cause the heat to swirl away from the building.

He switched the computerized thermometer to read the indoor temperature and it showed eighty degrees Fahrenheit. So far no one noticed the raise in temperature due to the panic of the moment. Everyone would need water soon so he looked through the unopened boxes to find something to drink with. Before he could find the glasses or cases of soda he found a box of plastic bottles and nipples for nursing calves. He didn't remember ordering them, but someone at the farm store must have sent them to him by mistake. The nipples were enormous compared to what a child would need, but Bill called Cherry away from the bicycle and told her to fill enough for everyone. She was looking a little over-heated from pedaling the bike to provide cleaner air.

"Where's the faucet?"

"Use the pump," and he gestured toward it.

"That thing?"

"Cherry! It's too hot to argue. All, right, here, let me pump and you hold the water bottles. After we fill one for each of us you cap them with the nipples."

"Who got these things? They're way too big."

"Cherry; Just hold them under the water!" Bill began to pump fast. He was hoping the water would somehow cool the floor and the air around them as it overflowed the bottles. Cherry squealed and dropped a bottle and Bill reached around the pump to hold another in place while he pumped.

"Focus, Cherry," he grumbled. "Soon, everyone will need water to drink."

"Yah, like the kids are going to go for nipples like these." But, she continued holding the bottles while Bill pumped.

"Cap them," said Bill as he walked back to the thermometer. It showed an indoor temperature of ninety degrees and over six hundred degrees outside.

"Becky, you, Ruth and Cherry put the kids into their beds and make sure everyone has a water bottle." He called Michael and Miriam over and explained the rise in temperature. The firestorm had pushed super-heated air ahead of itself and soon it would overheat the barn. He ordered them to water the plant beds so they wouldn't dry out and kill the new plants. He had only a week's growth on the seedlings, but didn't want to start over again at a later date. Every time-line now had an immediate need for success.

The three of them pumped water and hurriedly moved to the raised beds. Water that was spilled seemed to evaporate quickly. Bill checked the thermometer and inside it was now ninety nine degrees. A thundering, roaring sound swirled around the building.

"This is it!" He hissed. "The firestorm is on us now!" The sheet metal on the outside of the building screeched as it expanded and pushed against other pieces. The whole structure groaned against the heat and wind. Everyone looked around wondering if the building would hold up. Fear was upon everyone, even though no one could describe what they felt or what they feared would happen.

Bill noticed he was hot and was having trouble breathing. "Everyone get to bed and take a water bottle," he ordered. "The firestorm is burning up our oxygen supplies and we have to rest and conserve what little will be left for us."

They moved as best they could and the exertion made they even more breathless. They were gasping as they lay down. The kids instinctively began nursing on their water bottles.

"Good old H20," thought Bill. He wasn't sure the two parts oxygen in the water would help when there was less than what was needed in the air, but it was all they had at the moment. He and Miriam tumbled on top of their bed and started nursing on the water bottles too. They could see fear in the other's eyes, but it was fear for the safety of the others, more than for themselves. Miriam reached for his hand and he held hers to his heart.

The thundering roar began to quiet as quickly as it came on. The firestorm passed, but continued to draw the air from the barn. Everyone continued to gasp for oxygen and drink as much as they could. Slowly hypoxia caused them to want to sleep and some did.

It only took a minute for the storm to pass over, but it felt like an eternity. The air turbulence that followed caused a downdraft through the chimney that replenished the oxygen in the barn. Slowly they regained their senses and began to take stock of what had happened.

Bill struggled to his feet telling Miriam to rest as he got on the bicycle to bring more air through the water bath so they all could breath better. The air outside the barn was filled with ash from the volcano and the fires it started. The water bath could trap the particulate matter even though the smell of the fire came through also. Thankfully, there was no smell of animals caught outside as the fire was so intense it killed and incinerated them instantly. Bill pedaled at a pace that would bring clean air into the barn and also charge the batteries for the lights. They had been in the barn for less that two hours, but it had seemed like an eternity. The batteries hadn't reached a state of discharge, but the voltage regulator in the alternator wouldn't allow an overcharge.

Michael stumbled past Bill to check on the animals. The goats were struggling to stay up and the birds made a desperate sight.

Most were down in the dirt floor or convulsing about. Thankfully, the open door between the animal and human areas forced additional oxygen in to them. It didn't take long and both birds and animals were shaking off the effects of not being able to breath and were looking around to see if what happened was still a threat. It was still hot and they shared the water supplies as soon as they could get to the pans.

Michael left the door open and walked back to Bill. Miriam walked past to check on the others while the men talked about the proper speed of the bicycle for clean air and the generation of electricity. Slowly, the women and children gathered around Michael and Bill while he pedaled. They all had the sense of having come through the worst moments of their lives. Grieving would begin soon enough, but for now a feeling of having survived filled them. They stood around watching Bill while he forced clean air into the barn.

After a few minutes Bill announced the batteries were charged and there was enough air to breath for the moment. The batteries were keeping the lights on, but the barn was a little darker than they were used to. Bill sent them all off to check around the inside of the barn to look for any signs of damage. They moved slowly away from their little gathering at first. Michael went into the animal area, Bill to the area where the firewood was stored and the women walked around the living area.

"Why isn't this light working?" screamed Cherry.

"It's not a problem," called Bill from the other side of the barn. "It means we've lost all forms of electricity for now. The light will come on at six a.m. and six p.m. and stay on for three hours. It's computerized to be that way. Provided, of course, the fire storm didn't destroy the dam at Jim Falls.

"Oh great, that's a real comfort!" Muttered Cherry.

Michael returned from checking on the animals and their area. There didn't appear to be any damage he reported, but it was too dark to see much. Bill said the same about the front area.

"I'm glad we insulated the whole barn," said Bill. If we hadn't, it would have been impossible to keep the hay and the firewood from catching fire. We'd have died along with everyone and everything else."

"And you're sure that's a good thing?" Cherry asked as she and the other women walked up. Everything looked O.K. where we were. Of course we couldn't see and didn't know what to look for anyway."

"Thank you, Cherry. I'll take that as a positive report.

Bill looked at his new family and struggled for something to say. A good leader always had plans and those who follow him or her will continue to for as long as they believed that.

"All right; here's the story. Most of us know about the magma deposit in Yellowstone that is now the largest volcano the world has ever seen. No one expected it to do what it did and those who feared it didn't expected it to happen so soon. But, it did happen and the world as we know it is in for some major changes. I don't think we know even half of what remains to be seen. Right now though, we are safe and will begin the journey to a new and better life.

"I'm hungry, Grandpa!"

It was Kiia and soon after he spoke the other little ones did too. As soon as people feel safe, basic needs have to be met. Bill struggled to remember where any prepared food was. Miriam moved to a box near their bed and announced she knew where some food bars were. She found them and returned with the box to give each child something.

Cherry unwrapped the bars for her daughters telling them they would have more and better choices tomorrow.

"Starting tomorrow we will have cooked food for most meals just like we did back home. Since this is home now we will do the same, but it won't be the same. The food will be nourishing and we will be too busy to worry about what it is or how it tastes."

"Mommy, I got to go potty. Now!" Cherry's oldest announced what would be the next activity for the rest of the kids. Becky showed Cherry and the kids where the toilet was. The kids circled it to watch the others as kids will do.

"There doesn't appear to be any bathroom walls or bathroom lights to go with the bathroom," Cherry announced in a loud voice. "I trust that was just an oversight!"

Bill looked a Michael for an answer. There had been no time to buy additional construction supplies. Michael thought for a moment and suggested bringing some hay bales forward to make an 'L' shaped enclosure for some privacy. No door was available so both men did what they could with what they had.

Some of the animals hadn't bedded down as they still hadn't accepted this barn as home yet. They watched as Michael pulled bales off the top to hand to Bill. A couple bales broke and after the men left, the goats kicked the hay around and made bedding out of it. The birds had already started finding nesting places and just continued. All of them could see the feed and water pans under the twelve volt lights Bill had placed over them so they had returned to feeding and nesting.

Since the toilet had been installed close to the corner of the room the bales just needed to be out from the wall with a ninety degree turn to insure privacy. A door wasn't available so an opening had to be accepted as an alternative.

"Great," muttered Cherry. We'll add a shower/tub, a sink and then we will paper and paint."

Bill chose to ignore her muttering. He put his mind to planning a livable schedule for the next day and the rest of their days together. His first thought was to get this day over with as soon as possible.

"First of all," he called out. "We'll have the mothers get the kids ready for bed. There will be no meetings or decisions made until tomorrow so none of you will miss anything important. I'll get my prayer book out and we will have prayers at bed-time and just after waking in the morning.

To Miriam and Michael he inquired about the plants and animals having enough water for the night. They replied yes and that the plants received close to too much water when the heat began to rise earlier. Bill suggested they start a small fire and put some pails of water to heat in the fireplace for morning baths.

Michael filled three pails while Miriam started a small fire. Bill chose three cups of assorted beans from one of the galvanized cans and put them in a small pot to soak overnight. Rice would be boiled along with them. He had no idea how much to plan for and hoped he had enough.

The fire was lighted and the pails set as close as possible. A cover was placed on the pot of beans and it was placed just inside the fireplace. Bill retrieved an old prayer book from the box of things he'd brought from home weeks ago. He carried a low voltage light to plug into the grow-light circuit so he could read the night prayers. The adults joined together with their children. The kids were down, but far from asleep. He plugged in the light and faced them all.

"This has been a day none of us will ever forget. For reasons I cannot understand we have been chosen to be the ones in this area to survive whatever it is that has happened. I have an idea about what happened, but no more details than anyone else. We will have to stay here for as long as it takes the earth to recover from what has happened. I believe this to be a temporary although long term situation. It will require a commitment to responsibility for all of us. If we all pull together we will survive this and find ourselves someday with all we need to have a good life. I believe that because for some reason we were the ones chosen to survive. We are the ones to go on in this life.

I believe this so deeply that I will be your leader; in our daily work and most importantly, in our prayers. We will pray every day; In fact, we will pray in a formal way more than once a day. After night prayers there will be no more meetings, work or worry. We will take time to read for pleasure, play games and just relax.

With that in mind my new Family Of God, Let Us Pray."

Bill prayed more fervently than he could remember praying at any time of this life. When finished he said 'Good Night' to everyone and he and Miriam walked back to the corner where their bed was. It was a little darker there as the large mass fire place was between them and the grow-lights.

Miriam sat on his side of the bed while he sat down on a chair to remove his shoes. When he saw her sitting so quietly he moved toward her and began to remove her shoes.

"Oh, William," she said so sadly, "I can not undress for thee tonight. I do not even think I can sleep."

She quietly rose and walked the short distance to her dresser and pulled out a bonnet and a long sleeved dress. Once changed, she came back to the bed and lay on her side. Bill climbed in and lay close to her. She responded by moving under his arm.

"There is little I am sure of right now, Miriam. Two things come to mind. I am sure there is a God who is with us tonight, and I am sure I love you dearly."

"And I, thee, William. But I am much afraid."

"I know. Let us try to put our fears behind our faith. It is time for God to do what is needed. It is all his anyway."

They lay together quietly until they drifted off to sleep. In time they were sleeping on their sides with Miriam tight to Bill's back. Neither heard the sound of rain, but when it turned to hail the noise was enough to wake them.

Bill rolled out, waking her. He knew from the sound what it was. He wasn't prepared for the darkness he noticed. The time on his watch showed they had slept almost six hours and half the grow-lights had gone out. The batteries couldn't sustain six hours without a charge. He made a note to prepare a time-schedule so someone would be on the bicycle every three hours and this wouldn't happen again.

The other adults were awake and up within a few minutes of the beginning of the hail storm. Michael also noticed half the grow-lights were out and sat down at the bicycle. Bill crossed the barn to the wall where the thermometer was and was shocked at the enormous drop in temperature. It was fifty degrees both inside and out. The fire had burned itself out in their area and the earth had returned to the heat range appropriate for this time of the year.

He returned to the bicycle where the women had come to stand while Michael recharged the batteries. The air drawn in with the fan was bubbling in the water bath.

Bill could tell the air was so filled with ash they would not be able to breathe without drawing it through the water bath. The bath would have to be cleaned and refilled as often as the batteries were charged.

He explained the temperature drop to them and said he expected the temperature to drop even more when the sun wouldn't penetrate the ash that was in the air. Since he expected it to be much colder than he wanted to explain, he just directed Miriam to add wood to the hearth and rekindle the coals to a fire. The water flowing around the firebox would keep the floor warm no matter how cold it got. He gave directions to Becky to find a notebook he could use to keep a log and then asked them to return to bed. They agreed reluctantly, after making the men promise to return to bed soon. It would only take twenty to thirty minutes to recharge the batteries. It would take electricity to restart the lights that had gone out, but it would be less than three hours and the dam would begin it's three hour supply.

Bill sat for a while to begin the log. Things had happened so fast he could only estimate the time and sequence of things, but it made him feel better to do so. Against their wives' wishes, the men stayed up a little later to talk of schedules, responsibilities and the sudden cooling of the earth. Bill went to put another log on the fire and felt the floor had warmed considerably. He made a note about it and the men went to bed.

"William, thee has been a long time returning to bed."

"I know, Love. I'll try to be better later on." He hoped he didn't sound like he was lying.

They lay tightly together and she was even able to return a kiss. Their love made them relax, but before they could fall back to sleep the light came on and the grow-lights were restarted. It was time to get up and face the second day of the rest of their lives.

They both groaned and with a sigh rolled out of bed. Bill went to check the power remaining in the batteries. Since it would take more electricity to start a grow light than it did to keep it lit, he was determined to know as much as he could about keeping them lit. There would be no need to pedal the bicycle to charge them while the dam provided the three hours of electricity in the morning and the evening. But, if his theory was correct, someone would have to "pedal up" some electricity every three hours when the dam wasn't producing.

"William, I hate to interrupt thy note making, but would it be all right if I made oatmeal for breakfast this morning? And where is the sugar to sweeten it a little. I think one of the nanney goats is still lactating so we should have a little goat's milk to have with our oatmeal. Is it cold in here? Yes, I think it is a little cold in here, does thee agree?"

"Sweetheart; yes, oatmeal is all right, no there is no sugar, two of the goats are still giving milk and yes it is cold in here. I'll check the temps and then put a log on the fire."

He got up from the table and walked to the wall where the indoor/outdoor thermometer was. He gasped when he saw it was thirty degrees Fahrenheit outside and just sixty three degrees inside. Back at the table he recorded the temperatures and then checked the hearth.

The draft was set last night and was still drawing smoke from the smoldering coals. As the smoke was drawn up and out of the barn, a slight vacuum was caused and outside air was drawn in through the water bath so everyone could breathe well. A few sticks of kindling would be all that was necessary to get a fire going again and Bill added a couple of split logs also to make it burn hot.

At the bicycle he pulled the belt tensioner off the belt that drove the alternator. There was no need to make electricity now. He needed to pump fluid through the firebox and then through the floor to keep the room heated. The same belt also turned the squirrel cage blower that drew air down the second flue in the chimney and through the water bath. Air drawn in this way would be preheated in the chimney flue, cleansed by the water bath and humidified by it as well.

As he pedaled, Bill noticed the water bath had enough ash and soot in it to make a slurry that was getting difficult to get air through. The water bath would have to be cleaned and refilled with fresh water each time it was necessary to use the bicycle for any reason.

He continued to pedal because the air was still drawn in and the morning's activity would put a strain on the amount of clean air available when the kids awoke.

Michael came up to Bill and asked what he could do right away. Bill motioned to the water bath and said he didn't know what to do with the 'mud' that was now in it and he would pedal for only another few minutes as the air seemed clear for the time being. There were pails of bath water heating in the hearth so Michael went to change the water in the water bath.

"The little ones are awakening now," he said. In a strange environment, children don't sleep late. How shall we prepare the water for bathing?"

Bill got up from the bicycle and looked around. "There are some plastic buckets in the back somewhere. Let's get one for each of us here and label them so we're not exchanging germs with each other. I think cleanliness is going to be next to Godliness AND to Survival if we're all going to make it through this. Let's go look for the buckets. I think there are some sets of towels back there too." The men walked to the back of the room and started opening the boxes. The sounds of the kids wailing into their new surroundings made them want to hurry.

When they came to the boxes with the towels it was obvious a man picked them out. There was no continuity of colors or designs, only bath-towel, hand-towel and wash cloth sets.

The men looked them over and decided to assign similar colors to each family and not worry about who would like what. Bill hadn't bought a lot so each family member would have to make due with what they were given and make their towels last for as long as was necessary. Originally his plan was for eight people so he got four extra sets. He now had eleven people, two of whom were pregnant. Towel use would have to be monitored carefully.

"Should we wash these before putting them to good use?" asked Michael. "Do we have any soap?"

"Yes. I have two boxes of commercial detergent that weigh a hundred pounds a piece. The clerk said the stuff could be used to clean anything. But, I'm sure it's not enough to last for as long as we may be here. We're going to have to be pretty stingy about how much we use."

"Good morning, anybody! I've got two girls here who need a bath every morning. When is the bathtub going to be installed?"

Bill sighed. There would be no bathtub and precious little bath soap for as long as it would take to survive.

"Let's use the towels and clean them later. Use these three look-alikes for Cherry's family, these four sets for you and Ruth, and divide these four sets between Becky, Kiia, Miriam and me.

We'll have to remember which towels have been assigned to which family and try not to mix them. It'll be hard to keep everything and everyone clean with so little soap and I don't want to be trading germs between families."

Cherry called again to relate a full toilet and a shortage of toilet paper. Bill groaned and grimaced.

"I will have Ruth show her how our people make do," said Michael. "Hopefully she will quickly grow up."

Michael took the towels and divided them among the others and spent some time telling Ruth about Cherry's needs. Bill pumped a pail of water and took it to the toilet for her to flush it. The woman was a poster child for someone on the ragged edge of losing all self control. She was trying to be a good parent, but couldn't hide the fact she had never faced anything that required courage or patience. Bill poured the water into the tank and flushed it.

"From now on, whoever uses the toilet has to refill the pail for the next participant in our potty games," he said. "Michael and Ruth will show you bathing techniques for the time we are together here. Miriam is preparing breakfast. It won't be what you are used to, but it will be nourishing. I've got to check the thermometer and make the morning log entries before prayers and breakfast. Will you and the girls be O.K. till then?"

"Yes," she said in a resigned manner.

Becky and Kiia had already used the bathroom and were back in their quarters. Cherry took her girls back to their quarters and then joined Becky. Michael, Ruth and their girls walked by on the way to the bathroom. Michael carried the obligatory pail of water and went to refill the one left by Cherry. Ruth saw to her girls as both she and her husband needed to use the lone toilet also.

Bill hurried to the back of the room to find the small plastic pails to be used for bathing. He marked each of them with a name so no one else would use it and went to the fireplace to see how much water had been heated during the night. Miriam was there and she had the oat meal started.

"William, does thee think thee has soaked enough beans for the day?"

"I'm not sure, Love. With an equal amount of rice there should be a hearty meal for each of us at lunch time. We can start soaking an equal amount for supper soon because I have never liked soaking beans too long. They cook down to mush." Miriam nodded and Bill went to check the thermometer.

The inside temperature seemed to stabilize at seventy to seventy five degrees and that felt comfortable. Outside, it had dropped to twenty five degrees Fahrenheit and that worried him. The outside temperature was dropping fast. There was nothing that could be done about it so he went back to the table to enter the morning's log. He'd hardly finished when the others joined him at the table with an air of concern for what to do next.

Bill stood and with a serious look repeated what he thought had happened to bring them all together for the rest of time and quickly went on to domestic issues. He held up the "bath pails," as he called them. His instructions were simple; One pail per person, no sharing. Don't waste water, especially heated water. It takes too long to heat more. Do not share towels. It will be hard to clean things and we don't want to trade germs with anyone. As quickly as we can we will name things so everyone knows what we are talking about or asking for. We will have to have one language so communication will be easy.

"How many languages does he think we know?" Cherry asked Becky under her breath. Becky signaled her to remain silent.

"Ruth and I would like to keep our native tongue for each other," offered Michael. "She and the children are already schooled in English, so that won't be a problem."

"Thank you," replied Bill. "We will speak English to each other and soon enough have every object and operation named so we all know what is being referred to. Since breakfast is almost ready we will now have morning prayer, breakfast and then baths."

"If it would be all right, William," said Michael, "I would like to check on the animals before we eat." Bill appreciated his request because it told the rest Michael considered him the leader. Bill answered Michael in a way that both men understood this was not a dictatorship, but would be a partnership.

While Michael went to check on the animals, Bill and Becky set up the communal dining table and chairs. Ruth told Cherry to follow her and her girls to start the bathing. She poured enough warm water to fill half a bath pail.

"And, I'm supposed to get one of my kids into one of those things?"

Ruth silenced her with a stern look. "In my world we bathe the baby thusly." She began to set two hand towels before her daughters, Anna and Mary. The girls quickly removed their shoes and socks, their bonnets and then their long sleeved blue dresses. They stepped onto the hand towels and Ruth wetted their hair with the washcloth and then put the cloth into the bath pails. Anna and Mary then wrung the washcloths and washed their faces and down their fronts, leaving the washcloths in their pails when finished. Ruth then washed their backs and legs, leaving their butts for last. She wrapped the girls in their bath towels and then rinsed and wrung out the wash cloths. She poured the bath pails into the toilet and returned to her girls.

"Mama will bathe later," she told them. "Cherry, does thee have any questions about bathing?"

"None," she replied, looking away and scratching her head. She wasn't about to argue with Ruth about anything right now. Her girls were clinging tightly to her and were easily persuaded to accept a bath from a bucket.

It would be a long time before they would have any understanding of what had just happened to them all. Cherry took them to the hearth and filled the two plastic buckets that had their names on them.

She returned to their sleeping area and set the buckets before her girls. They sill had little or no inhibitions and undressed as Anna and Mary had. Cherry assisted her youngest, Lilly, while Rose was old enough to do for herself. Becky was just finishing Kiia's bath. The boy had been amused by the thought of a small bucket of water being his bath, but entered into the fun of the things as soon as his mother said it was all right to play at bathing. Both mothers finished their children, promised to bathe themselves later and dressed them in the clothes they had worn the day before.

Michael came in from seeing to the animals with a small pail of goat's milk. He brought it to the table and whispered to Bill that one of the adult quail had injured itself in the fearsome activities last night. He had finished its life, dressed it and left it in a cold place so it could be used for a soup that evening. The old goat he'd castrated a few days before the disaster was showing signs of trauma and shock and if he continued Michael said he would butcher it. At least there would be some meat for the first few days of their confinement in the barn.

Miriam brought the pot of boiled oat meal to the table. Bill had retrieved one of the expensive looking silver sets and some bowls.

"William. Such expensive silver for the poor of the earth?"

"I'm sorry, Miriam. This is what I bought in a weak moment so this will have to do. God won't mind how we eat. And I won't mind either, especially if no one wastes."

"William? Why would anyone waste?"

"Sweetheart! I really don't care why anyone would waste. I just know that for reasons I can't remember I chose to change the lives of everyone in this room. I'm going to change their diets, their lifestyles, their futures and since I took them from what happened I even changed their pasts. They are no longer a part of everyone and everything that was a part of them."

Michael had been watching the conversation between Miriam and Bill and he sensed it was time to walk over. He held up Bill's prayer book and asked if it was time to pray or begin breakfast.

Bill was startled at Michael's question, but he nodded and took the prayer book. He called everyone to the table and prayed a short blessing. After it he asked if anyone would like to add more. No one offered and it seemed the first meal together as a new family caused the adults feel the loss of their loved ones and renewed their fear of the future. No one seemed interested in eating so Bill took the initiative.

"Since the kids are all 5 and under, put a half a cup of oatmeal in their bowls with a quarter cup of goat's milk. The adults get a cup of oats with a half cup of milk. If there is enough for seconds, start with the kids. Pour an equal amount of the leftover milk in the small tumblers for drinking.

"William? I have made enough for all and the Nannies have provided enough milk for breakfast."

"Good," he said absently. "Try to save enough milk to bake at least one loaf of bread a day." If he had taken time to listen to himself he wouldn't have recognized his speech. He'd retreated inside himself like he did back in the old firefighting days when he forced fear outside himself and worked at saving life and property. The others didn't really notice him and brought the kids to the table.

Miriam scooped the oatmeal and milk into the bowls and got it in front of the kids as fast as she could. Their mothers fussed about no high chairs or booster seats or table napkins while the kids looked into their breakfast bowls with expressions that suggested yesterday's disaster was no match for today's breakfast. Bill sidetracked everyone's apprehensions with a before meal prayer and then he began eating.

"But, Momma," wailed Lilly, "This isn't what we usually eat."

"I know, dear," replied Cherry. "Just do the best you can. And then take it up with Kiia's Grandpa later."

The remark surprised Bill. He'd never really had time for Cherry because of her open and casual sexual behavior. He'd accepted the friendship that existed between her and his daughter and dismissed her from his life as someone he just didn't want to have for a friend. The tone of her voice suggested she wasn't ready to overlook his indifference toward her even in an emergency situation.

The remark didn't go unnoticed by the other adults either. The fear and uncertainty of their new lifestyle was still overwhelming them and personality conflicts only gave them something else to worry about. They kept their interest in their breakfast and made compliments to Miriam for her cooking and Michael for thinking to milk the goats.

Bill and Michael focused their attention on their bowls while trying to come to grips with what could become a real divisive attitude. They were clinking their spoons against their bowls trying to get every last morsel when they became aware of the women staring at them.

"Is it getting cold in here, or is it just me?" Cherry asked no one in particular. "Because it just seems to me that it is getting cold in here." She paused for a moment. "Of course, it could just be me, but I think it is getting cold in here"

"Cherry!" Bill hesitated a moment to compose himself. "I think it is getting cooler in here too. I checked the outside temp when we got up and I will check it now. I am going to keep a log of daily temperatures and meaningful activities."

"Is that something only you can do or can someone else do it too? She was really getting her nose up. "I mean, would it hurt anything if someone else walked over and took a peek at the thermometer?"

In spite of his tensions, Bill managed to chuckle at her remarks. Once again, he assured her the temperatures would be taken as much as twice daily and the fire would be tended as needed. He used the next few minutes to outline the need for a daily schedule of work assignments. A division of responsibilities would also be necessary as the person cooking should not be mixing fertilizer and cultivating the plants in the raised beds as well.

With that in mind, Miriam and Becky suggested they take the cooking responsibilities. Ruth and Cherry agreed to take child care, education and laundry with everyone agreeing to be full time parents all day, every day. The kids were made to understand the adults would take time for their needs whenever they arose. Michael would continue as Healer and would assume all animal husbandry duties.

Bill would keep the log and add note-worthy additions suggested from the others. Since the growing of vegetables in the raised beds was his idea he would be responsible for cultivation, harvesting and any replanting. Miriam, Michael and Ruth asked if they could help in the gardens from time to time. Since their lives had been rooted in farming for generations Bill agreed. He knew their expertise was beyond his and the joy of growing things would please anyone interested in gardening.

They would share equally in cleaning assignments although there was a frightening lack of supplies. The two boxes of soap they did have would have to be rationed for the laundry and dish washing. Bill felt a teaspoon only for each load of laundry and an half of a teaspoon for dish washing. He suggested that and it wasn't accepted well by the women, but they agreed to try it until they had a feeling about how long the soap would last as compared to how long they believed they would be in the barn.

Bill believed the batteries would keep the low voltage lights on for at least four hours so he began a schedule for the minimum amount of time that would have to be spent on the bicycle charging them. Since the electricity from the dam was available at six a.m. and six p.m. for three hours each, he let the 120 volt battery charger provide the necessary charge for six and nine in the am and pm. The bicycle with its 12 volt alternator would have to be used at noon and 3 pm and at midnight and 3 am. If the adults adhered to a ridged schedule the lights would always be on and their vegetables would grow well.

The kids were getting a little fidgety and he suggested a break from their planning. He asked the mothers check the stores for games and toys to keep the little one occupied.

"Am I still the only one who feels cold?" It was Cherry again and she had only her summer top and shorts on from the day before. Bill had noticed it was cooler than when they got up so he suggested she check the thermometer with him.

The outside temperature had dropped to one degree above zero, Fahrenheit and the interior temperature was now at 55 degrees. It was a radical drop in outside temperature, but Bill was impressed with the barn's insulation that allowed it to retain heat. At the outside wall, he could hear the wind had risen in intensity again. He had nothing to tell him the wind speed other than how it sounded against the barn.

Cherry paid little attention to how to switch the thermometer from inside to outside readings so Bill simply agreed with her that it had gotten colder and they should move closer to the fireplace and throw on another log. He didn't want to start a bad habit of throwing on logs with no thought of rationing them, but it satisfied Cherry for the time being. She watched him carefully place a log on the now cheerful fire and folded her arms across herself till she felt warmer.

Ruth had brought the dolls she had made for her twins Anna and Mary. Cherry's daughters, Lily and Rose had gone with Becky, Kiia and Miriam to look through boxes for a suitable toy. Ruth returned to the table immediately when she saw Bill return and speak quietly to Michael.

When she stood by her husband Bill realized all the adults would need to know everything important right away. This was not the type of emergency where only officers would share information and then expect others to follow their lead.

Bill cleared his throat and spoke loudly enough for the women searching for toys to hear.

He told them the outside temperature had dropped significantly, as he had expected when the volcanic ash began to block the sun. How cold it would get remained to be discovered, and the inside temperature could be controlled with wise use of the fire wood. The bicycle that charged the batteries and brought clean air into the room could also pump water through the fireplace and into the pipes in the concrete floor. The water pump could be turned by hand between the times the other jobs were being done and it might be necessary to do so if they wanted to keep the room comfortable.

The other kids returned to the table with toys to play with and while they were all occupied Bill went on. The mud made from bringing ash in with the air needed to breathe would have to be removed every three hours if they were to remain healthy. How to get rid of the mud would be a problem that had to be solved quickly.

Michael suggested he remove the mud to the dirt floor in the animal area where it could freeze on the dirt floor before being thrown out the small door to the outside. He would make a small form to hold it till it froze into a manageable size before being thrown out. Since no one could know how toxic it would be, a quick disposal would be a good idea. Michael rose to try out his plan and all the kids took his movement to protest the cooler temperatures.

Bill sighed with the prospect of dealing with problems that hadn't been expected. Neither Becky nor Cherry could have planned for any changes in seasons as they were in the truck at the time of the volcanic eruptions. They were in their summer clothing. He asked Miriam and Ruth what they might have to help the others.

"I have only inside clothing for my husband and girls," said Ruth, "nothing for wearing outside."

"I have nothing for outside either," responded Miriam.

"All right," said Bill. "Here is my decision. I'll hand pump some more water through the fireplace while Michael cleans and refills the water bath. Miriam, if you and Ruth would look through any and all clothing to see how we can keep everyone warm it would be a good idea."

The light by the load center went off and it caught everyone's attention. Fear showed plainly in their eyes. Again, Bill told them it would be turned off three hours after it came on and they would have to get used to it. There would be enough light to keep the plants growing and for every one to find their way around.

"Let's get going. The faster we work, the more we can get done," he joked. He turned toward the pump on the fireplace and began to turn it.

It took about a half an hour for the floor to feel noticeable warmer and then he returned to the table.

Cherry had moved to the fireplace with the kids to keep them all warm. She gave a cold look to Bill as he walked by. The women had returned to the table with what looked like a lot less clothing than was needed. Miriam was studying a new hooded sweatshirt Bill had thrown in with his things. She had one arm crossed in front of her, her other hand holding her chin and her toe tapped rapidly, although quietly.

"Damn," thought Bill. "I thought they only did that when they were mad at some poor man."

"Ruth," she said thoughtfully, "Dost thou think we could cut this garment apart and use it for a pattern.

After all, we already make a hooded cape for the winter and I have seen a Catholic Monk with a hooded garment the covered him to his shoes. Two such garments would be simple to make and surely keep us warm."

"Yes. I can see how such a sewing project would work. But, do we have any thread and fabric to do this."

"William? Thee have gotten so much for me in the near past. Hast thou any fabric to keep our children warm?"

Bill stammered, "I have some fabric for table linens, and a lot of thread. In fact, I bought a great deal of thread for reasons I can't even remember. I remember getting a lot of fishing line to use for thread if the real stuff ran out; but, no fabric."

"Did I not see a great many blankets and sheets when we made up the beds last night? Ruth asked. "It seems to me I did."

"As did I, Ruth. If thee would bring three blankets and sheets to the table we will measure one and see what we can sew. William would thee and Michael move our sewing machines into a better light that we might begin our task?"

Bill and Michael agreed to do so and helped move first one and then the other machine. Michael then pumped a pail of water to refill the water bath. Bill showed him how to release the tension on the alternator belt so a person could pedal the bicycle to bring in fresh air and also drive the water pump to heat more water and run it through the pipes in the floor. There was no way to know how often to pump water through the floor other than to judge how comfortable everyone was.

As Michael pedaled air was drawn down the pipe that was installed next to the flue that took the fire smoke up and outside.

The pipes were close enough in the chimney for the incoming air to be heated before entering the water bath and then the room. This was imperative as the outside temperature continued to drop rapidly and the colder air would make heating the barn nearly impossible.

The only issue to contend with was the positive increase of air pressure in the barn made the fire burn faster as the smoke was forced up and out the chimney. This caused a faster consumption of fire wood and could not be allowed.

As the water in the bath turned muddy Michael stopped pedaling and Bill threw a thick log on the fire so it could turn to coals and a flame could be built up later when needed.

The women began to open the cabinets to set up the sewing machines and Bill turned his attention to the plants in his raised beds. They'd received enough water the night before when the temperature spiked during the firestorm. He walked up and down by the beds to check the height of the grow lights over the seedlings. He wanted to maintain about a three inch distance between the plant tops and the lights. It was important the plants didn't try to "reach" toward the artificial sun and grow spindly rather than strong.

There was no need for cultivating or weeding as the seedlings had barely reached two inches in height. Bill walked around all six beds noting where seedlings hadn't come up and areas where too many had germinated. Originally he had planned to thin out some areas and plant to the bare areas, but with Michael needing space for his medicinal plants he decided to wait. The two men would survey the small growing area and decided where to plant new things and where to thin out existing plants so there would be enough room for them all to grow well.

As he walked around the raised beds, Bill noticed how warm it felt close to the floor.

The heated concrete radiated warmth, but as the heat rose it cooled significantly about waist high. The room was large and the extreme cold that was becoming apparent outside would make heating the area evenly next to impossible. He glanced toward the fireplace where Becky, Cherry and the kids sat to stay warm. The women were wearing shorts and tank tops and the kids about the same. They'd gone from summer to cold winter in less than two days with no time to plan or pack what they needed.

It took Bill about a half an hour to scrutinize his plants and then he rejoined the women to see how the sewing plans were coming. They had marked the first blanket and a sheet and Miriam was cutting them. Ruth's eyes followed the plated scissors Bill had given to Miriam and in an instant he understood why the Amish limited unnecessary extravagance in their lives. It hurt her to see such beautiful things when she could never have anything like them. Miriam cut carefully and then set the fabric before Ruth so they could gage the sizes against the people they were sewing for.

"Perhaps," said Miriam, "thee would like to cut pattern pieces while I sew," and handed her the beautifully plated scissors.

Ruth's smile showed her gratitude for the chance to hold and use something so beautiful. She went right to work. The women had sewn for so many years they knew what they wanted and about what size to cut the fabric for each child and adult. Ruth made chalk marks around the pieces, cut them and handed them to Miriam who began to pin them together and then sew them. Ruth made few marks as she and Miriam had made patterns and clothing all their adult lives. Using the plated scissors pleased her.

When the first hooded cape was sewn, Ruth called her Anna over and tried it on for size.

The fit was good and since there was only one garment a healthy childish jealousy captured the others and they all wanted one. The women cut and sewed as quickly as they could and before the light came on at six pm the four girls were similarly attired and happy. Each hooded cape had a soft cotton sheet for a liner under the wool blanket it was made from.

Kiia wasn't sure he wanted the same thing the girls were wearing as he didn't see his grandfather wearing something like theirs. The women traded places and Miriam cut his a little different and soon he was wearing something that resembled a monk's hooded alb. Bill admired it and when Miriam said she would sew something like it for his grandfather he beamed and ran to show himself to his mother.

When the light came on at six pm, Becky said she would boil the rice and beans if Miriam and Ruth would keep sewing. The women agreed and Bill and Michael fed and watered the animals. They had shared the responsibility of pedaling the bicycle to circulate water through the floor and bring in fresh air. The fire was replenished with two logs and the pots neared boiling. Everyone had been so busy they'd forgotten they had only two meals this day. Usually there would be three as they were used to, but a natural flow to things hadn't come to them yet. However, hunger overcame them all and they were ready to eat before the food was cooked. It didn't take long for the kids to begin whining and the adults made a mental note and promised to stay on time for the next meal.

The animals were feeding and their water was staying thawed as the dishes were set on the heated concrete that extended into their area. They had plenty of hay, but preferred the feed grains and ate what and when they preferred.

The men came back in and Bill went to check the thermometer. Outside it was now thirty degrees below zero Fahrenheit and the wind could be heard everywhere inside. Everyone had been too busy to notice until now. The feeling of fear returned with the sound of the wind. It seemed to swirl around the building causing an occasional "pop" or "crack" in the wood studs that made up the outside walls. There didn't seem to be any groaning or weakening sounds in the structure, just the sound of a high wind. The strength of the building was a source of comfort for the little band of survivors.

Since water was always being warmed in the fireplace, Becky had a pot of beans and rice heated to boiling quickly. There would be enough for a large helping for everyone, despite the lack of seasonings and condiments. Such would be the beginning of their new diet. It would be nutritious as it had been for a large part of the world's population for hundreds of years, but sparse for the people who now made it their diet. Hunger made it acceptable, but sighs were easily heard.

Bill led the prayer before eating as he would for the whole time they would be together. During the meal he ventured to talk about the feelings everyone must be having.

"Fear," he said, "will become less strong in the future as we began to trust in our ability to accept the changes in our lives and triumph over our adversities. I realize how difficult it will be to talk of loved one who are not here. When the time is right we can and will talk of them. It will not cause us to lose what little we have or cause another misfortune if we think of them and speak of them." His breathing became difficult and his voice shook, "but, think of them and speak of them we will; and we must. Just not right now."

The others stopped eating as he spoke. They suffered in silence and then took up their spoons again and finished their portions. The kids spoke openly about wanting something else to eat, especially sweets and bread. Everyone looked to Bill for a moment.

"Bread will be baked tomorrow. As far as sweets go, it will be a while before we can grow beets and make beet sugar."

The twins, Anna and Mary, expressed a dislike for beet sugar instead of cane sugar and were quietly shushed by their mother.

"I don't like it either!" Spoke up Kiia. "Did I ever have beet 'whatsis?" He asked his mother.

"Yes," Lied his mother. "I'm surprised you don't remember how much you liked it."

He searched his little-boy-mind and not finding anything to the contrary of what his mother just told him went back to eating. Everyone finished their beans and rice and washed it all down with a small tumbler of goat's milk. No one felt well at such a radical change in their diet, but no one got ill either.

Everyone bussed their own dishes to the end of the table. The kids were trained to do so also. Kiia was still a little young, but when he saw his grandfather do so he concluded it was a fun thing to do. Becky washed the dishes and stored them on the fireplace mantle as no shelves had been built.

Miriam and Ruth went back to sewing and Cherry remarked she was tired of knotting a blanket around her neck to stay warm. The Amish women assured her the next cape and bonnet would be hers.

"Just what I need to be stylish," she muttered and went off to check out the wash machine. Bill had given her the instruction book which she looked at and promptly discarded.

"What's there to know?" she demanded. "Put slop in the top; turn the crank till I gag; dump the water in the toilet; pump rinse water in the top till my back breaks; turn the crank till it kills me and then die of old age waiting for you to put up the cloths line. Sounds simple to me."

"Cloths line," groaned Bill.

"Yes; cloths line," echoed Cherry. "I'll bet you didn't think of that either, did you?"

"As a matter of fact," he retorted, "I did too. A line drier is somewhere in the storage area and we will find it tomorrow. Wash the towels and lay them over the chairs and anything else you can find for now." He moved away from her before she could come up with any other questions or comments.

He walked back to the storage area to look for the portable cloths line and pole. He'd seen it when he brought the Wash Machine to the barn. It was in a tall thin box and he found it on the floor where it had fallen behind boxes that had been moved to locate something else. It only took a moment to unpack it and he carefully kept the cardboard box in case it was needed for something else. There'd be no replacing it if it were destroyed before a new need was discovered.

"I found it right away," he said as he set it before her.

"Please put it between my beds and those of the Amish," Cherry replied without looking up from turning the wash machine. "I'd like a little more privacy for myself and my girls."

Bill put it between the beds and since it afforded little to no privacy he said he and Michael would put up a hay bale wall by tomorrow at the latest. It had gotten so cold in the barn he needed to wait until Miriam and Ruth finished sewing warmer clothing for the men before they could work out there. He returned to the fire place to make plans with Michael.

There remained the matter of covering the midnight and three am charging of the batteries. Michael said he or Ruth would take the three am time because he was used to rising early for prayers and for animal care at the farm. Bill agreed as he preferred to take the last charging before he went to bed. The women would take the night charging only if either man got sick.

Miriam had ground some wheat in the hand grinder and was ready to make bread in the morning. She said she wanted to bake after the noon charging because there would be a good fire at that time and the hearth would be hot enough to bake good bread. Bill marveled at how easy such things came to her and was proud Becky was so eager to learn from her. Becky took the noon bike ride and Cherry the three pm ride.

The light blinked off at nine pm and the kids immediately rushed from play to their parents. Bill hoped it would soon stop scaring everyone, but for now it helped set a pattern for behavior. Ruth asked if there would be enough water for evening baths rather than in the morning. Bill agreed and said bathing the kids would be up to the parents. The pails would be filled and placed in the large hearth whenever they were empty.

Cherry announced the end of the first cloths washing and anyone who needed to use the toilet should come forward and do so while there was rinse water to fill the tank. In the future she would time her cloths washing so the soapy water would be put in the toilet tank to clean the toilet when flushed.

Bill made a mental note that Cherry finally said something positive and took the initiative to do the right thing. If the parents didn't have to carry water to the toilet before the kids used it they might also learn to flush it when they finished using it.

Miriam and Ruth announced the completion of the two monks-albs for the men and called for them to come try them on. Since both men were tall enough to feel the air begin to cool as it rose to the ceiling they were glad for something warm to wear. The albs would be essential for wearing in the barn to care for the animals. Ruth put the plated scissors in their decorative box and gave them to Miriam who placed them on top of her sewing machine for future use.

Ruth turned to the care of her daughters while Miriam cleaned up the scraps of blankets and sheets used to sew the warmer clothing. Everything that could be saved had to be saved. Most of the towels were still wet from the first washing so baths were planned for later when a laundry schedule would provide clean dry towels and washcloths. Kiia said a night without a bath was certainly a nice change.

The kids went to bed quickly although they kept an eye on their parents constantly. So much had happened in the last two days they all had moments of great insecurity. The portable white lights had been used for sewing so the mothers spent a few minutes telling bedtime stories instead of reading. Their presence overcame childhood fears and sleep came quickly.

The parents congregated back at the dining table for lack of any other reasons. They knew what they had lost and knew they would never forget what had happened. Fear was still their primary emotion, but sorrow and grief were close behind. Their confidence that the building could keep them alive would come next

The full impact of their grief would come to the forefront later. Now, the need to appear confident before their children was so great they didn't have time to experience their own feelings.

When together at the table late at night they could look at each other with a wild eyed fear and searched each other's eyes for courage, leadership and hope. They would have to deal with their fears and struggle with new identities in an unknown world. The kids were too young to be alert to the outside as long as they had their parents to trust for their childhood securities.

After watching the others study each other Bill spoke. He talked of the day's activities, early cooperation and success in getting through day-two.

"I think we should use the term barn for the area where the animals are. House or home will refer to the area we live in. The hearth will be the fireplace area and will include any references to a kitchen.

Tomorrow we will begin to organize the area where the food and miscellaneous items are kept and we'll just call that area 'stores.' Once organized, only those cooking will be allowed there and any supply needs will have to be approved by me before going there. What we have is all we will have, barring the birth of any birds or animals. These terms and others necessary for us to have a common language will be recorded and remembered. Any questions?"

"Is it cold in here again?"

"Yes, Cherry. It is cooler in here again. I checked the outside temp again and it is fifty degrees below zero, Fahrenheit. That's very cold, and the cold and the wind have combined to create some serious climatic anomalies. There is nothing we can do about what happens outside.

Inside we can move heat through the floor to stay as comfortable as we can. Whenever we add wood to the hearth to cook we will spend time on the bicycle to save as much heat as possible."

"By the way, if you're told…asked…to spend time on the bicycle it will be referred to as 'take a ride'. You'll pedal at twelve to fourteen volts at the alternator for twenty minutes. This will be enough time to charge the batteries, bring fresh air in through the water bath and flow coolant through the firebox and into the floor. I realize we are heating the coolant, but it is a type of antifreeze mixture that will stop corrosion from building up in our primitive heating system. That's why I calling it coolant. I've written these terms in the log and anyone can read the log when I'm not adding to it. No changes will be allowed! After all, it will be a brief history of our time spent here."

"Michael, you were the last one in the barn. How are the animals doing in the cold?"

"The goats are nimble and have gone to the top of the hay bales near the ceiling where it is a few degrees warmer than the floor. They have burrowed into the hay and have places to sleep. The quail nest on the ground usually and have made nests a little advanced to what they usually make. They have them on the narrow portion of heated concrete near the inside wall. The water stays thawed on that concrete too. I think they will have few problems surviving. Their instincts will serve them well."

"Miriam, are you and Becky ready to cook again tomorrow?"

"William, we have beans soaking for tomorrow and a portion of rice set out to cook with them at noon and evening. The oat meal has been ground for breakfast and will only need to be boiled."

"Becky, the food was good today."

"Thank you, but I hope you have something better planned for the future. Beans and rice will get old fast."

"I don't have any plans beyond whatever herbs and spices we have or can grow. It will take eight to ten weeks to get any veggies grown to supplement what we have seen so far. Tomorrow we will have the Quail Michael butchered and unless the old Billy goat looks worse in the near future that will be the last of our meat for a while."

Miriam and Ruth; The hooded capes and albs are just what we need, but very soon Michael and I will need an additional type of cape or Mexican type of Serape for working in the barn. Every one will need at least one additional outfit of some kind. Of course, there won't be the time constraint you worked under today."

Both women smiled weakly and nodded. Their fingers ached from sewing so quickly and they were happy for a break.

"Unless anyone has anything else of importance tonight, let's call it a day. I'll rest a little and get up to take a ride at midnight."

"I'm still cold."

"Cherry, I am afraid our heating capability is at maximum right now. We'll bank the fire each night so there are coals to reignite in the morning. Cooler temperatures are going to be normal from now on. As long as we have fresh air, batteries and enough warmth to keep our plants growing that will be all we can expect. Anything else?" Hearing nothing, he led the night prayers and declared the second day to be over.

The adults turned and slowly made the short walk back to their sleeping quarters. Unlike children who can derive great comfort from the presence of their parents, there is no one for an adult other than their own concept and commitment to a higher power.

Bill could only hope Becky had as strong a commitment as he and the Amish did. He was sure Cherry had little or no faith, but secretly hoped she would some day soon.

Alone in their beds they were alone with themselves. Anything their minds brought to the forefront was what they either fought to change or were the victim of. The reality of their lost loved ones and lifestyle, fear of the future, fear of the barn collapsing before the wind and cold, fear of no medical attention in the event of an illness or accident or anything else imaginable was all there. Faith and prayer were the only things that could stand up to such fears. It was the first of many nights when someone could be heard crying themselves to sleep.

The wind could be heard all night long. It wasn't so loud, as it was ominous. It was as if somewhere between the bowels of the earth and the highest of heavens that all of nature was trying to sweep away all the indignities the earth and heaven had suffered. The cold would freeze the outer edges of the wood and the sap still contained in some of the studs would freeze and contract at a different rate from the dry wood beside it and the stud would crack with a loud report.

At first, the adults would snap awake and then after remembering the non-dangerous noise fall back into an uneasy sleep. The kids might stir, but their slumber was secure and they didn't wake up.

The generator at the dam had charged the batteries well and when Bill rose at midnight all twelve volt lights were on. He emptied the slurry from the water bath and poured it over the fence into Michael's form and hurried back into the warmth. He touched the large mass fire place as he passed it and it still held good warmth. A fresh pail of water was added to the water bath and he took a ride for twenty five minutes.

Twenty minutes would have been enough, but Bill took no chances where safety was concerned. Twenty minutes generated enough electricity and pumped enough coolant through the hearth to heat the floor. They were safe and warm, for now. When he turned in, Miriam rolled next to him. Life was good in their corner of the world.

Michael rolled out for the three a.m. ride and to check the animals. He did the same things Bill had done and tended to the animal's need for feed and water. He always made a quick check of the animals to make sure they were well in their beds before rejoining his wife in their warm bed. He had slept almost six hours and would now sleep for another two. It wasn't the best routine, but it fit what needed to be done. The others slept as best they could between nightmares and restless worry.

The electricity came on at six a.m. again and somehow the light that came with it awoke the survivors. There was no reason for it to do so. Perhaps it was just the mystery of everything lost that made them want to see the effects of electricity and live around its accessibility. What ever it was, they rose when the light went on at six a.m. and put to bed their children and the day's problems when it went off at nine p.m.

The soundless light brought the line to the toilet, to the pump for water and to the hearth for warm water for bathing, heat and breakfast. Bill checked the temperature inside and out, turned the hand crank to bring in clean air for breathing and wrote the log for each morning.

Breakfast would become the same every day; Oatmeal with goat's milk. Lunch and dinner would also be the same thing each day; Beans, Rice and very little goat's milk. Today would be the first time they would have a half or whole slice of sourdough bread. There would be no butter until a churn could be built later.

The amount of milk used for butter or served with oatmeal would be determined by the health and productivity of the small herd of goats. The herd would ultimately increase as time went on, but for now every ounce was rationed. Male goats were to be eaten as the herd proved itself to have an adequate number of studs to keep the she-goats pregnant.

But, again this morning as many mornings to come, the little family gathered at table for prayers and a boring breakfast. The kids had already developed the habit of eating and then waiting and watching Bill to see what the day would bring. The adults did too with no one realizing they were doing it. Bill was soon aware of this and would begin prayers right after eating. Announcements were minimal and the chores had been divided so the adults knew what to do. Fear drove everyone, but when there seemed to be a change in the wind, a hail storm or a sound from the building, everyone looked up and stopped what they were doing. Bill would too, then sigh and go back to work. This was enough of a comfort to the others that they followed him and returned to their assigned duties.

The raised beds were rolled back and forth under the three sets of grow lights so they could each experience eight hours of direct light, eight hours of light simulating the lesser amount of light experienced in the early and late hours of the day and eight hours of night. The plants, in turn rewarded their benefactors with a noticeable growth in the first three days of their captivity. Still, there would be no harvest for over two months, but it filled everyone with hope to see a healthy growth.

Play is a universal activity for kids, so they had no trouble adapting to each other's interests. Old toys would soon be forgotten and anything new to them plus their imagination would keep them happy. Becky, Ruth and Cherry had accepted the roles of primary care givers and the others had no trouble remembering to offer loving care to all of the kids.

All ready the kids had discovered the importance of the raised beds and wanted to watch the plant growth. The men planned to break up some pallets and hammer together a pair of step stools so they could watch the progress of the plants.

Lilly, Cherry's oldest, whispered a question to her mother. Cherry looked for Bill and called across the house.

"Hey, Bill. Lilly wants to know who is taking care of her cat."

"I believe your mother is, isn't she?" Replied Bill. He had so much on his mind at any given time he didn't want to get into discussions that he felt should be taken care of by parents. He was too busy at one of the plant beds to look up and see the glare that Cherry shot his way. He knew it was coming, so why acknowledge it.

"And when will we see grandma again?" Cherry had never been one to face things, but she was smart enough to know she'd better learn fast now since there were no options for running away from anything.

Bill stopped for a moment to think. He looked at Cherry and Lilly.

"Perhaps after this winter, but not before. What do you think, Cherry?"

She spoke quietly to Lilly and then turned her toward the other kids. She shot another glare at Bill who pretended not to see.

"William?" It was Miriam's soft voice. "Have we other than this one strange broom and two mops for cleaning the floor?"

"No, Love. Only a push broom and two mops," he replied quietly. He still wanted to hold her in his arms whenever she was near, but didn't because the others were watching. "I didn't know what all I would need, and there was just no time to get more."

"What do you suggest?"

"Well," he sighed. "We will do the best we can with what we have. No one can ask any more."

Miriam turned and walked back to the hearth. Bill looked around the room to see where everyone was and what they were doing. It wasn't a matter of checking up or spying as much as it was watching out for everyone's interests. After he had seen everyone he realized a sad feeling of being afraid of losing any of them had come over him. Everyone, including himself had lost family and friends and he couldn't bear having something go wrong and losing a single member of his new family.

"William, dost thou think we could move a few more plants and add a few more things I think we will need?"

"Yes, Michael. I think there will be room for something medicinal." He looked at the sets Michael held and gestured toward one of the beds. Both men walked to the bed and began to move some seedlings and plant Michael's sets. Kiia watched the men for a moment and then darted back into the stores area and came back to the beds. He could barely reach into the bed, but managed to push a seed into the corner of two of the beds. Before the men finished, he turned and ran back to where the kids were having a pre-school.

"Kiia, how did you get your hands so dirty?"

"Don't know, Mommy."

"Bill!"

"Yes Cherry." Bill looked up from his planting hoping she would be in a good mood.

"Tell me there is more than one box of computer paper for art class. And then kindly direct me to where the computer is so Becky can begin teaching that too."

"Uh, well, there is only one box of paper. Ten reams in all. There was no time to get more. And, uh, computer training will just have to wait. Try to conserve the paper."

He went back to what he was doing. The last thing he wanted was to have a computer set up and someone get on the internet. If there was anyone around close enough to invade or attack them he didn't want to give away their hiding place. Michael glanced up at Cherry, and the way she glared at Bill made him uneasy as Amish women didn't act like that; or, at least Ruth didn't.

"Dad? What's all this chalk for if there isn't a blackboard for the kids to draw on?"

"Honey, I didn't have time to get a chalk board. Try drawing on the floor. You can't hurt the concrete."

"Dad? We sweep and wash the floor regularly."

"Look at it this way, you will never run out of places to draw if you clean regularly. Besides, it's warmer on the floor than anywhere else right now."

The wind continued to howl and the barn continued to creak and groan as it did. There was always the reminder that it was no longer possible to go outside. Bill kept the log up to date and the assigned jobs kept them all as busy as he could keep them.

He pumped some water for the watering can and began to "irrigate" his crops. He wasn't worried about the quality of the water because so many people had been drinking it since he bought the farm. He poured the water and it flowed from side to side and corner to corner. Kiia's corner surprise would be a happy one for everyone and keep them guessing from seedling to first fruits. Right now, since no one had seen him plant the seeds, his secret was safe. They germinated right away and began their growth.

The first week ended and even though it had felt like an eternity it was still only seven days. The wind and cold continued and one evening the wind blew something into the outside wall. It was a muffled crash and then a scraping sound as if something was clawing its way across the side of the building. Everyone gasped as if they expected a fearful being had come to break in and deliver to them all the unreal yet imaginable terrors that must exist outside. Once the wind had blown it away from the building it was not heard from again. Everyone stopped what they were doing to breath hard and quell the tightness across their hearts.

"It was nothing!" Said Bill. "I'm surprised the wind hadn't blown something against the building before this."

As they all looked to him their smiles were weak and tears of relief ran down their cheeks. Cherry was pale, but the first to respond.

"Well, I was hoping it was some well-hung dude looking for me. You know, without me it has to be pretty boring out there for men like that!"

"Cherry," responded Ruth. "That kind of talk is inappropriate in front of the children."

"Well, Miss Purity Pants, just where do you think these children came from? I'm sure the stork doesn't leave them under a rose bush in your neighborhood either." Cherry took menacing steps toward Ruth.

"As a midwife, I am well aware of the conception and bearing of children. And as a mother I am also aware of what is and isn't appropriate speech in front of children."

Cherry threw down the book she had been reading and stormed over to Ruth.

The kids looked up at Ruth with worried expressions and the other four adults moved to stand between the two women. Bill was the only one of a non-pacifist nature who had any training in self defense so he stepped in front of Cherry with a stern determination to do whatever was necessary to settle her down.

Ruth was defenseless as a violent action or reaction was not a part of her way of life. Bill got between them quickly. Michael was there also and put his arms around his wife in a protective and loving embrace. He jumped back as she screamed and doubled over. In the excitement her time had come. Miriam and Michael helped her to her bed and Becky came forward to lead Cherry to her's.

In the next twelve hours all worry about the survival lifestyle they were living disappeared. Ruth was without her mother, her midwife and any of the supports of her peaceful community. She was about the business of birthing her third child. Michael was a valiant husband with his attention and the potions he knew how to make and serve. He calmed her and took away as much pain as his natural healing ways could. Miriam had only her experience to help with. Ruth bore her child as stoically as she could so as not to frighten her children.

Across the hay bale partition Becky had her hands full with Cherry who constantly wailed her apologies and screamed in sympathy when she perceived Ruth's most difficult moments. The children of both women sat shoulder to shoulder on Kiia's bunk sensing this was one of those grown up things they would endure someday. Bill sat at the hearth with Kiia wishing the boy was old enough to share a beer. Instead the two prepared the evening meal and fed those who could eat. In the wee hours of the morning baby Rachel was born. Tears of joy and laughter born of that night's stresses were on everyone's face.

New life had come into the world and with it came a feeling that this little family would not disappear as had so many others in the cataclysm. A confident feeling was born that night with baby Rachel. Bill's "Family of God" became just that and they all knew they would somehow survive. Cherry clutched her belly and moaned her way to sleep.

In the morning everyone awoke at the usual time. Except this time, the electric light didn't come on to signal the dawn. Bill checked to see if it had burned out and the filaments looked fine. He recorded the temperature in the log noticing it was at fifty five degrees below zero Fahrenheit. The only assumption he could make was the cold had finally frozen to the bottom of the Eau Claire River and there was no water to flow through the generator turbines. They would have to make do with their grow lights and four white lights that would work off the batteries. One of the white lights was in the barn over the animal's dishes; one in stores; and the other two were used for sewing and their little school.

Bill went into the stores area to retrieve the last white light. He noted the location of the six extra bulbs in case they were needed. In the house he put the fourth light on Miriam's sewing machine and turned on the other two for morning baths.

Ruth had awakened, nursed Rachel and was sharing her presence with her sisters. Michael brought the bath pails with warm water and moved a light into their sleeping area.

Cherry led her daughters to the toilet and then back for their bath pails. She carried her own and Rose's while Lily followed with hers.

"Mommy, I can carry my own. If someone fills it for me I can take a bath alone too," she exclaimed in their room.

"Great. When you can run the washing machine you can get the towels for yourself too." She put the pails on the floor and set out the towels.

"All right, ladies, let us now dunk our donuts, or bathe our bums, or whatever the new language says to do." Suddenly, she looked around. "Hey," she shrieked across the room, "why isn't the light on?"

"Explanation at breakfast, Cherry. In the mean time, can we keep the decibel level low enough for a baby to sleep?" He hoped he didn't sound as loud and grumpy as he feared he did.

"OK!" Came the loud reply. In a lower tone she told Lily to ask Kiia's grandpa when he would be serving bacon, eggs and orange juice. It wasn't low enough as Kiia cheered about the new menu. Becky shushed him and sent him out for a good morning hug from his grandpa. She finished her bath and came out when the others did.

Bill waited on the morning prayers until Michael came in from the barn with the goat's milk. He'd had a busy morning and was catching up. After prayers, everyone asked about Ruth and Rachel, and Michael assured them his family was fine and then took Ruth's breakfast to her.

Bill explained to everyone why he thought the electricity was off. Since there probably wouldn't be any let up in the cold temperatures for a long time he suggested the twelve volt lights would have to do.

"We'll fall back on our instincts and just get up when we think it is six a.m. by the dam's time. We did it today and we should be able to do it for as long as is necessary."

Cherry wasn't thrilled about the time idea and Bill wasn't too pleased with having to explain to Lily why there would be no bacon, eggs and orange juice for breakfast. He was tempted to say he would assist her mother through the front door to go to the store, but knew it would settle nothing.

Lily was a bright, intuitive child and accepted Bill's explanation of the unchanging menu. A bond between them started and as Bill looked at the four kids at the table he felt a glow of happiness that had fled with the cataclysm. These four kids, and Rachel in her mother's arms, were worth his every effort to stay positive and happy. He was determined to be the father and grandfather figure to all the kids in his Family of God.

"I went for a ride at midnight and six. Since we must now fill in for the lack of electricity, who will take the nine o'clock ride?" Miriam volunteered with a little hesitancy because she had never been on a bicycle before. Her determination to try impressed Bill so he let her have the time slot. "That leaves six and nine p.m." Michael took the six p.m. and Becky requested the nine p.m. ride.

"Kiia is still ready for bed at eight thirty and I can easily take that one."

Bill sent everyone to wash up after breakfast and then to their duties; school for the kids and cleaning for the adults. He went to work on the raised beds and the barrel plants. It didn't take long for him to see a new seedling in two of the beds. Volunteers he called them because he didn't know how they came to be growing with everything else he and Michael planted. He recognized them as a type of vine and considered pulling them out right away as they would take up a lot of room for few fruits.

Michael came over after changing the water bath on the air intake. Both men looked at the new seedlings and Bill explained why he wanted to pull them as weeds. Both men knew the seedlings were watermelons and would need a lot of room, but Michael encouraged

Bill to let them grow. He reasoned they would be a welcome treat in a few months.

Kiia saw the two men talking at the corner of the bed and came running over.

"What, grandpa?"

Bill picked up his grandson and hugged him as he always did. He explained the seriousness of having an unwanted plant that could take light and nourishment from the others that would provide food.

"But, Grandpa, I planted that," and twisted around to point at the other bed, "and that one too!"

"You did?" Bill exclaimed. "Well, then we should keep them. Do you know what you planted?"

"No, I just wanted to help."

Both Bill and Michael had a good laugh about the boy's enthusiasm. It was obvious Michael was enjoying the antics of a little boy mixed in with the rest of their "all girls" family.

"Well, Kiia," Michael said, "We will call these Kiia's Surprise Plants and let them grow till we all know what they are. Then," he burst out loudly, "we will eat them all up!"

Kiia let out an excited little boy laugh and agreed. The girls came running over to see what the excitement was. When told, they all wanted to plant something. The men had their hands full trying to get everyone back to school and only accomplished that with a promise to bring out some seed packages for a school project.

Back in the stores the men found the package of watermelon seeds that Kiia had opened and closed it. They selected a number of vegetable seeds and went back to the school. Needless to say, the girls rejected the choices and asked for flower seeds. All four of them wanted to plant something and an extra plant for baby Rachel.

Chagrined, the men went back to the stores and reorganized the seed packages. They selected all the flower choices, but stayed to talk a moment.

Bill brought up the issue of how clean or toxic the slurry taken from the air intake water bath might be. A good test might be to plant some seeds in a pail of the stuff to see if it would sustain life. There were few pails left, plastic or metal, but the idea was acceptable to both of them. Unfortunately, it was not for the girls. They wanted to plant flowers and plant them now; not after a bucket was filled up.

So, after lunch that day, a different flower was planted for each of the five girls. The women declined as they knew how valuable the gardens were going to be later when there would be an ongoing harvest. In a few months there would be a Marigold with the Broccoli, a Pansy with the Peas, a Petunia in the Onion patch, a stately Sun Flower in a Tomato barrel and a Zinnia for Rachel with the Blue Berries.

Bill and Michael prepared two of the extra plastic pails for a seedling test. There was very little soil left in stores after filling the seed beds but they mixed some in with the slurry from the air bath. Three cucumber seeds were planted in one pail and three squash in the other. They were placed on the edge of the Tomato barrels so they wouldn't take up soil or block any light. If they grew, the vines would be trained to run along the barrel tops and around the floor. If, after a few months the slurry proved to be non-toxic and able to nourish plant life they would be able to pour it into the raised beds to sustain plant growth there.

Over the next few weeks everyone watched the growth of the new flowers and mostly watched the growth of Rachel. No one mentioned the need for inoculations, but everyone prayed quietly for her good health. Natural cures would have to work for her and anyone else who caught anything.

The days turned to weeks and slowly the constant fear turned to constant vigilance.

Everyone expected to survive the cataclysm, but knew they had to be constantly on guard to be clean and careful about everything they did. An injury might not be healed without a hospital setting. An infection could ravage a person's immune system and alter or take a life. With little soap, and that reserved for washing dishes and laundry, hand washing with water only had to be frequent and as thorough as possible.

Another issue of great importance became a reality with the ripening of the vegetables taken from Miriam's garden. She and Bill had time to salvage a few tomatoes, some herbs and the fruit trees and shrubs they had gathered a few days before they had to enter the barn. After a month they had recovered from the shock of being transplanted and some fruit was beginning to ripen. Bill had to "lay down the law" about eating outside of the meals they prepared. One person could eat a tomato that could flavor a soup for the entire community. When the Strawberries and Blueberries ripened they would be a nice desert for one person, or two or three berries for each person. It had to be understood and agreed upon that no one could take it upon themselves to eat other than at the appointed meal times. This was a real issue as everyone was now tired of the same old flavors of the oatmeal, beans and rice. They were nutritious meals to be sure, but by now boring. The vegetables needed another month to produce and Bill didn't want anything lost to the group as a whole.

"Well, I don't know why we have to be so picky about what and when we eat. My God, I'm losing weight already! Do we have a scale here at the Hotel Hay Bale?"

"No scale, Cherry. And I must say your weight loss is noticeable. He didn't want to say anymore because she still needed to lose another fifty pounds. Besides, Bill reasoned, God still punishes liars and flatterers.

Cherry accepted Bill's remark as honest. In fact everyone had lost some weight since they entered their new lifestyle. There was less to eat and more exercise than they had all experienced in the past. Hard work had kept the Amish thin, but extra exercise is what took off the fat in all cultures. The bicycle did more for them than generate electricity, heat the place and bring in fresh air.

Two weeks later, another decision had to be made. The strawberries had begun to ripen and there were enough for everyone to have three each for desert after the evening meal. Becky washed them and put them in a bowl at the center of the table. After nearly two months of beans and rice, the chance to have fruit was the highlight of the day.

"Uh, who gets that big ripe looking one?"

"Cherry, there are three apiece and we can just place three on each person's plate and…"

"But, who gets the biggest and best looking ones? I haven't had a treat for so long I have a real bad need for something like this."

"I would like my girls to have the best of what is given to my family." Said Ruth and looked to Michael.

"I agree." He replied.

"I think the same way about Kiia and I," replied Becky. "He can have the better of the six given to us."

"William? I would like my three added to whatever is divided between the children."

"No Miriam. There are three berries for each person in our family. As Spiritual Leader of this family I will make the distribution and my decision will be final. He stood up and took a tongs and the desert bowl and began.

In an attempt to stop any more complaining he started with the large one on Cherry's plate and worked his way around the table trying to keep an even distribution of large and small and most ripe.

"My decision is final," Bill said as he sat down.

"Ruth has six in front of her."

"There are three for her and three for Rachel and three for every child, woman and man in this family! My decision is final!"

"I have a one time solution that might fit this situation." Ruth said. "Since Rachel isn't able to enjoy her share I will give one of hers to each of her sisters and one to you Cherry," and placed the best two with Anna and Mary.

"Oh, you didn't have to do that," blushed Cherry as she grabbed her four and packed them in her mouth.

From the fire in Ruth's eyes there was a real possibility she was nearing a change in her religious attitudes.

"As tempted as I am to say Grace again for such a nice desert, I think I will forgo that and enjoy…" Michael picked up one of his berries and bit into it. He savored the flavor for a moment and then pushed the last of it along with the little green leaves into his mouth and everyone followed his lead. For a few minutes everyone experienced a joy that strawberries couldn't have given them two months ago.

Becky said there would be more in a few days. The treat soothed them all and their spirits were higher than they had been for some time.

After their evening meal, Michael pulled Bill aside. "The young Billy has impregnated one of the nannies and there is no need to nurse the gruff old Billy along. He is no longer able to breed and the herd's instincts no longer trust him as a leader."

"All right. Butcher him when you are ready. I think meat at a few meals will help keep our morale up."

"Yes," replied Michael. "We neutered him about two months ago and he should provide some tender meals." He turned to get two butchering knives from the hearth area and threw a newly sewn cape around his shoulders before going into the barn. Miriam and Ruth had finished sewing for the time being to the benefit of all. The heat was constant, but a little cooler than they all wanted. The wool garments kept everyone warm enough and allowed enough movement so work and play could be done. The extra cape was necessary for Michael to work in the barn as it was largely unheated. The small amount of heated concrete extended only a foot into the barn; it was just enough to keep the water pans thawed, yet not enough to heat the area significantly. The animals survived on the minimal heat and natural bedding. Michael's presence several times a day was welcomed by the goats as they were domesticated animals.

It didn't take Michael long to butcher the animal and dispose of the unusable parts through the small door that used to lead to the now burned away goat pen. He had stopped crouching to look out. The extreme cold and fearsome darkness made him want to shovel out any unwanted material quickly. That he did and then he pulled the sheet metal door closed and replaced the Styrofoam panel. A little snow and a lot of ash always blew in, but Michael shoveled as much back to the door as he could and the rest had to settle as it would.

There had been no sign of snakes or rodents or even insect infestations. The extreme heat of the fire storm killed everything that hadn't had time to seek shelter, and the heavy rain and ash fallout drove insects down where the quickly lowering temperature froze them.

Michael butchered quickly and set the cuts on a bale where they froze solid. It was important to estimate small portions as extra food eaten today meant less to eat tomorrow. He'd left a small portion of the Quail he butchered earlier and there had been no signs of anything eating it. Assured there was no predators or insects to compete for their meals he felt secure in his home made natural freezer. He picked up his knives and took them inside to boil them clean.

Miriam had a pot ready to boil when he returned to the hearth. He told her to expect meat for dinner the next night and then shook off the cape and stood close to the fire. It didn't take long for the barn-cold to penetrate his layered wool garments and he was glad to be inside. The fur was thick on the goats and the quail looked "full-feathered" as he put it and they all looked healthy despite the extreme cold in the barn. There was every reason to believe they would have meat occasionally for as long as it was necessary to live as they were.

Becky found the bicycle for the nine o'clock ride and everyone else started getting ready for bed. Kiia spent time with Bill and Miriam while his mother rode and they got him ready for sleep. In a little over two months they had all adapted to the new rituals. It was apparent the kids felt comfortable with their parents in this new lifestyle. There were still the memories of other family members and an occasional question or comment about them, but fear was no longer the major emotion in their lives. They accepted life inside as long as they were young and well cared for.

The adults found themselves in lighthearted moments occasionally and tried not to dwell on their losses and the unfathomable future. It was perhaps, their efforts to provide for themselves and their children that let them believe they could be happy again and live the carefree life style they had been accustomed to in the past. Whatever the reason, the grief that still haunted them was punctured by occasional happy moments and their lives went on. Except for some issues, of course.

"You know, Becky," Cherry shouted from across the room, "it feels like a Saturday night to me and we should go out tonight. I mean, I haven't been laid in months and..."

"CHERRY!" Shouted the adults.

"Well, come on!" she shot back. "I'm stuck in this Hay Bale Hotel with two old married men and one little boy. Not exactly my life-style if you know what I mean!"

"CHERRY!" This time Becky could be heard with the other adults. "You are taking in too much territory by talking about my son!"

"Oh, I'm not suggesting anything. It's just that I've been cooped up in here and this just isn't my lifestyle and I, I…" she turned and ran to her bed in tears.

"Becky," called Bill. "There is a lot about what has happened I can't explain and the future is even more of a mystery to me. But, I am very sure that the government has a few places scattered around the country where there are survivors just like us."

"Are you sure?" Becky asked with a hopeful look.

"Sure?" Replied Bill. "In all my taxpaying years I have never known the government to be short of men in the military. Why right now I'd bet money there are men in the Army, Navy, Air Force and the Marines holed up somewhere just waiting for a couple of good looking women to come out of hiding and be their dreams come true."

"How much money do you have to bet?"

"Cherry, cry yourself to sleep and let me worry about this!" snapped Bill. He was in no mood for Cherry's twisted logic about anything that might affect Becky or Kiia.

"Are you sure, Dad?"

"Yes. I really believe there are places here in America where food and manpower have been hidden and protected in case of an emergency like we are surviving too. Now, you have finished the nine o'clock ride. If you will help Miriam get Lilly and Rose ready for bed I will spend some time with Kiia and get him tucked in."

It didn't take long to get the kids to bed as they had accepted that regimen as well as their parents. Kiia was a joy to his grandfather at these moments and the two couldn't get enough time together. When Becky and Miriam checked in with Bill he had Kiia well on his way to sleep. He spent a few minutes reassuring Becky there would be a good young man in her life, but all in God's good time.

"William? It would seem thee is only sleeping between the twelve and six a.m. rides and I know that to be insufficient. Please retire with me as I have spent too much of my life alone." She took his arm and pulled him toward their bed. He was too tired from their ordeal to resist. He easily slept till the midnight ride, but the exercise that usually refreshed him left him with his headache. Miriam welcomed him back to their bed and lay close while he slept. They awoke for the six o'clock ride and the beginning of a new day.

Bill replenished the electricity and clean air while Miriam boiled the oatmeal. After breakfast and prayers Bill surveyed his Family of God. Cherry's eyes were still red from crying all night and everyone else looked as if their own stresses had wreaked havoc with their emotions.

I've finished the log for today and there are no significant changes outside. Since it is Sunday, I declare an end to all unnecessary work. We will ride for the electricity and fresh air, see to the animals and tend to our children. Other than that, Sundays will be a day of prayer and resting. And, it has occurred to me," Bill added, "we have been working too hard and resting too little." There was a general assent and Cherry rose and went straight back to her bed. The other adults chuckled to themselves and agreed to rest more on Sundays.

Bill reaffirmed the need to keep the rides on time as no one knew if they could restart the grow lights if they were allowed to go out with dead batteries. The only thing Bill was sure of is that it took a lot more electricity to start the lights than it did to keep them lit. Everyone agreed to keep their rides uppermost in their minds and finished what they had to do before retiring to their rooms. There was little objection from the kids as they too had suffered sleep interruptions from storms and the adults getting up for their rides.

Bill stayed with Miriam to finish the dishes and clean up the table. They went to their room and for the first time since the storm she stopped to undress before slipping into bed from his side.

Her instincts awoke her on time for the nine a.m. ride and other than Becky making the noon and Cherry making the three p.m. rides everyone slept till the evening meal.

After dinner, the animals were tended and all attention was directed toward the kids. An evening of play was light hearted, but when Becky started the nine p.m. ride everyone moved to their beds. Sleep came to all, but the wind and hail always managed to interrupt someone's sleep.

The days passed quickly as the survival activities still took everyone's time and attention. The plants began producing well after they had been inside three months.

The additional food was nice, but the variety it offered was better. Everyone's appetite had shrunk with their stomachs and waistlines had come down too. There was no problem with anyone being overly hungry now.

Bill surveyed the food supply and felt his original estimate of a two year supply of staples would easily last. If the storms didn't abate they would have some meat and the newly grown vegetables to last as long as necessary. He hoped the atmosphere could cleanse itself in less than two years, but if it couldn't he still had hope for survival.

After three months in the building, nearly all plants were bearing fruit. The tomatoes were as prolific as Bill had hoped. They flavored many soups and stews and occasionally could be eaten alone. All the vegetables were producing, but there just wasn't enough garden space to grow enough sugar beets to boil down into sweetener. A small number were rotated into the beds, but the lack of sweeteners had started to take the sweet taste away from everyone's palate.

Michael had tied Kiia's mystery vine to the edge of the beds and the blossoms were large and strong. Bill wasn't sure if there would actually be fruit on the vines as there were no Bees to pollinate the blossoms. He talked it over with Miriam because he was afraid Kiia would be terribly disappointed if his plants provided nothing. Miriam looked at the plants the next day.

She removed her bonnet and let down her braids. She bent low and touched a braid into the male blossom and then fertilized the female one. She did this at both beds where Kiia had his "secret" plants. To make sure there was pollination she brought pollen from one table to the other and then looked proudly at Bill.

"This has worked well for me in the past. There was a time when I was known for growing some of the best vine plants in our clan." She beamed as she tied up her braids and replaced her bonnet. Bill watched her walk toward the bicycle for her nine a.m. ride. She glanced back at him and saw love and pride in his eyes. Two simple people cast into the roles of leaders at a pivotal time in human history.

It didn't take long for the adults to recognize Kiia's plants as being watermelons and the boy was ecstatic about being the one to have planted them. He began to pester everyone about when to harvest them. Actually, harvesting them wasn't as important to his little mind as was his ability to enjoy their flavor. In a month the first two out of six were ripe and a Sunday afternoon picnic was planned.

Bill asked Michael to "Harvest" three quail if there were enough adult birds to do so. This was a frightening decision as there would be no more to eat for a few months until more eggs were laid, hatched and grown to size. One bird could make a pot of soup or stew for the whole family, or flavor a mixture of beans and rice for a day. But the need for a picnic was great and three males were selected by Michael for roasting.

The meal was served on blankets over a particularly warm place in the floor. The usual staples of beans and rice were there as well as broccoli, string beans, sugar snap peas, cherry tomatoes and a piece of freshly baked bread without butter or jam. Tea was served hot or cold depending on preference, although there was no Tea and imagination had to fill in for flavor.

There were enough beans and rice for everyone and the serving size of everything else was in one quarter to one half cup amounts. But, the desert made up for whatever was lacking in quantity and quality of meal.

Bill had ordered the strawberries picked and served because he believed the plants were about to go dormant. Everyone got eight berries along with a nice sized piece of watermelon. Serving sizes were dictated by stomach size and age, not appetite. The desert made the meal. Everyone was excited with a natural sugar high.

Becky had discovered Bill's old guitar in the stores area and had been quietly practicing for the last two months. She had studied the guitar in her early teens and had sung in her church's choir. Cherry had a love for music and had studied her voice until she discovered "fun with hormones" was easier that practicing music. The two women led the singing of spiritual music and they all let the children dance and sway to the hymns.

Bill watched over his family as they enjoyed their picnic. They had been in the barn for over four months now and he was suddenly aware of how slowly the time had passed since the firestorm. He felt a cold dark cloud descend over himself. In the beginning he was so strong in his belief that he could save his family and thereby assure a portion of humanity would triumph over adversity. Now he wondered if he hadn't committed a crime against them by letting them survive at the expense of all their loved ones. An evil coldness seemed to be trying to envelop him and he struggled against it. He picked up his empty plate and silverware and mumbled something about starting to clean up so no one stepped on and broke the table settings.

Miriam saw a change in him and said picking up was a good idea. She followed him to the hearth and they put their dishes into the wash water. Then she pushed him into their room.

"William. William! I see thy fear. I feel a cold dark place descending over thee. It has been the same for all of us. But we have shaken it away with thy leadership.

Thee has been the one to lead us in prayer; the one who assures us of the presence of God; who gives us the confidence to go about our daily duties and see to each other's needs. I have watched thee do the simplest things well for all of us. No one knew what to do and we even forgot how to do the simplest things for daily life."

She was shaking him now, as much as a small woman could shake her husband. "It was thee who did the small things, the simple things that fed us, that showed us how to do what we were capable of and had forgotten in our fear. William! Thee has shown us that our God still exists and even though we know nothing of why this happened or what the future will be, we are all sure you have been the one selected to lead us. You should not; you cannot allow the cold darkness to overpower you. William! You cannot choose anything but a strong path of leadership."

Bill crushed her to himself and held her tighter than he could ever remember doing so. He crushed the fear out of both of them and tried not to cry. She felt him wracked by quiet sobbing, but it passed in due time as his strength of resolve returned to him. This was the first time he had felt such a powerful negative force in his life and it nearly destroyed him. He'd followed what he believed was his path and hadn't even thought about any personal difficulties. But, leadership is a lonely post and must be guarded from unseen evils even more so than physical maladies.

"Oh, my God," he repeated over and over. "I didn't even see this coming. I had no idea how powerful fear and depression could be. I can't let the others see me like this."

"William, I will tell them thee is taking a pleasant Sunday afternoon nap and we are to pick up the dishes and finish enjoying our evening."

"Yes, yes," he replied. "Tell them I am going to rest a while and then be up for the midnight and six a.m. rides."

Miriam led him to their bed and helped him in.

"My God, I'm tired," he mumbled. Sleep came to him quickly and deeply. He wasn't aware of the time passing, but woke when it was time for the midnight ride. Miriam stirred, but he touched her cheek and told her to rest. She fell back into a deep sleep knowing things were well and she was safe.

Bill walked into the dimly lit hearth area. Everyone else was asleep and the white lights had been turned off to save the batteries. He felt the cold darkness, but it was no longer hovering over him. Knowing it would always be somewhere around but have no power over him gave him strength. He checked the water bath and the belt tension to the alternator and sat down to pedal for twenty minutes. So far the batteries were still strong and no lights had burned out. The plants were growing well and his family was fed. Life was good. After his ride he made his way back to bed. Miriam slumbered while he got in between the covers. He pulled the covers up to his chin with his beard over them.

"I must look like a proper Amish Husband." He thought. Sleep came to him quickly.

"BILL-YUMMM!"

Bill shot out of bed and turned to ask his wife why she woke him. He was sure he didn't over sleep his six a.m. ride.

"BILL-YUMMMaaaaach…"

"Oh, my. It must be Cherry's time. Yes, I believe it to be so. I must check with Ruth and we will see to her needs." She quickly rose from their bed. "Oh, and William, please don't forget to dress. This isn't a trip to the wood pile, you know."

"By God," he thought, "I'll pile some wood on that woman's head if she ever screams me awake like that again."

He pulled on his old cargo shorts and a tee shirt and then the wool alb Miriam had made to keep him warm. Lilly and Rose came running around the hay bale wall and jumped into bed behind him.

"Oh good, it's still warm"

"Will mommy be all right?" came Rose's muffled voice from beneath the covers.

"Oh, yes," came her big sister's authoritative reply. "I just hope this doesn't mean another baby. One more was enough for me."

Bill decided not to enter that conversation as he agreed with Lilly, but knew the eventual outcome of the screaming. He walked out to the bicycle for the six a.m. ride. Michael had finished the early feeding of the animals and was waiting by the hearth. He was his clan's healer, but this was not yet a question of healing. Ruth was the midwife of the clan and she had everything under control. Except Cherry's screaming, unfortunately.

They offered each other a good morning and Michael said he had started boiling some sort of root that would give Cherry some pain relief if she could keep it down. Bill asked for some pain relief for their ears when Cherry let go another scream. Michael winced and laughed at Bill's remark. Bill mounted the bicycle for the six a.m. ride.

"My God! You would think a woman wouldn't have sex again after the first birth if it hurts that much.

"True," replied Michael. "But, I think there is a natural sort of amnesia about such things as a part of the returning sex drive. Of course, that is not a medical fact." He poured a cup of the root coffee for each of them and took the rest to Cherry.

"BILL-YUM, YOU SORRY SONOFABITCH! If you think you are ever going to touch me again you are crazier than you think I am!"

"Does she have to keep yelling at me?"

"Oh, I think that is the name of her illicit impregnator. I believe you English call them a "significant other."

"Among other things. But, what's in a name? Hey, speaking about names, do you know I don't even know your last name?"

"Oh? I didn't know that." There was a long pause as they finished drinking their root coffee.

"William? It has occurred to me that you have never called me by my last name. Does thee not think that odd?"

"If I knew your last name I would consider it odd. Not your last name, but...you know."

They looked at each other for a moment trying to figure out what the other meant. Cherry shrieked again, but the men just looked around wondering where that far-off noise came from and then poured more root coffee.

"Well, it is the same as my father's last name."

"I don't think that is so unusual. By the way, what was your father's last name?"

"You knew him."

"Huh?"

"Yes."

"Well, then what was your father's name?"

"Yocum."

"Yocum...Yocum...hmmm. Yes I seem to remember a good friend named Moses with that same last name."

"Yes. That was my father. He was the Bishop who married you and my Aunt Miriam."

"Your Aunt Miriam is my wife?" Bill thought for a minute. "Hey, who is that Amos guy?"

"He is my older brother." He paused while they listened to Cherry scream for a while. Becky approached the men.

"Dad, do you know you have been on that bicycle for over an hour?" Don't you think it is time to do something else?"

"Well, yes. I'd like to suggest someone boil out these coffee cups before any of the kids get a hold of them."

Becky took the cups from both men with a bewildered look and put them in the pot to be washed. The men ambled over to the raised beds to check on the crops. Cherry screamed until just before bed time and then Miriam came out to announce the arrival of baby Hyacinth, another flower girl for Cherry's non-existent weddings.

It occurred to Bill he didn't know Cherry's last name. Either that or he had forgotten it. Either way he was sure he would remember to never let Michael make another pot of coffee.

The children were ushered in to meet the new baby and Lilly realized her worst fears had come true, but said her new sister was beautiful and was thrilled when her Mom let her hold her. Kiia wasn't impressed and requested a truck to play with.

Bill and Michael took the next few days of rides so the women could rest. Becky wouldn't give up her rides as she was beginning to like the exercise. After two days of rest Miriam and Ruth reclaimed their rides for health reasons and Cherry was forced back into the saddle a month later. The babies thrived and were loved by all. Rachel showed quicker than average progress at every age and Hyacinth was so perfect a baby that Bill questioned whether she really was Cherry's.

Time continued at its own pace and if no one drew attention to the calendar it didn't seem to be as agonizingly slow as it was. Work was a bearable necessity because the consequences of losing even one mature plant, or worse yet a battery pack or grow light, was frightening. Tending the plants was easy for all because the vitamin D necessary for good emotional health was available from the white lights and the grow lights. After his own short bout with depression Bill was quick to watch the others so they could be helped immediately, if necessary.

Their diet was spartan to say the least, but it kept everyone healthy. After eight months Becky and Cherry were heard to remark they were sure that had reached their best High School weight. Cherry was a little disappointed she had to "hide" her shape under a cape and hood, but a day of feeling cold made the cape more acceptable.

Bill observed a phenomenon that disturbed him at first and then he just accepted. It seemed everyone had gotten familiar with their rituals and just went about their duties without any conversation. The idea of knowing when to start and stop an activity or when another needed any amount of help was so ingrained in them now they just moved around to help or complete a task without being asked. Dialogue had nearly disappeared. Even the kids had quit arguing.

One night after dinner Bill went into stores and found the harmonicas he had picked up in an impulse purchase. He all ready had an older Meisterklasse he could wail out a tune on and he surprised the kids with it. Kiia went into orbit when he remembered his Grandfather could make music. Bill gave a harmonica to him and also to Rose who was already showing signs of being a real tomboy. Michael wasn't sure he wanted one and refused with the option of praying on the matter later. Music wasn't something his clan had anything to do with.

As an option to singing, playing the guitar or harmonica, Bill suggested recitals or recitations of scripture and other inspirational writings. Ruth and Michael agreed immediately and even said Miriam had been known for a good speaking and praying voice. Miriam responded with a blush and nodded.

"All right then. Here is my plan. Since we can get our work done easily by suppertime we will spend the evenings entertaining and instructing each other with songs, inspirational music, scripture and good literature. Everyone will participate to the best of their ability. Does that sound like a good plan?"

Before anyone could agree a loud crash in the back of the barn startled everyone. It bought with it every fear they had managed to conquer over the last eight months. Fear showed in everyone's eyes.

Bill's training in Fire and Rescue took over. He knew he had to rely first on his instincts and then on his training after the situation had been assessed.

"Miriam! Bring me the twelve volt flash light that is charging on the middle inverter. Michael! Let's get our capes on before going out into the cold." They rushed to the back door that lead to the barn and pulled up their hoods and tied the capes around their necks.

Miriam rushed up with the flash light that had a strong beam after being on the charger for so long. She watched with horror as her husband and her nephew opened the door to the barn and stepped through.

"Keep this door closed. We can open it ourselves when we come back in."

Michael closed the door hard before the women could protest. Bill flashed the light around the barn and saw the animals and birds were in their nests and bedding. They showed more fear of the light than of whatever had caused the crashing sound.

"The animals don't show any signs of being afraid of a predator so I think we can quickly rule out any large animals. Stay close to my right side because I have to go further into the barn to check things out."

Michael was a healer, not a soldier, but he was a brave man and love for his family made it easy to go forward to protect them. He closed the animal gate that kept the goats from the passage way they had just come through. Bill flashed the light around looking for signs of damage or forcible entry.

"There, William. Just past the goat door to the outside."

Bill flashed the light to that area and saw a large crack in the sheetrock above the bales of hay. Whatever hit the outside had made a dent inward, but the hay stacked against the wall absorbed it.

"Help me open the small goat door so I can look outside. We have to know how bad the outside wall has been damaged. Hold the light for me. I'll call for it when I need it."

Michael held the light as Bill moved the Styrofoam, the oak bar holding the outside door and finally the outside door. Michael handed him the light and he leaned out into the wind.

The wind tore through his two layers of wool and the cold began to bite at his skin. The ash made breathing next to impossible. He flashed the light toward the area of damage and pulled himself in immediately. It took both men to pull the sheet metal door in place and bar it. The Styrofoam went in place easily and Bill needed Michael's help to get up and scurry for the gate and passageway back into the warmth of the house.

The women were pale with fear when they saw the ill effects that the men showed after only a few seconds of leaning outside the building to see the damage. They pushed the men to the hearth and Becky threw some extra logs on the fire. Cherry mounted the bicycle with Hyacinth in her arms and pedaled up some heat and fresh air for the house.

"It's not as bad as it sounded," rasped Bill.

"Oh, William, thee is frostbit and thee sounds like thee has caught thy death of a cold."

Bill smiled weakly and shook his head. "Michael and I are well. Let me tell you what I saw. It appears that some time between the firestorm and now the wind picked up a small private plane and kept it aloft. Somehow it spiraled down and ultimately landed against our northeast wall. There is a break in the sheet metal, but not big enough to compromise the structure. The windows of the plane are all broken out and it would have been impossible for anyone to be alive in it or to fly it or ride it down to the ground. The wind could pick it up again and it could be gone soon. When the weather warms up we will have to repair the wall before the spring rains. What do you think, Michael?"

"I agree with thy assessment, William." And to the others he announced the building was still secure and the animals were safe.

"And now woman," Bill said to his wife, "how about pouring a cup of tea for your still cold husband?"

Miriam looked to Michael. "Has thee a potion to keep my husband from catching his death from the cold?"

I know which herbs he will need," spoke Ruth and she went to get them. Miriam drew water from the pail closest to the fire and filled two cups. Becky pulled out two chairs for the men to sit down. Ruth came back with herbs to help with chest colds and another for a tea which would calm nerves before going to bed. She gave a small amount to the kids so they would sleep well too. It was the second time they had used any of their herbal medicine.

Both men stayed close to the fire and drank their tea. Michael had no injuries from the cold, but Bill had frost bite on his face from looking out at the airplane. He also had the effects of frost bite in his lungs. It wasn't bad enough to kill him, but he would experience a chest cold for a week before feeling well again. The incident drove the fear of the unknown back into all of them and they would never take their safety for granted again. Bill announced he was warmed again and asked everyone to go to their beds. He couldn't stop a small cough as his lungs did need to bring up some moisture and ash that came from the outside.

They made their way to their beds, thankful for their safety. The fact they were all still alive gave them hope in their ability to go on. Bill and Miriam didn't see Lilly follow them to their bed. She watched with a child's fascination at something she didn't understand yet. Miriam undressed and pulled William's clothing off also. She slipped into bed from his side holding him. There was no danger of being cold she thought, but Lilly saw Miriam wrap herself around him under the covers to give him her body heat.

Lilly stood there in the darkness for a few more minutes thinking about having been present to the birth of two babies and nearly losing the Patriarch of their Family.

It was too much for a child not yet seven, but it left her feeling stronger than she could comprehend. Quietly, she slipped away and went to her bed.

The extra sleep from going to bed early made it easy for Bill to getup for his rides. It took a week for him to clear his lungs and for the skin on his face to heal from the cold. His healing and the birth of the two babies gave confidence to his family as it symbolized their ability to rise above injuries and illness and carry on.

Time continued to move slowly, but it wasn't as noticeable as it was at first. When Bill announced they had been in the barn for a little short of a year, everyone expressed interest in a celebration.

Bill agreed and everyone else started suggesting things to do. Becky and Cherry wanted to take the music portion of a show and promised to write at least one new song. If it was all right with their parents they promised a "home school" show. A small adult chorus would sing if there was time to rehearse something "tried and true." Bill and Michael promised to finish the plans for a churn so there would be butter for their fresh bread. The strawberries and blueberries were in blossom and would provide jam about the same time.

Michael said a male goat would be ready for butcher soon and there would be meat for the celebration. As usual, there would be enough milk from the female goats, but not enough to try to make butter and ice cream as well. Not every idea was possible, but the thoughts of a party brightened everyone's face. Bill agreed with every idea that seemed possible and everyone began plans for their part of the party.

"In the mean time," he said, "we have to keep up our daily chores. Let's not get too far ahead of ourselves."

Everyone agreed, but the party idea was foremost in their thinking from that time on. All plants were watered, weeded and cared for with the idea of having a little extra food for the special day. Becky and Cherry changed the school curriculum to include more music and recitations. Miriam and Ruth scoured the stores area for anything they could sew up that would look festive.

In the last eleven months Bill had kept everyone so busy they were able to control their fears and boredom. There was, to be sure, a feeling of desperation in everyone, but they were able to keep it under control. The party plans added to a sense of control they needed to have. Everyday chores took on a new excitement.

When the One Year Anniversary came they were surprised at all they had accomplished. There was a small amount of butter for their bread; beets had been boiled for a sweetener and jam was available for the first time in a year. The male goat had enjoyed his added rations and unwittingly provided a great treat. The kids sang and did their recitations while the adults cheered and clapped as if they'd never seen a better show. They, in turn, sang and danced and made the kids laugh.

At nine p.m. the kids were put to bed and the adults went down too. Bill made the "Nine-ride" and then checked the temperature before making the log entries for the day. At the thermometer he tapped it lightly and the reading didn't change. It was odd because it usually read fifty to fifty-five degrees below zero, Fahrenheit. Tonight it read forty-five degrees below zero.

After the first week it was consistently the same and Bill wasn't sure he wanted to record the change. He did record it, but made a point to keep it to himself. He didn't want to arouse any false hopes in the others.

At night, when he reached his bed Miriam was already asleep. That was good because he would not have been able to keep the temperature rise a secret if she had asked. It was too soon to tell anyone unless it happened several times again. In the morning he checked the thermometer before he took his morning ride. The temperature was still at forty five degrees below zero! He made the entry, closed the book and then began his ride. The others began to get up and a new day was started.

In the evening, the temperature was down to forty four degrees and Bill rushed back to the table to enter the difference in the log. Miriam noticed his excitement and asked about it. The increase in temperature was too important to keep a secret any longer.

He told her and she gasped. The others noticed their excitement and came to the hearth for an explanation. Bill told them and had to do so three times before the significance sunk in. They asked questions about how soon it would get back to normal and how soon before it would be safe to go outside. No one asked how soon they would be able to check on their loved ones. The thought of finding everyone they loved dead or missing was something they couldn't deal with. They had gotten used to living with the unknown and the sick fear that went with all they had gone through. Reality beyond what they already knew in the barn was too much to consider right now.

Bill calmed them as best he could and cautioned them about premature speculations about spring. He was right to do so. It took another three months before the temperature would get up to zero degrees Fahrenheit.

The other adults talked about what their lives would be like when they finally were free of the barn. Talk always centered on a life style similar to what they had before the cataclysm. Bill knew everything would be different.

Life would not only be different, but maybe even more difficult than what it had been. He feared their disappointment so much he talked with them about it that night. There was no guarantee of electricity, running water and nice homes to live in. He went so far as to predict a life style similar to what the Amish had chosen and nothing at all like what had gone on around the developed world. The family was so elated at the record Zero Degrees it was hard to calm them.

Bill bid them all a good night and Becky took the nine p.m. ride. When he got to bed after writing in the log he couldn't go to sleep. He was very unsettled about the increase in temperature. There was no way he could know how everyone would fare after the earth had repaired itself. The fear he had felt when they first entered the barn and began a survival lifestyle was easier to control than his fears about the next lifestyle change. He knew what he had to do to keep the cold out and the crops growing, but what would the outside life demand of them?

It took a long time for him to fall asleep and when he awoke he didn't feel like he'd slept at all. He went straight to the bike and made his ride. When he went to check on the temperature he forgot to look at it. The electric light was on! It was on for the first time in over a year. He stared at it until he was aware of going blind if he didn't look away. When he stumbled back to the hearth his wife noticed him and went white with fear at his confusion.

After some thought he told her he believed the earth's temperature had managed to melt the river's ice from the bottom up and enough water was able to go through the dam to begin generating electricity again.

Miriam shrieked and hugged him. The others came immediately and noticed the light before they could ask about Miriam's joyful shriek. They stared at it as if they were seeing a long lost friend.

Bill took a moment and explained the possibility of the earth's warmth coming up from the bottom of the river and melting enough ice for water to flow through the turbines again. No one cared about his explanation as the thought of one day getting out of the barn was the only thought on their minds.

"This doesn't mean we will be going outside in the near future," Bill interrupted their thoughts. "This may be just another weather anomaly that could change anytime. It could be a long time before we see the outside again."

It had been fifteen months since the cataclysm and this ray of hope changed everything for them. No longer was there a feeling of a never ending nightmare. The thought was now of surviving unless there was another disaster. The wind still howled around the barn and no one was able to go outside. There was no clothing for such frigid exploration. Bill and Michael stuck their heads out the goat pen door and the wind and cold bit into them so bad they closed up right away.

"I would say the wind chill is still far below the zero that is registered on our thermometer," Bill observed.

"Aye," replied Michael. "I noticed the air is not clean yet, despite the snow and hail that has fallen for over a year.

If it hadn't been for the sandstone bluff behind the barn the snow would be piled above the roof by now. The swirling wind kept the drifts away from this side of the building."

"I know," said Bill. "Let's see if we can open the passage way." The men carefully opened the passage way and it was blocked as if snow had been blown against it. They reinstalled the oak beam the barred the door and the Styrofoam and made no plans to try again until they noticed a better change in temperature.

The temperature continued to climb for the next four months and then Bill logged temperatures in the mid thirties every day. The sound of rain falling on the tin roof could not be mistaken, but it got tiresome when it happened so often. It was nearly a month before the wind stopped howling and the rain quite pelting the roof and sides of the metal barn. It had been nearly nineteen months and the mood was of impatience for a spring day and a chance to get outside. Tempers that had been calmed by fear and the need to cooperate for survival had begun to show them selves again. Bill hoped to get some time outside before anyone said or did something mean or cruel.

Michael kept reporting on what he could or could not see when he opened the goat pen door to throw out slurry or what little garbage they generated. They could no longer count on cooler temperatures to freeze their meager supply of meat and actually had to throw some of it out one day.

By the Twentieth month Michael was able to report enough light to see there was little snow and some drifts that he thought were made up of ice. It was still too windy to venture out.

The intermittent rain storms were too severe to allow a brave explorer to be caught outside yet. But, Michael surmised it wouldn't be too long before exploration could begin.

Bill kept the log up to date and continually came up with activities that would keep everyone's mind off going outside. He wasn't sure he was accomplishing the later, but he tried.

At the end of the twenty-second month he ordered the opening of the passage way again. It was just after the morning light had gone off and the thermometer showed fifty five degrees Fahrenheit. He and Michael carefully removed the Styrofoam and then swung the door open. It squeaked from lack of use, but swung open all the way. They pushed the steel panel on the outside and huddled around the opening and looked out. No one wanted to move outside at first, but Kiia slipped between the adults and jumped out.

"Hey, where's the house?"

Everyone pushed out all at once. They stayed close to each other and close to the open door. The house was totally burned away and only the field stones that had made up its foundation could be seen.

"Grandpa! What happened to your truck?"

Bill looked and it was a sorry sight. The heat had burned everything flammable from it. The aluminum cast wheels had been burned as well as the tires, upholstery and even the paint. The remaining body was rusted and what was left of the glass was singed black.

"I guess we won't be going anywhere for a while, Kiia. Unless, of course we walk."

"Oh, no!" Michael groaned and the others looked in the direction he was. They all had forgotten that his horse wouldn't be taken up to its barn and all that was left of it and the buggy was the bit from the harness, the four steel rims and an assortment of fasteners.

All were lying close to each other. The animal couldn't have suffered as the firestorm was so hot it perished immediately.

Their gaze went from the remnants of the buggy to the hill where the Amish Community had lived. The trip uphill had to be made, but fear made the decision to go difficult. As they stood there looking toward the hilltop a clap of thunder and the return of the wind signaled another thunderstorm and Bill turned them all toward the door. Once inside the door was closed, but the insulation and steel cover wasn't used.

"As soon as we can count on several hours of good weather we will go up the hill," said Bill. "For right now, let's get back to work."

Michael suggested planting more seeds and moving to the garden a few seedlings already started inside. Bill agreed and suggested waiting until the weather settled down a little. The wind and rain had been a little severe for a while, but Bill expected it to moderate before the end of the day. He was right. Shortly after the noon ride it became silent outside and Bill ordered the door opened again.

Chapter 17
Time

Nothing could make time pass any faster than it had for the past few months. Bill constantly worked on time schedules so everyone was kept busy and had time off as well. School for the kids was paramount and in the evenings everyone participated in music, hymn singing and skits. It became easy to get each other laughing despite the occasional scares the weather brought to them.

Bill kept their prayer life constant and was pleased every time he heard someone refer to their little group as the Family of God. It was an identity that brought calmness to them in the most difficult of times.

If a plant showed signs of dying or becoming dormant it caused a stab of fear in them. Any loss of food production was a cause of concern. Michael and Bill kept a small area of the raised beds for starting new plants so it was easy and quick to replace the non-producing ones.

Plants that went dormant like the strawberries and blue berries were easy to explain and accept. The apples hadn't started bearing yet so there was no loss there. But, any sign of blight resulted in a plant being uprooted and the surrounding soil dug out and boiled before being relegated to the compost heap. No chances could be taken that might result in the loss of other plants. So, there were seeds planted regularly and discarded at any sign of blight.

Bill called Michael over for a quick consult. They talked about transplanting some plants, seedlings and seeds outside. They selected some dormant strawberries and blue berries to begin with. A trip to the stores area produced seeds that would survive a cool spring and the men chose a few of each to start with. Then they dug up a half dozen plants and put them in pails to take outside.

The women had been watching and although they had guessed what was gong on couldn't resist asking. They caught the excitement of the moment and suggested some changes. Everyone's opinions were equal in importance and changes were made. Bill cautioned everyone about waiting for the right time in nature's erratic weather patterns, but shortly after the noon ride a "quiet" was noticed outside the barn and Bill ordered the door opened again.

They all stepped outside looking around for the predators they feared, but knew couldn't exist after the fire storm and months of extreme cold. It was as safe as they had hoped it would be and moved quickly to the area that was once Miriam's garden. She directed them to the areas she wanted things planted in and they planted joyfully.

It didn't take long to do what was good as the storm clouds blew in quickly and they scampered for the safety of the barn. Inside, they listened as the wind and rain whipped the building as it had when it was so cold.

A few hours later it was quiet again and Bill opened the door so everyone could run out. The plants and seedlings were beaten down by the rain, but showed no sign of being unable to recover. The soil had been fertile before the firestorm and the addition of several inches of ash didn't hurt at all. The seeds were not washed out of the planting rows and a little over a week later were seedlings.

While everyone watched the seedling's progress Bill had them all planting half of every seed type they had. He wasn't worried about over planting any of the Hybrid types as they couldn't set seeds for replanting anyway. Half of the non-hybrid seeds he kept in the stores in case the weather caused a crop failure. The joy of being outside again was intoxicating for everyone and they overdid everything they planned.

They'd walked down to the small lake and despite the black ash on the bottom it looked the same. Some water vegetation had all ready come back and fish could be seen swimming around. Bill announced a day of fishing and swimming for the next day and promised a change in diet if the fish would bite. The promise was accepted and they went back to planting. Bill went back to the barn with Kiia and brought back the three fishing poles he had and they all went down to the lake. Unfortunately, the fish wouldn't rise to the artificial baits they had.

The Strawberries had been put in the rows that they had been taken from and the blueberry shrubs as well. It didn't take long to clean up the fields as the firestorm had burned them clean and the only things the wind had been able to blow in were all metal.

There were posts, light beams, sheet metal and assorted sizes of chain link and wire fence. The pen for the goats was rebuilt from the chain link fence and posts, and the beams and sheet metal were used to keep the strawberry plants growing in rows. In two weeks they had completed the planting of their seeds, shrubs and trees. The weather chased them back inside daily, but the storms were not as intense as they had been and they could have stayed outside if they didn't mind getting wet. The winds still made it difficult to build something or move around the gardens so running back inside was an easy decision.

But, the issue of when to go up the hill to check out the Amish Farm Country had to be resolved. It was a sunny morning when a very hesitant group of survivors began the trek up the hill. When they came out of the barn there was nothing else to be seen but foundations and that was all they expected to see on the hill. The kids ran around the adults as they walked up. The Firestorm had burned the tar, but the road base was still there and it was a quick walk. Their worst fears were realized at the top of the hill. There was nothing on the horizon but stone foundations and whatever steel fences that had been erected years earlier.

Michael, Ruth and their children walked alone to their farm while Bill, Miriam and the others went to what remained of the farm Moses had spent his life on. Each group reached their respective farms about the same time. Bill instructed his group they were not to go inside the foundation of the home. Whatever might have been left was there to be sifted through by archeologists in the future. To him it was the burial site of his friends and his wife's family. He held her as she wept quietly over her childhood home. She agreed with William that no one should try to find usable things at this time. Her grief at losing her brother and his family was equaled by her guilt over being a survivor.

Steel rims marked the spot where their buggy sat when the Firestorm came through and steel bands marked where wooden water barrels had been. There was nothing in the barn area that would make life any better for them so they decided not to look for anything there either. It was a sorry time for all of them and after a few hours of looking around and mourning he called them all together for the walk home. A mild storm caught them half way down the hill, but aside from a good drenching they arrived home safely.

Miriam busied herself at the hearth rekindling the fire. She had a good fire going in a few minutes and they all huddled close to dry off. Becky continued the noon ride to recharge the batteries and pump hot water through the floor. The grow lights were still in use although their use would be discontinued soon when the plants began to flourish in the natural sunlight.

The bread dough Miriam had set to rise was put to bake on the hot ledge in the hearth and a portion was left to make the next dough rise. Beans were boiled and vegetables harvested for their lunch. Bill led the prayers as he always did and they ate. It was a solemn time for all, but a feeling of closure was there also. There was no one left from their families around them. It was too long a walk to take Cherry to her mother's house, but she knew there was no one alive there either. Bill promised her they would go into Augusta as soon as they could. She had nodded and said nothing. Lilly had put together the thoughts necessary to understand the loss of her family, but the other children hadn't the resources to figure such things.

"What do you say we go fishing this afternoon?" Bill asked out loud to no one in particular. "A big fish fry tonight would be a real treat. We could braise some fillets, some potatoes and veggies and…"

"A good idea, William," responded Michael. "And after dinner tonight let us begin to plan a wake service and funeral for our lost families."

The adults nodded and spoke their assent of Michael's suggestion and the kids looked around with questioning eyes. They'd become used to responding to planning sessions, but had no idea what was going to be talked about this evening.

Bill closed the lunch with a short prayer and while the women cleaned up the men got out the fishing tackle. The little family made their way past the goat pen to the lake. At the last minute, without thinking, Bill picked up the spade and a large pail and followed behind. It was a pleasant walk in the early afternoon. The plants and seedlings looked fresh and strong and that pleased them. God willing, there would be a bountiful harvest in the fall and life would go on.

The lake was a peaceful sight and Michael lead them around to what he thought would be the best place to fish. They rigged the three fishing poles so the women could fish with the kids and the two men made "throw lines" to get out to deeper water. Bill took a few minutes to dig in the soil and was surprised to find earth worms. They had gone deep when the cold came and had survived below the frost line. Thinking there would be plenty more elsewhere he picked them up and replaced the artificial baits they were using. The fish responded magically. There was laughter and cheers as bigger fish than they had hoped for were caught. Smaller ones that would have been kept two years ago were tossed back in and called "bait size." They had the most fun ever since they had been able to get out of the barn. When the large pail was full they knew they had to stop fishing. There was no way they could eat all of them in one sitting so they picked up their things and headed back home.

Miriam suggested they walk through the garden once again so she could check on her new plants. Another day in direct sunshine had stimulated growth in them and they looked strong.

"William?" She said in a troubled tone. "I hear a strange type of thunder. We must be quick about getting back inside."

"Miriam, that's not thunder," Bill replied as he strained to hear the sound better. "If I didn't know better, I would say it was a helicopter; two of them, in fact." He put the bucket of fish down and began to look around. By their sound, he believed they had to be close. He was right.

They came in from across the lake and turned to come around the sandstone bluff.

Both machines banked and turned steeply until both of them hung in the sky as if they were looking back at Bill's Family of God. They hovered while both parties stared at the other. Miriam and Ruth clung to their husbands as the children did the same to their mothers. The kids whined in fear looking to their parents for a different way to respond to these two strange noise making machines that hovered before them.

The radio operator of the one of the choppers called his headquarters to announce the finding of the first survivors they had found in their surveillance flight. They had been flying and bivouacking for two weeks checking out "hot Spots" in the North-Central part of the country. The eruption of the magma deposit in Wyoming had ultimately caused movements in the Teutonic plates which caused smaller volcanoes and hot geysers and springs around the country. Their orders were to check these "hot spots" to see what they were and to try to determine if they presented a danger to what little human life was left in the United States of America.

The radio fairly rattled with talk back and forth about the discovered life in the West Central area of Wisconsin. Officers were called to the radio at headquarters and gave advice on how to approach the survivors, what weapons to take and even what languages these strange survivors might speak. The instructions were numerous and became so close to an overkill situation that the Flight Commander ordered the choppers to land in what had been the driveway. The two helicopters moved slowly to the area near the burned out foundation and Bill's burned out truck. They landed easily and the engines were slowed so the rotors began to stop turning. The flight commander stepped out and two heavily armed soldiers got out of the back of each chopper. The five men approached the Family of God and stopped about ten paces from them.

They must have been a strange sight to each group. The Family was barefoot and clothed in their woolen garments made from Army Blankets. The women had pulled their hoods over their hair in a manner of modesty and the girls did so too. The men and Kiia were bare headed and surveyed the soldiers in their combat gear.

"I am Captain Marcus Olsen, Flight Commander of the Fourth Expeditionary Flight of the Transional Government of the United States of America."

"I am William Thomas, Patriarch of the Family of God;" and with a smile added, "Resident of the City of Augusta, State of Wisconsin and the good old U. S. of A."

He and the Captain looked at each other for a moment and then the soldier started to smile also.

"How many civilians are in your family, and how many in this area? Are there any Combatants, er, soldiers in this area?"

"There are thirteen members of our family, and we know of no other civilians or soldiers in this area."

Cherry moved over to Becky and whispered to her something about these soldiers really are men.

"I want one." She whispered.

"I get the Captain," Becky whispered back.

"O.K. Then I get the rest of them."

"Agreed."

Miriam released her hold on her husbands arm and moved a step toward the Captain. "We are forgetting our manners. Will thee stay for dinner and perhaps, for the night?"

"A kind offer Ma'am. We accept. Please excuse us while we perform a required military maneuver." He raised two fingers and motioned toward the passageway of the barn. Two of the soldiers broke away and ran toward the barn. They stopped at the door and one of them held up his hand to stop the other and then opened the door before he could kick it in. They lit the lights on their rifles and pushed in. They could be heard rushing around inside and were back out in less than two minutes.

"No civilians, Sir. Just a couple little animals in the back room, Sir."

"Judging from the animals in the pen I'd say they were goats, Conklin. You didn't have those in the Bronx, did you?"

"No, Sir."

"Basically, they're harmless. But don't bend over in front of the ones with horns."

"Yes, Sir."

"Thank you for your invitation, Ma'am. We accept your offer of hospitality and will offer the same back. Conklin, have the men secure the choppers for the night and have Sparks bring the hand held radio to me as soon as he finishes his report to HQ."

Let's clean these fish and then go inside," said Bill.

"Yes, Sir," said the Captain. "And, Conklin, have the men dress down and report for food preparation as soon as possible." And to Bill he said, "I'll follow you, Sir."

A feeling of relaxation came over all and they went inside to bring out the knives for filleting the fish. The Captain didn't have to tell the soldiers to hurry because they had been eating from sealed pouches for nearly two years and a fresh home cooked meal was too good to be true. They set the screw anchors and began to tie down the choppers. The radio operator made his report and when HQ demanded more information and all he had to say was the Captain was doing further investigations. He signed off quickly, pulled out the portable radio and headed for the barn.

Inside, Bill and Michael showed the Captain around and explained what they had been doing and why they did it. He was impressed at their ingenuity and said the military at Cheyenne Mountain in Colorado had more than enough dehydrated and canned foodstuffs. They grew nothing.

He asked a number of questions and then asked Bill for everyone's ages and who they were related to. It was for his report, he said. Bill filled him in as best he could and was interrupted by a knock at the passageway. The sound of anyone knocking startled the Family because no on had done so for the last two years.

"I'll get it," Sang out Cherry as she glided out of her private area. She had rolled up the sleeves and shortened the cape by tying a waist sash. All I all, she was showing a lot more skin than she had for a long time.

She swung open the door and gushed at the seven soldiers who looked at her as if they were seeing a woman for the first time.

"Oh, do come in!" She gestured with her arm in a sweeping motion. "We are so glad to see you." The soldiers smiled widely and offered thanks and open stares at her bare legs.

Conklin reported to the Captain that the tie down was complete and Sparks handed him the portable radio. They kept their eyes on Cherry and smiled like grinning idiots. The Captain took the radio and couldn't help smiling at his now-captive men. He turned on the hand held radio expecting to have poor to no reception, but was surprised by the strength of the satellite signal. The operator at headquarters was calling in a semi-hysterical tone.

The Captain responded to the call and had the operator's attention.

"Ten-Four, Captain. Stand by for your old man; I mean The Old Man; I mean…" there was a rustling sound and then a new voice was heard.

"This is General Olson, Commander of the Army of the Provisional Government of the United States of America. Who am I addressing?"

The Captain responded and it was obvious they were father and son. They conversed about the flight and the finding of civilians. Then, the General asked for personal information about the newly found Family of God. The Captain described Bill, Miriam, Michael and Ruth and the children. When he announced there were two unmarried women in the Family an eruption of cheers from Cheyenne Mountain drowned out the General and his radio operator. They could be heard ordering a silence that was slow in coming.

"Ten-Four, son…I mean, Captain. We now have two hundred and sixty seven men including the two new ones; forty married women and a total of six unmarried women." The loud cheering drowned out the General again. The seven men with the Captain lost control and joined in the raucous cheering.

"Conklin," yelled the Captain. "Have the men fall in for Kitchen Police." He glared at them for their lack of discipline. He returned to the radio to report the safety of his soldiers and aircraft as well as the newly found survivors. After answering a few more questions he reported a loss of battery power and said he would prepare a report for the next morning. Then, he shut it off.

When order was restored the men went outside to clean the fish and Cherry went with them. She spent the next few minutes complimenting biceps, stances, statures, fish cleaning techniques and was generally ecstatic about being around men again. Inside, the Captain was looking around the living quarters until he spotted Becky. The three women still had their hoods up, but he recognized her immediately. She was boiling water for rice, beans and enough vegetables for twenty one people, some of whom would probably eat like caged animals. He walked over to her and offered to help, if he could.

Becky blushed at the attention of the first man to notice her since the death of her husband. Kiia looked up at the tall Captain.

"I'll be five soon," he said. "Won't I Mom?"

"Yes, you will, Son," she replied. "Do you think you could ask your Grandfather to cut enough Broccoli and other veggies for dinner?"

The boy nodded and scampered off toward his Grandfather who was already cutting Broccoli spears and harvesting pole beans. Kiia and his Grandfather talked and harvested while the Captain and Becky alternately talked and embarrassed themselves as new lovers are wont to do.

Bill brought a pan of veggies to Becky and quickly moved to Miriam and asked if there was enough starter to bake bread for their guests. She nodded and smiled at Bill because she had been watching Becky and the Captain too. There were three oval loaves prepared and when she lifted two of them Bill picked up the other and they put them on the ledge in the hearth to bake. Becky and the Captain put the food in the pails to boil and went with Kiia to see how the fish cleaning was going.

Cherry was still gushing over the men and generally holding things up. At the sight of the Captain they settled down, got to work and finished quickly. Conklin finished up first and reported to the Captain.

"Mission accomplished, Sir," he said with a smile. "And as a point of interest, Sir, did you see that photograph of the old Ford Coupe in there? It looked like the type of old car you like, Sir."

"Thank you, Conklin. I'll take a look at the photo if the occasion allows it. If you think the men can get the fish inside to be cooked without tripping all over the woman, now would be the time." He turned with Becky and Kiia and went back inside. Becky told him a little about the old 34 Coupe and suggested he ask her Dad about where he had put it for safekeeping. She hadn't seen it go into the basement at the car lot so she wasn't sure where it was.

The soldier who cooked for the Expeditionary Force took the lead and offered his services to Miriam and Becky.

They prepared the fish over the open coals by frying, baking and a large pot of stew. There were spices in one of the helicopters which the soldiers shared and a meal fit for a king was enjoyed by all.

In the course of conversation the Captain mentioned the photograph of the old Ford Coupe to Bill who smiled and talked about his favorite project openly. After describing the condition it was in when put in storage he said it would be great to see it again, if in fact, it had survived the firestorm.

The Captain offered to make an expeditionary flight with one chopper first thing in the morning if Bill was interested. He was and described the dealership building in Augusta. If the firestorm hadn't reduced it to a useless powder there was a chance the old Coupe was still intact. They made the idea a plan and finished their meal.

Once again the radio became a constant interruption and the Captain tried to satisfy the headquarters' insatiable requests for information. In the end, General Olson ordered a flight from Cheyenne Mountain to Augusta to arrive in the morning. He expected his arrival to be before noon and hoped to meet the "survivors" for a formal interrogation. The Captain acknowledged reception of the estimated arrival time and signed off for the rest of the night.

Bill and his family continued their usual activities and prayers for the rest of the evening. The soldiers joined in as they were totally impressed with how well this small family lived compared to the military regimen back at the mountain. The kids warmed up to the soldiers and they in turn found it easy to entertain them. At lights out the soldiers offered to take the midnight, three a.m. and six a.m. rides, but the Captain ordered a late night swim in the lake and then a return to their usual bivouac sleeping outside. No one was more disappointed in the bivouac than Cherry.

In the morning, Bill took the first ride and the adults got up to start the day at the same time. The soldiers had promised to exchange MRE's (Meals, Ready to Eat) for the Family's natural food and cooking at breakfast time. The Family was determined to keep it's rituals despite having guests. The soldiers came in after prayers to eat. They quickly requested admittance to prayer time and any other rituals the Family practiced. Bill conferred with his family and they agreed; although the Amish members were a little hesitant. Cherry assured them she and Becky could keep the soldiers occupied and there was nothing to worry about. Cherry's assurance only made them worry more.

Captain Olsen ordered two of his crew to his chopper for a short reconnaissance flight to search the City of Augusta. The other three men under the direction of Lieutenant Conklin would police the garden and lake area and file a suitable report; the barn being off limits. The orders were acceptable to everyone except Cherry who kept her action plans to herself.

After breakfast the chopper lifted off and landed at the car dealership in less time than it took to warm it up. The rows of cars and trucks were still there, only they were as badly burned up as Bill's new truck was. The walls of the building still stood because of the thickness of their construction. The windows and roof were gone as well as everything inside. The fire doors leading to the basement were made of steel and were intact, although slightly warped from the firestorm.

One of the soldiers found a pry bar and the other got some flashlights from the chopper. Between the four of them they got the doors open easily and slowly walked down into the darkness of the basement. They came across the first of Andy's antique cars and it was still intact. The heat must have been intense, but the walls and ceiling of the basement remained intact and there was no burn damage. Bill's 1934 Ford three-window Coupe was where he parked it and it still shone under nearly two years of dust. They rolled it over to the up ramp where the sun penetrated through the open fire doors. While Bill spent time checking it out with the Captain, the two soldiers went to check for an underground gas tank and some gas cans. The underground tanks were easy to find and a portable pump from the chopper produced a tank of gas for the old coupe. The pilot and the other soldier flew back after the Coupe had been started and the basement storage area had been closed again. The tar on the roads had been incinerated by the firestorm and the concrete roads had been reduced to powder, but the road bed was still there and it was an easy drive back to the farm.

For Bill, it was a dream come true to be driving his old Coupe again. Captain Olson was happy to be riding in a car that probably couldn't be found anywhere else on their burned out planet. Back at the farm everyone was smiling when they drove in. Kiia went into orbit at the sight of his Grandfather's old car. He'd had too many good times in it to forget about it.

The soldiers went down to the lake for a short swim and then came back to check out the choppers before the General and his staff arrived. It was good idea to do so because shortly before noon a propeller driven commuter plane circled the farm and set down on the roadbed. The pilot taxied up to the farm's driveway and turned it to a takeoff heading before shutting down the two engines.

The General deplaned without the usual security precautions and walked/marched down the driveway to meet his son and the survivors of what everyone thought was an impossible situation. His pride in his son and the pleasure of meeting the Family of God was obvious. The difference in the blanket clad family and the sharply dressed General in his dress uniform took a few minutes adjust to. They studied each other and then smiled as Captain Olson completed the introductions. The women, except Cherry, had their hoods up in the presence of the General and his flight crew. Their modesty impressed him and Cherry amused him.

Bill and Michael opened the sliding doors at the front of the barn to let in light and fresh air. The general and his men accepted a short tour and one of the flight crew took several pictures. During the tour the General spoke quietly to his son and he left the building. Miriam asked the General to sit down with them and enjoy lunch and prayers. He accepted the offer with a smile and said the soldiers would enjoy their MRE's outside after his Aide brought him a briefcase. He sat down with the Family and after prayers his Aide returned to surrender the case and left. The meal was good and impressed the General immensely.

After they had eaten, General Olson asked Bill if he could explain the situation that existed after the cataclysm. Without waiting for an answer he began. "To this date, no Expeditionary Team has found human survivors, only a few animals in similar steel barns that were equipped with automated feeding and watering systems. Death had come quickly and mercifully to everything after volcanoes erupted around the world." He went on to offer them medical care and treatment and military protection.

He pulled the briefcase onto his lap and opened it. After looking at the files for a moment he called his Aide and told him he was about to start and he would need him soon thereafter.

"Bill," he started, "You have an impressive history in Fire Protection and Emergency Services. Your training and awards have been well documented.

Our new world will need your expertise." He surprised the other adults when he pulled out files with each of their names on them.

"Mr. Yocum, your file tells me you are a Healer, trained in your family's traditions. That's good! In spite of us having a good supply of medicines for many things, your knowledge of natural healing techniques will be very important and useful to us.

"Missus Yokum, your file has only one page, but the information is as important as your husband's. A midwife is of incredible importance to us. We have only forty married women right now and all of the young ones are pregnant; some of them are due soon. You are already needed badly.

Rebecca Thomas; I have the police reports on your late husband's untimely death and your current scholastic achievements in Computer Sciences. You have no idea how important your skills are to us now.

Cherry Johnson; your file is empty for some reason, but I'm sure we will find a place for you somewhere in our new world. And, of course, all of you and all of your children will be appreciated and cared-for with us."

He turned and on cue his Aide came into the barn. Behind him came the rest of the Flight Crew and Captain Olson with his two chopper crews. All the soldiers had returned to full battle gear and were armed as if to go to war!

"To continue," said the General, "it has been the decision of the Provisional Government of the United States of America that any and all survivors of the recent cataclysm be repatriated to the Cheyenne Mountain area for medical and educational analysis and then placement into the best possible position for the protection and advancement of our government.

In accordance with my orders, we will be leaving this location with you in approximately one hour. My soldiers will help you with your packing if need be. There is room on the plane for all of you. We will change to a larger jet powered aircraft in the Minneapolis/Saint Paul area and be at the Mountain before dawn. There will be a lot of people there happy to see all of you. I'll wait for you in the aircraft." He closed the briefcase, got up and left the building. The soldiers stayed behind.

The family sat in shocked silence. Miriam leaned heavily against Bill and moaned; "We shall never see our home again. We are lost in the hands of those who have the power to control us." Bill held her tightly and tried to say something right. All he could think of is this was the very thing he feared at the beginning of their stay in the barn. He knew he couldn't fight against these armed soldiers; he'd accepted his life's mission to be the saving of lives and property, not taking lives.

"You will always be safe with us," offered Captain Olson softly. "I promise you; you will be well cared-for and have meaningful work."

Bill looked at him with every intention of protesting, but having been a Commander of men in emergency situations he knew he had better be ready to leave in an hour or face an unpleasant consequence. He shifted Miriam's weight so he could see her and console her.

"William, what of our plants and animals?

"Missus Thomas," said the Captain, "we will bring the animals in the choppers and the plants will be put outside to grow as best they will. Everything will work out. You'll see."

Then, to the others; "It's time to start packing."

Slowly and numbly they got up from the table and went to their rooms. There was not an abundance of clothing to take and there were few possessions as there was never time to make or build anything in their need to survive. A few pillow cases were all that was needed and the adults didn't need soldiers to help carry anything. It was more difficult to sooth the children's fears than it was to make the move. They left the barn in less than an hour and boarded the commuter plane. Bill threw the car's key to Captain Olson and asked him to park it in the barn and lock up before leaving. They boarded the Commuter Plane in fearful obedience. The engines were started and the plane lifted off and didn't circle the farm. No one could look back.

Epilogue

It had been more than sixteen years since anyone had set foot in the garden Miriam had tended and loved. A young woman in the uniform of the Transitional Government of the United States of America walked carefully among the plants that had survived. As she walked she stopped to pull a weed or straighten up a plant. Her love for the land and making a living on it is apparent. Her name is Rachel and she was born a little more than sixteen years ago in the house part of the barn that protected the Family of God. That was a long time ago and she was here now as more than a visitor. This was the place and the lifestyle she asked for and hoped to live for the rest of her life.

She had moved back to her birthplace with her husband Kiia Thomas, to work the farm that had been in her Aunt's family for generations. Life had been good at Cheyenne Mountain where she and her family had been taken against their will years ago. It was a good life, but there was a shortage of women there.

If a young woman wanted to live alone with the love of her life instead of being available to several men she had to get away. Kiia felt the same way and as he fulfilled his active military obligation they stubbornly sought reassignment to the farm. There had been a shortage of fresh vegetables and meat at the Mountain and since the farm had been productive years ago it was a necessary decision for the government to move them. Of course, since Kiia's mother was married to the newly promoted General Olson it wasn't quite as difficult as one might think.

They had been on the farm only two weeks now and had made a great improvement to the sixteen years of unsupervised growing. Kiia's Grandfather had carefully planted some non-hybrid plants and they had continued to flower and reseed themselves. The orderly rows were no longer there, but the rear-tine tiller they were given cut new walk-ways and the crops were thinned and replanted. The government plane was supposed to fly in every month with provisions and gasoline for the tiller, some of which Kiia used for Bills 1934 Coupe. It was a simple life and the solitude suited both of them. If they could raise and send back enough to feed other small outposts they would be able to stay.

As she walked among the plants she spoke quietly into a recorder. Education had become a high priority to the survivors of the Cataclysm and they were determined to keep the knowledge of the past even if there were not enough people to sustain prior lifestyles. Her assignment, along with the farm work, was to record the history of the Family of God into which she had been born.

"I want to start with what my Mother and Father told me about the move from the farm to the "Mountain".

"Both of my parents were given important jobs in the medical department even though they had what was considered a primitive education from the Amish. But, both were skilled and intelligent; my mother as a midwife and my father as a healer. The transition from primitive farming to the "Mountain" Community wasn't as bad as they feared on the flights to Colorado. With a little more than four hundred people in the community there was ample time for study, work and prayer. After a few weeks both my Mother and Father fit in well. In fact I would say they thrived in their environment.

Becky, Kiia's mom, married the then Captain Marcus Olson shortly after the move. He is good to her and to Kiia also. He's been a good father, a good role model for my husband and an excellent military leader even though we live in a world at peace. From little on I was attracted to Kiia and watched him as I grew. He was a happy child and embraced challenges with confidence. He has two brothers and a sister now and even though the Transitional Government wants more children per family, I think that is as many as Becky and Marc want.

Cherry is another story. There were too many available men at the "Mountain" even for her. She took one look at the assembled soldiers when we arrived and promptly proposed to the seven men who had flown in with Captain Olson. Everyone laughed when they heard about it, but the T-Gov approved it as they were only interested in an expanding population at that time. With seven husbands she has had nine more babies since Hyacinth was born on the farm. All three of her girls from The Family are married and that will be a blessing. With so few girls and so many men we have to struggle for education and an identity that makes us more than sex objects and baby makers.

The T-Gov doesn't make that easy as they are pushing for early marriage for all girls and as many babies as possible.

My sisters, Anna and Mary are married also although I wonder how happy they are. As Twins they have always been emotionally strong and self supporting without the need for someone else to validate them. They married good men who seem a little intimidated by their independence. So far each has only one child and there is pressure on them to have more. Time will tell.

William and Miriam didn't live very long after the move to the "Mountain." I never knew them and my parents tell me there really wasn't a place for them. I'm told William was a man born to leadership, but the military and the Transitional Government ran everything and they made no room for anyone else. Miriam, they say, was a woman of the land, simple in needs and a motherly type. There was land being farmed at the time, but the land and animals were cared for by the men. There was little for either of them to do even though they were the strength of our Family of God.

It seemed they attracted everyone who was unhappy with their lot in life at the "Mountain." Anyone with a sad story or a bad case of the blues descended on both of them. Mother said they could be seen everywhere with someone who was lonely or crying or angry. Father said their goodness was so great everyone expected them to carry their troubles as well as their own. It became too much and they died within weeks of each other with a type of fever. My parents said it was the burden of too much unhappiness added to their own that killed them. Few people at the "Mountain" even knew what they'd lost when William and Miriam died."

Rachel moved back and forth around the plants making sure each had enough sun and space to grow. She kept notes on how well each plant grew when close to one species or how poorly they did near another. Her notes would make a big difference in horticulture in the future.

Kiia struggled daily to build fences around the garden. When the Family was forced to leave they were told the goats would be flown to the "Mountain" in the helicopters. Unfortunately, this was just a ploy to aid in an early departure. The soldiers had been ordered to release the goats into the wild and empty all the galvanized cans that still held seeds or feed grains. This left enough forage for the goats and feed for the quail. After the cataclysm, the earth "greened" over quickly and they began to wander to favorite feeding and breeding grounds. With no predators both species had been prolific and an effort had to be made to keep them out of the gardens needed for human consumption.

Suddenly, she noticed someone lurking in the apple orchard. She took a long look and was sure she was right. It was Kiia and he was crouched between two trees.

"I wonder," she thought, "if he has something on his newly married mind." She continued her work in the garden and when she got close to the orchard, Kiia jumped up with a laughing shout and ran toward her.

'Kiia!" She squealed. They were happy in their new marriage and love play was fulfilling to them. She turned to run and led a merry chase around the bluff and down to the lake. He overtook her in the shallows where the sun still warmed the water. They kissed and teased and held each other as only lovers could. Their uniforms were thrown together on the shore and they continued their love play in the shallows.

When the moment was right they returned to the shore and lay on their clothing. Nine months later the twins William and Miriam were born.